MW01001088

THE FALL

MICHAEL S. VASSEL

This book is dedicated to Linda Jean Vassel.

Mom,

I know it wasn't always easy being a single parent, but you made it look like it was. You were always there for us. You worked your ass off from 8 to 6, sometimes six days a week, only to come home to two arguing preteens. That took guts – and more than a little alcohol – to deal with on a daily basis. I don't know how you kept your sanity intact, or your anger at bay, but you did. And you did it in style.

I will always remember our vacations to Catawba Island and Hawaii, and how you made every day – every outing – a boatload of crazy fun.

Thank you for always being there for us.

And thank you for always helping me with my homework. God, how I hated "showing my work."

I still do, yet … this …

Love you!

Cover art: Arash Jahani – arashjahani.com

ISBN: 978-1-09838-396-1 (Print)
ISBN: 978-1-09838-397-8 (eBook)

PROLOGUE

"Hey! Green light! Sweet! Okay ... now that I have *you* working, where do I start?"

"God, where *do* I start? Where do I fucking ..."

"Sorry about that. User error. Wait one."

"Alright ... so, if you're hearing this, you must've found this digital recorder ... and apparently charged it. Which means you're probably human. So, I guess ... good on you."

"And sorry in advance for all the stopping and starting of the message. I tend to do that a lot. My mind often wanders nowadays. Probably too much. So, please excuse me. I don't mean to offend anyone. Assuming someone is listening to this now. Wow! That's stupid. They'd have to be listening, else …"

"So, let me start with why I'm recording this message. I'm recording this to tell the story of what happened. Or at least what happened to me. I'm sure there's others … other perspectives, that is. I can't be the only one. Can I?"

"Well, before I go down that rabbit hole, I better start telling you my tale. And a personal tale usually starts with an introduction. So, hi, whoever you are. My name is Paul. Paul Davidson. Paulie to my close friends … and family. I've even been called the Paulster. Not that anyone calls me that anymore. Well, not since high school anyways."

"Just so you know, I'm not originally from here. Here being Vancouver. In fact, I'm not even from Canada. Believe it or not, I'm actually from the United States. Ohio. Cleveland, to be exact. The mistake on the lake, they once called it. But I'm sure no one's calling it that now."

"Assuming you're listening to this in my bedroom, near the window, you'll find a map on the wall to your … err … right. A map I've had for quite a while now. And if you're looking at it, you'll find a big green arrow pointing to Cleveland. And a blue line sketched throughout the map that marks my trip to where I am … well, where we are now."

"Yeah, I know. It's not a direct route. Not quite as the bird flies … not even close. But, if you follow the line, you'll probably guess why. Big cities, you know."

"Okay, I don't want to get too far ahead. I really want to relay my journey to you from the start. I think … I think that's important. I hope someone else thinks it's important, at least. You know … someday."

"Because … well … if you're hearing this … I guess … I guess that means I'm probably dead."

"It's a weird thing to think about, isn't it!? You know, the idea of being dead. Going to the great beyond. Because, I would've never thought that I'd ever *be* dead. Maybe it's that feeling of invincibility you have as a kid that never went away? Oh, you know the one. The one that, no matter how high something is … or dangerous something is … you feel like you can climb it. Or drink it. Or outrun it. In fact, I would've never thought in a million years I'd be doing this … this recording. It seems so strange …"

"I mean, the whole time, this entire time, I never gave up. Not for one second. Not for one …"

"Because, when this all started, I figured it'd just blow over, you know!? That there'd be … something … like, a cure … but … well …"

"Oh, and lastly, sorry for having the music blaring while I tell you my tale. The music helps me think. It keeps me thinking straight … on track. Right now, I've got on … what? Oh yeah, The Police … *Message in a Bottle.* Great song. Kinda fitting, now that I think about it."

"Hey, I promise I won't break into song again. Or at least I'll try not to. Doesn't mean I won't though. Music has helped to keep my sanity over the last … well … I guess my lifetime. And it's gotten me this far, so ..."

"Anyway, without further ado or gilding of the lily, here goes my story. Or what there is of it, anyway."

"It all started around the Fall of 2022 … you know, after we all thought we were clear of the coronavirus. And it all happened kind of … slowly. As slow as an autumn leaf falling from a tree."

CHAPTER 1

"Hey, Hun? Did you see this?" I heard Lorie shout from the living room. I was in the middle of brushing my teeth, so I didn't reply right away. It didn't take long for a follow up.

"Hun?"

After spitting a mouthful of toothpaste into the sink, I returned a resounding and a little annoyed, "I'm here! What's up?"

What followed was a notable pause in the air. It wasn't long before a reply came, though.

"Did you see this ... on the news?"

"I'm in the middle of brushing my teeth! Can it wait?" I called back.

I listened for some sort of reply – a rebuttal, calling me a name or some such – but nothing came. So, after wiping my mouth, I headed downstairs. Lorie was in the kitchen packing her lunch. I went in to join her and also to make my morning coffee. She didn't meet my eyes at first. I knew I needed to say something.

"I'm sorry … I was full of toothpaste. What's up?" I asked, trying to sound apologetic.

She ignored me while she walked over to the fridge. Opening it, she leaned in then answered, "I was asking if you saw the news?"

Still trying to sound remorseful, I asked, "No, why? What's going on?"

After righting herself, she turned towards me and gave me a curious look. I knew why.

As part of my normal morning routine, I usually had the TV running in the bedroom. That morning was an exception. I'd been listening to an audiobook. You know how it is. You get close to the end and you just don't want to set it down. Stop playing it, in this case. I was about fifteen minutes from the end. Those I killed while exercising and readying my work clothes for the day.

"No, the TV was off. Why? What's up?" I repeated, that time without guilt. Her eyebrows raised and she let out a huff.

"They're saying that, for the first time in … well … ever, there's been a decline in human births."

I narrowed my eyes, not knowing why this was a big deal … especially to her, or us. It wasn't like we were trying to have a kid. We'd both decided early on in our marriage that we didn't want any. Call us selfish or whatever. It just didn't seem to make sense. At least not at that time.

It took a moment, but I got what she was on about. We were both educated people. We'd both taken history, and – more importantly – science. And, of course, we both watched the news. You'd practically have to live under a rock or be raised by wolves not to realize the planet was exploding with people. I didn't know exact numbers, but I knew the population was well over eight billion, and a billion of that had been born in the last decade or so. I think I read somewhere that the population would be over ten billion before the middle of the century. Crazy growth … like a plague. My quick guess was it was probably just a fluke.

"Don't you think that's weird?" she asked, eyebrows re-raised. "The guys on the news seem all concerned about it."

Mine raised to match hers as I thought, then I offered a smirk. "Are the Christians on Faux News freaking again?"

She scowled. She hated when I referred to Fox News as Faux. Her dad was a die-hard Republican that exclusively watched one channel and one channel only.

Keeping it out of the mainstream, he said.

Burying your head in the sand, was always my retort. Although I'd never say that to him, or to any of the other Fox Folks I knew.

Lorie's hands went to her hips. "No! I was watching CNN, asshole. I flipped on the local news and they said the same thing."

Before I could say anything else, or even offer an apology, she turned and strode towards the bedroom.

"Sorry! I was only kidding!" I shouted. I swore I heard a huff in return.

But that was our way, really. Going back and forth like that. We were both sarcastic mother fuckers. Me especially. Not a day went by that we didn't throw shots over the wall to each other. It made for an interesting banter – and a *very* interesting marriage.

Knowing I wouldn't hear more from her until she was ready to leave for work, I turned, walked to the front door, grabbed my shoes, then sat down in front of the TV while I put them on.

Sure as shit, the TV was turned to Faux. I knew she'd probably just switched the stations to gaslight me. It was something she'd done before, which was no big deal, and kind of funny. I glanced towards the bedroom, hoping she was standing in the doorway so I could flip her off. Unfortunately, she wasn't.

Stopping mid shod, I reached for the controller and typed in 1202, the four digits that took me to the other side of the coin - CNN. As always, I waited until the screen displayed their logo before I set down the controller. Hey, I've been known to fat finger a digit or three in my time.

After a moment, the reporters on screen started discussing what Lorie had been going on about.

"Yes Ken, Scientists are baffled, for sure," some lady named Karen - or at least she looked like a Karen - said before the screen switched. Her face was replaced with a timeline, showing the world's population rise over the last twenty years. As expected, the line shot up like a Navy fighter jet. That is, until it hit the last two years. The first of those showed a leveling off, the second marked a slight decline.

"Does this have anything to do with the Coronavirus, Karen?" Ken asked. As soon as the words were out of his mouth, a smaller picture of Karen appeared in the lower right-hand corner.

"I'm told there are some contributing factors, Ken. But not enough to explain the severe drop in births seen in the last six months," she replied. His head bobbed as if hanging on every word.

"Maybe it's from all the social distancing?" he laughed, hoping for some response from her. She only hinted a smile.

Ken turned back to us, his viewers. "Well, thank you Karen."

She gave her thanks and her little window disappeared.

"See what I mean?" Lorie blurted from behind. Her sudden appearance made me lurch.

"That births are down?" I asked, turning towards her. She was shaking her head.

"It's more than that. It's that people have been dying at a higher rate. Higher rate of suicides too."

I narrowed my eyes again. "Where did ya get that?"

"It's all over the news, Hun. Every news agency is reporting the same."

Part of me wanted to doubt her, but most of me knew she kept her nose to the grindstone that was the news outlets. Morning and night – when I wasn't watching one of my sci-fi shows – she watched the 'relevant' news. This included listening to PBS on the way to and from work. I really didn't know how she did it. That much 'reality' would drive me nuts. That's why I constantly had my head buried in a novel or eyes affixed to a sci-fi or fantasy. After all, reality was *really* depressing. All the shootings and stabbings and general anger between humans really got me down. I seriously didn't need all that negativity that in my life. But that's one of the places where we differed.

"I'm telling you, life is really changing out there. People are just ..." she paused, then said. "Just ... weird."

I gave her a shrug. I knew what she'd meant though. Over the last few years society had changed. The social distancing wasn't just in the spaces between people. It was in their attitudes towards one another. More than just between the rich and poor, white or black. People's friendships and relationships had been distancing. You could see it in … well … everything.

"Oh shit! I'm going to be late!" Lorie announced, double checking her watch. I barely had time to put on my other shoe and get off the couch before she enveloped me, stealing her morning hug and kiss. In a heartbeat she was out the door. And as soon as her car was out of the drive, I shut off the TV, finished cleaning up the morning dishes, then hit the door myself.

Driving to work that day I avoided the news. I always did. It was just too damn depressing. Instead, I listened to a mix of Slipknot, Avenged Sevenfold, and New Found Glory. My normal getting ready for work music. Listening to angry tunes in the morning before having to sit at my desk all day always seemed to help alleviate the pain – even if it was only a little bit.

I didn't think about the morning conversation at all that day. I'd like to blame it on the heavy workload. But, to be honest, that wasn't it. In fact, if anything, the workload was light for a Wednesday – usually my busiest day.

No, to be honest, the reason I didn't think about the conversation was because it was becoming increasingly hard to believe in the news. There was so much fake news out there making things like that morning's report seem blown out of proportion. I figured that, in a week's time, there'd be a new news report that would contradict it. That the population figures were taken from a hot spot in Northeast Bumfuck where people had moved out, causing the change.

So, like most things, I ignored it and concentrated on the work in front of me. The work that kept our bills paid. The work that, although tedious, helped the days and weeks go by.

When I got home that night, I did my usual thing. That is, I changed, sent Lorie a text telling her I was heading out, then hit the road for a pre-dinner run.

As I ran and listened to some 90's and 2000's music, the thoughts of the day – those of spreadsheets, PowerPoints, and the like, slowly drained from my head. All thoughts of morning news and society were also kept at bay as Slipknot and Mudvayne screamed at me, cleansing my mind like water run through a Purell filter.

By the time I rounded the last corner on my return home, my mind was void of all negativity. The only thoughts that remained were that of the spaghetti I planned on having for dinner and how great the shower would feel when I got back.

My mind was so clear, in fact, that I almost missed it – almost stepped on it, I should say. There, on the sidewalk almost in the middle of the path, was a bird. It was lying on its side. Featherless. Unmoving. Dead as a doornail.

"Shit!" I exclaimed as I jumped to avoid crushing it. And I was successful but, as I landed, I came down weird on my ankle. Wincing in pain, I bounced awkwardly to a stop.

I walked around for a minute, as one does, feeling out the pain – making sure my ankle was still good to go if you know what I mean. My feeling-it-out course inevitably took me back to the dead bird several times.

On my last route, having verified my joint was up to snuff, I couldn't help but stop and look down at the poor creature. As you can guess, probably having seen one yourself, what I saw was a grotesque oddity. Without feathers, the wings seemed malformed. And the head – a head that was sprawled sideways at an unusual angle – looked too large for the body beneath it. The beak was cracked open slightly, leaving the impression that something had crawled into it. Or, if I dared to stay, something might just crawl out.

The worst part about this disturbing sight, if I was made to choose one, were its eyes – the protruding lidless eyes. Drawn wide and covered with a milky white sheen, they looked upon nothing, and yet maybe saw everything. Once though, those eyes had seen nothing but the world as new. Now though … now they were only bleak reminders of a creature that used to be.

Curiously haunting arrows pointing toward something that'd gone terribly wrong.

I'm not sure how long I stared at it, or how long I would've, actually. Thankfully my smart watch buzzed, telling me that dinner was nearly ready and that I should get my ass home on the double.

Those were Lorie's words, obviously.

Turning, I started walking away from the scene. As I did, I tried putting this unwanted image out of my mind. My walk eventually turned into a jog, then ultimately into a run. I arrived at home a few minutes later … although I knew a portion of me would never again leave that unforgettable spot.

After showering I joined Lorie in the kitchen. Dinner was ninety percent finished. All that was left to do was to plate the food and move to the living room.

We watched TV while we ate, and by TV, I mean Netflix. It was our preferred option over the depressing news or late afternoon repeating sitcoms most networks showed.

It wasn't until later, after the plates were cleared – and Lorie and I had adult beverages in hand – that we shared the highlights of our days.

"So, it looks like I may not have a job soon," Lorie announced, making me stop mid-swig. Before I could ask, she continued.

"Sales are down network wide, and they're looking at closing half our stores."

I tried to look stunned about the store closings, but I wasn't. I'd heard the scuttlebutt – the entire nation had. Retail stores like Sears and JC Penny's had been on the decline for years. It was the way of the world, it seemed. Why go to a store when you could just as easily buy stuff online.

I pursed my lips as I thought, then asked the obvious question. "But why would that affect your job? You're IT."

She let out a sigh. "We were told today that profits are down. Less people are buying, even online. Long story short, they basically told us that they don't need to keep an entire IT staff if online keeps declining."

"But what about new product lines? Someone has to configure that shit!" I barked, perturbed, as a million thoughts about paying bills and her looking for a new job ran through my head.

Lorie only shrugged. I could tell by her look she was as perplexed as me. These same thoughts were running through her head as well. I instantly felt like a bad husband.

Taking a deep breath to calm myself, I waited a few seconds before I asked, “When do you think you'll get the news?”

“I'm not sure. I heard a rumor. They're saying two weeks. Maybe a month.”

I slowly nodded. It was all I could do.

“I heard they're laying off half,” she said.

“Half? Half of what?” I asked. She again shrugged.

“Maybe half of the company?”

My eyes widened, and I wanted to say something – scream something. But I thought better of it. Instead I leaned over and put my hand on her knee.

“Well, that sucks, Babe. I'm so, so sorry.”

She nodded and patted my hand as she tried to smile. After a moment she turned towards the TV. I did the same.

We both sat there for a minute, silent, as we considered our options. With my paycheck alone, we could get by. If I cut out my 401k contribution, that is. I figured she'd get some sort of severance. And there was always unemployment. Sure, we could get by. Maybe we'd have to cut back a little here or there, but we could get by easily.

Turning towards her, I smiled and matched her shrug. “Well, it is what it is. We'll make do.”

Lorie gave me a smile, and I knew she believed me. Hell, my tone almost made me believe myself. Almost. Then, as if touched by a muse, a sudden thought popped into my head.

“Hey, I was just thinking,” I smiled. “Our anniversary is in two weeks. What do you say we make it an earlier one this year?”

She gave me a confused look.

"You know, instead of waiting, why don't we move it up. Celebrate it this coming weekend instead?"

Her eyes darted around for a moment as she thought. "But … I haven't had a chance to get you a present. I planned on going Saturday …"

I held up my hand cutting her off. "Instead of spending money on each other, why don't we maybe spend the weekend at that winery on the east side … you know, the one in Geneva?"

Her eyes widened and a smile – an actual smile this time – suddenly alit her face.

"You mean The Kilderkin?" she said. I nodded.

"This weekend?" she said. I nodded again. Her smile grew tenfold. "It's supposed to be beautiful this weekend!"

"That's if I can get a reservation," I replied. Lorie started nodding enthusiastically.

Seeing her delight, I let out a chuckle, then reached for my phone. "Okay, I'll go online and see what I get."

Putting her arm in mine – which made it a little difficult to search – Lorie watched on as I pulled up the site and perused the rooms. Sure enough, they had one King room available. And there was a "special offer" on the table. So, I nabbed it.

As soon as I booked it and placed the phone down, Lorie pulled me into a huge kiss. And, well, it didn't stop there.

It only goes to prove the time-tested wisdom, a motto I've quoted at least a hundred times, "Happy wife, happy life."

Well, at least most of the time, anyway.

CHAPTER 2

Okay, before I go on, I'll share a little history on The Kilderkin. You know, why it popped into my head. Then … and now.

First of all, it's where Lorie and I first met. And if that wasn't enough, it's also where we got married. Stopping to think about it though, it's really more than those two things.

Even though I was born and raised on Cleveland's westside, I believe that region – Geneva-on-the-Lake and its surroundings – is the best place to vacation. In the Fall – my favorite time of year – the look of the trees and lake, combined with the old world feel of the wineries, relaxes me and centers me in ways no other place on earth can do.

I guess that kind of makes me a Fall person. Not that I like the cold, though. But it's in my blood, you know. Just like it's in every true Clevelander's.

If I had a choice though, I'd probably be a snowbird – knowing how much I dislike the bitter cold and empty feeling of Winter. That

I could deal with. Living in Cleveland until the leaves change and fall. But as soon as the first snow, I'd be on a plane heading to parts south, or – if I had my druthers – maybe California.

Sorry. Got lost there for a moment. Let me continue. I'll pick up just after getting out of work on Friday.

We both ran late, as usual, putzing around the apartment while we packed. So, it was nearly 8 p.m. by the time we arrived at the winery. That trip, like the others in the past, we valeted the car, checked in, dropped the bags in the room, then – after freshening up a bit – we hit the restaurant to get in a meal before the kitchen closed. After that, well, we 'retired' to the room to celebrate ... if you get my drift.

The next morning, we both woke early, just before sunrise. As we normally did, we quickly cleaned ourselves up, got dressed, grabbed our jackets, then headed to the lobby for coffee. Once we had caffeine in hand, we walked out the back door and found seats on the patio just as the sun started to pique over the vineyard.

"Oh, ma' God!" Lorie exclaimed as soon as we were seated. I was just speechless.

"It's so amazing out here, isn't it?" she asked. I nodded.

"It is every time."

She shook her head. "No, I mean, like, right now. I mean, look at the trees! They're so ... so ..."

"Vibrant," I replied. She returned a slow nod.

"More than last year, don't you think?"

Part of me wanted to shrug, knowing I felt like this every time I saw these surroundings. Yet part of me – maybe the wishful side of me – wanted to enthusiastically agree. The light making its way through the trees, highlighting every leaf, every twig. The dew drops in the grass sparkling as rays from the morning sun hit them. All of it left me with a feeling of awe. Captivated by everything I saw.

Okay, okay. I know. Big ex-military guy here losing his shit over some grass and trees. Sounds girly, I know. But I don't care. I've earned my man-card over and over again. And if I wanted to gawk at a majestic morning, so be it. I am who I am. I've never pretended to be anything other than that.

You good with that!? Okay. Good.

Anyway, getting back to it, Lorie and I sat down and watched the sunrise while we drank our java. It only took a minute or three before the glamour wore off. She was the first to noticed it.

"Hun … do you …" she started, then paused.

Leaving me the opening, I smirked, "Need to fart? Nah, all good here. Left it back in the room."

I was hoping for a smile, or maybe even a small laugh. I only got a perturbed glare.

"No, asshole! Be serious!" she blurted, then glanced around. Eventually, she met my eyes.

"Does something seem weird to you?"

I narrowed my eyes at her, then looked around to the spots she had. I didn't see what she was talking about. But, in the back of my mind, I knew something felt off. At first, I thought it was her just getting into my head, like she was about to spring some sort of joke. Or maybe, just maybe, even a fart of her own. She'd been known to do that, you know. Both get in my head and fart. So, I just looked back to her. Yet, instead of a grin – or a scrunched just-about-to-fart-face – I saw only a questioning look.

Then it suddenly hit me. It hit her at the same time. There was a distinct silence in the air.

"Birds … where are the birds?" she uttered as she looked from tree to tree. I started doing the same.

"Hun, do you know what I mean?" she asked. I slowly nodded.

"Yeah … that's weird, huh!?"

"More than weird," she replied.

I turned to her. "Maybe we missed something? Like maybe someone set off something."

She met my eyes. "Like what? Fireworks?"

"No," I huffed. "Like maybe they were mowing the lawn … or running a leaf blower before we came out. Those usually make birds stop."

"Yeah … maybe," she replied unconvinced. "But if that was the case …"

"I know," I broke in. "Those things usually only shut them up for a few seconds or so. Early morning birds …"

"Are usually loud … and constant," she said, finishing my thought.

We both stared from tree to tree for a bit, trying to see any activity. Yet try as we might, there was nothing. No movement. No noise. Nothing.

Absolutely nothing.

Then we both saw it. A single bird. A red-headed woodpecker I guessed, based on its size and red cowl. It darted out of one of the trees to our left. It swooped and flitted for a bit across the grounds in front of us, then headed towards the trees to our right. Then just as quickly as it had appeared, it was gone. Lost within the foliage.

"Well, that's something at least," I remarked. She shrugged. I did as well.

Looking down at my cup, I noticed I only had a gulp left. I quickly took care of it then waggled it so she could see.

"I'm out … you?"

She looked down at her own then announced, "I could use a refill."

With weak smiles, we both rose and walked back into the winery. After getting fill-ups, we headed back to the room.

The eeriness we both felt that morning stayed with us the rest of that day.

That afternoon we scheduled a visit through the winery. If you've ever been on one, I'm sure this is nothing new. Lorie and I – along with a dozen others – followed a tour guide as she showed us the magic behind the curtain.

Having finished our penance, we finally came to the highlight of the tour – the wine tasting. We were sat at picnic tables outside and handed pieces of paper with the eight wines listed. Then we were asked to select four, and only four, of them.

Now, normally Lorie and I would split these, her and I both taking four different ones so we could sample all they had to offer. Out of those there were always two or three that just didn't fit our bill. The rejects we usually set to the side and shared the ones we liked. That time though, instead of choosing a spread, we both picked what we knew we'd like off the bat and drank to our heart's content.

We were well on our way to inebriation, mostly through our glasses, when we were finally approached by one of the staff.

"How are you enjoying this year's selection?" Grant – that weekend's steward – asked as he suddenly appeared out of nowhere. His unexpected arrival made Lorie gasp. Then, like a frightened rabbit, she jumped from her chair and rounded the table, practically running to my side.

"I'm sorry! I didn't mean to ..." Grant started but stopped seeing Lorie's reaction. Noticing the shock on his face, I turned to her. She was standing next to me, shaking, her face pale as a ghost's.

Reaching out to her, I tried to touch her hand, hoping to soothe her. But instead of calming her, she flinched away from me the moment I made contact.

"Babe, are you okay?" I asked, pulling my hand back. She didn't respond right away. Her eyes stayed wide, staring at Grant, looking scared out of her wits. And it wasn't until I said "Babe" again – a little louder the second time – that she finally turned towards me. Even then – with a look of total fear alighting her face – it still took her a few seconds to answer.

"Yeah ... yeah. I'm okay. I was just ... I was just lost in my thoughts, I guess."

"I'm really sorry, Mrs. Davidson. I didn't mean to ... to ..."

"It's okay, Grant ... really. I was just out of it," she said, her eyes not leaving me.

Grant turned to me, looking for acknowledgment of her statement. I glanced between him and Lorie a couple times before I replied.

"Yeah, we're okay. We were just deep in a conversation. You know how it is."

Grant gave me an unbelieving nod but accepted the explanation for what it was. As the tension in the air eased, he motioned to our empty glasses.

"Can I get you anything else?"

"No, we're all good. We were just getting ready to leave," I replied, rising to stand next to Lorie. Grant offered a halfhearted smile.

"Okay … well … again, I'm sorry if I … umm …"

"It's all good," I interrupted, waving him off. I then reached out for Lorie once again. That time she let me take her hand.

Without another word, Grant gave a small bow, then turned and walked off. A moment later we did the same. It wasn't until we were well away from the tables that I questioned Lorie about her reaction. It took her a moment of soul searching before she could offer an excuse.

"I'm … I'm not exactly sure. When he was just suddenly there next to me … I … I don't know. Something in me just told me to get up and get away."

"To get away?" I asked. She nodded.

"It was like I wasn't myself. It felt like I was viewing the whole thing from someone else's body. You know, like through a window."

I gazed at her questioningly, but she didn't notice.

"Before I knew it, I was standing at your side. And, well …"

Lorie paused then, both in speech and pace. Turning to me, she squeezed my hand.

"I'm really sorry, Babe. I feel so embarrassed. I've just never felt like that before."

Before she could say more, I returned her squeeze and shook my head. "Don't feel bad. We all get scared from time to time."

She gave a half nod, humoring me I guessed. I raised her hand, kissed it, then looked deep into her eyes.

"And hey, he did just suddenly appear … and he *is* creepy as fuck."

My comment, having brushed away the moment, made her smile. With a slight tug I restarted our progress back to the room.

Once back, she took a nap while I watched some TV. We didn't reemerge until it was dinnertime.

Instead of hitting the bar like we always did, we opted for the full meal deal. You know, appetizers, salads, and the like. We even ordered a bottle of the red blend – the one we were both partial to. And when that was finished, we ordered another.

What can I say!? The meal was great, and we got toasted. Who could ask for more!?

Even though we were stuffed, and well on our way to a massive hangover, I ordered Crème Brulee for two. As we waited for the delight, I drunkenly went on a rant about something … I don't even remember what now. You know, one of those things you've complained about a hundred times, but you'll still complain about a hundred more? You get the picture, I'm sure.

So engrossed in my rant, I didn't notice Lorie's face at first. It wasn't until I begged her for an answer a second time that I noticed how still she was. Her eyes, bugged out like the earlier encounter with Grant, now stared over my shoulder towards something across the room.

"Babe, what gives?" I asked, preparing to turn. Her arm lunged across the table, fastening onto my forearm in a vicelike grip.

"Don't turn around!" she begged. "Pretend you don't notice!"

"Notice? Don't notice what?" I asked, because I really didn't.

"Can we leave?" she announced out of nowhere. No sooner did the words leave her lips then I heard something behind me. *The* something she'd asked me not to notice. But it was impossible to ignore.

"Oh yeah! Fuck you!" a voice said – yelled, really. As soon as the words hit my ears, I couldn't help but turn around. There, behind me, standing close to the bar where we'd normally be sitting, were two guys standing face to face. Their noses were within inches of each other's, and they were arguing at the tops of their lungs.

"Fuck me? No! Fuck you, asshole!" one of them shouted as he took up a position next to an open seat – the only open seat at the bar.

The guy – who immediately became Fuck You number one in my mind – was probably about six-foot tall, if I had to guess. He had his hand on the open seat and had blocked the other guy from sitting down by swiveling the back towards him. That guy was an only slightly shorter version of Fuck You number one that I instantly dubbed Fuck You number two.

Again, only in my mind.

"I was just sitting there, asshole!" Two said as he tried to wiggle his way in between the guy and the seat. Both inched a little closer.

"No, you weren't. No one was sitting here when I walked in the door," F.U. number one said. F.U. number two's eyes narrowed. They were filling to the brim with anger.

"When was that? Like a minute ago?" he yelled, then pointed at the bar. "If you don't believe me, look at the drink right there!"

F.U. number one scoffed. "Oh, you mean that empty glass? That doesn't mean jack shit. It probably belonged to someone else and you're just claiming it so you can sit down."

Just then I felt a tug on my arm.

"Babe. Can … can we ga-go now? I don't want to be here," Lorie said. I ignored the request without turning. The yelling match was too good to ignore.

Now, I'm normally not a rubber-necker. But for some reason this encounter made me watch. Deep down, I needed to know how it was going to end.

"Oh yeah! Well you can ask the bartender! She served it to me," F.U. number two yelled, hoping to get the bartender, Krystal, to settle the argument. Instead of settling it though, she turned and walked away. A moment later she was nowhere to be found.

"Well, obviously that was her way of agreeing with me!" one said, again facing two. "Now I suggest you back the fuck off before I make you."

"Oh, make me, huh!?" two barked as he nodded his head.

After that, everything happened fast.

The next thing I knew – the next thing the entire bar knew – number one had a blade in his hand. The minute everyone in and around the bar noticed, they simultaneously jumped back a foot or two. It was crazy to see, kind of like watching the oil and soapy water trick. I'm sure you've seen it. Everyone from the closest to the farthest seemed to move in unison, backing away from the Fuck Yous and their impending altercation.

Number two, seeing the blade suddenly appear, took a quick step back, knocking the bar stool behind him to the floor. Nervously glancing from side to side, he found what he was looking for. Seeing an almost empty beer bottle on the bar, he latched onto it and in one fluid motion smashed it, creating a jagged fighting weapon.

Part of me wished I had popcorn at that moment. You know the meme of Michael Jackson from Thriller where he's spooning popcorn into his mouth and smiling. Well, had I had popcorn, that would've been me. Yet, another part of me wanted to rush forward and help. Obviously the first instinct took over. Like you, I'm very allergic to getting stabbed by either bottle or knife.

Because everyone was backing away from the altercation, my view became blocked. At first, I tried moving my head from side to side to see the melee. But it was no good. There were too many bodies. So, I decided to stand.

As I rose, I was instantly pulled back into my chair. Coming down awkwardly, my ass hit the side of the chair causing a small stab of pain in my right butt cheek. Wincing, I turned with a snarl. There, across the table from me, was a shaking and crying Lorie. Her eyes, filled with tears, were unrelentingly pleading. Suddenly all thoughts of anger and excitement left me.

"Babe, are you okay?" I asked, quickly reaching out for her. As I did, she released her grip on me and abruptly moved backward. A moment later she was standing.

"I … I want to go … I na-na-need to go!" she uttered. Her voice was broken and wavering as if she was about to collapse.

Completely forgetting about everything else in the world, I stood and rushed to be at her side. Seeing my approach, she turned and moved rapidly through the restaurant towards the back door.

"Babe, wait up!" I called, hoping she'd wait for me. It was as if she was in another world – a world that suddenly didn't include me, or the fight going on behind us.

A moment after she was through the door, I was as well. I followed her as she made her way through the corridors of the Inn, making a beeline towards our room.

Catching her about midway up the stairs, I didn't try to slow her. I just moved to her side, grasped her free hand, and rushed with her up the stairs. I only briefly let go of her to open the door to our room. Once we were safely inside, I closed, locked, and deadbolted the door as she moved to the farthest side of the room.

Okay, here's the thing. Lorie was always kind of skittish. She hated fights – never wanting to watch boxing or MMA bouts – and especially the blood, spit, and sweat that came with them. It's something I'd gotten used to over the few years we'd spent together. But that – that reaction to the barfight – was unusual for her.

Turning to her, I took a moment – and a deep breath – before I moved into the room. The moment I started, I stopped at what I saw. Lorie was at the far side of the room, facing the wall, fists clenched as if she was about to try and break through it.

Not wanting to unhinge her any further, I slowly moved forward.

"Honey ... are you okay?" I asked as I rounded the bed and approached. I knew she knew I was there, closing, but she never responded.

"Babe?" I questioned again, stopping my approach when I was about maybe three feet from her. Hearing my voice, I saw her ear prick slightly. Then, without any notice, she started banging her head against the wall.

Shocked at that reaction, I stood there for a few seconds as she thumped her head into the wall. Awareness finally hitting me, I rushed forward and grabbed both her arms. After dragging her away from the wall, I pulled her into me.

Shaking, she struggled to free herself from my grasp. Within moments though, she seemed to calm, eventually collapsing into my arms. That's when the waterworks completely let loose.

"Aww, Babe. I'm so, so sorry you had to witness that," I said, holding her and moving the two of us to the bed. The moment we sat, she buried her face in my shoulder and continued to sob. Pulling her closer, I started kissing her forehead and rubbing her back, hoping to settle her. It helped a bit, but only just a little. Regardless, I continued to try.

Okay, I hate to admit this, but that's ... that's when it got weird.

As I sat there, rubbing her back and kissing her forehead, something about that moment ... excited me. Now, I don't know if it was the adrenalin running through my system, or her smell, or her vulnerability, but something about that moment got me aroused. Suddenly all I could think about was pushing her onto the bed, ripping off her clothes, and penetrating her. Thrusting into her. Violently making love to her.

Part of me – a very dark part of me – wanted to make her scream.

My mind suddenly turned to how I could make that happen. I wondered how I could get her backwards. How I could get her clothes off. How I could make her turn this scared side of her into passion.

I quickly came up with a plan.

First, I started rubbing her back hard. After a few seconds of that, I grabbed the back of her blouse, untucked it from her pants, then moved my hand to her bare skin. Once our flesh met, I started caressing her back from bra strap to just under her pants. As I did this, I moved my lips from her forehead to her cheeks, kissing each to remove her tears.

While my lips went from cheek to cheek, I backed away slightly to move my free hand to her left side. Massaging there for a moment, I stuck my hand under her blouse, then slowly worked it back and forth, up and down, until it was just touching the bottom of her bra. Within a moment I worked my thumb under it, firmly caressing the underside of her breast. Hearing what I thought was a moan, I moved my lips from her cheeks, intent on kissing her.

But that's when she put it to a stop.

Shoving me back until our eyes met, she gave me an imploring stare.

"Paul, I … I want to go home," she announced.

As if waking from a dream, I stared at her, blinking, not fully understanding her request.

"Can we go home? I want to go home," she repeated. It took me a moment to respond. Most of my brain was … well … elsewhere, in that moment.

"You … want to … go … home?" I managed. Pushing further away from me, she nodded emphatically.

"Why do you …" I started, thinking about the logistics. "But it's, like, the middle of the night, Babe."

"I don't care … this place … this place scares me. I want to go home … where it's safe."

I couldn't help but stare at her like she was speaking Latin, or maybe even Klingon. I just couldn't believe the words coming out of her mouth. In my mind we were making love until the sun came up – which wasn't too, too far off. But in hers …

"Can we? Can we leave?" she asked, then stood. After fixing her bra and re-tucking her blouse, she moved to her travel bag and started packing … as if I'd already said yes.

"But, Babe," I implored. "It's a weekend package. A package we paid for in advance! We just can't …"

I stopped when I realized she wasn't listening to me. Her hands were moving feverishly between counter and bag, floor and bag, desk and bag, picking up everything she'd meticulously laid out.

Watching this, I was stunned in disbelief. I couldn't fathom why she wanted to pass on the lovemaking. Why she wanted to leave.

I wanted to say more to her. I wanted to say something to stop her and make her change her mind. But I couldn't think of anything. Not one thing.

Which, as it turned out, was probably for the best.

As she stopped for a moment, searching the room for more of her paraphernalia, I noticed her hands. They were shaking. Uncontrollably trembling.

Seeing that … that level of fear, I instantly changed my mind.

"Okay," I said, then rose. "Let me gather my things."

Although I didn't want to, I knew I sounded pissed. Because, really, I was. My cock was still rock hard, and adrenalin was still coursing through my veins. How could I not be at least a little upset!?

It didn't take long to gather my gear. I didn't bring much – I never do. Within five minutes we were both packed. And less than a minute later – after calling to have our car brought around – we were out the door.

On the way down to the lobby we passed a few policemen and a couple EMTs with a gurney. We knew where they were headed and why. It didn't slow our pace one bit.

It took a few minutes for our car to arrive. While we waited, I talked to the valet and explained the situation – that we'd gotten an emergency call from our landlord, telling us about a water leak in our apartment and that we needed to head home. I think he believed me, although more than once he stared at Lorie for confirmation. She only seemed to stare past the emergency vehicles off into the lot, waiting for the boat to sanity land to arrive.

After helping Lorie into her side of the car, I made my way around the back and to my door, tipped the valet, then got in. As I reached for the shifter, I paused for a moment as I looked towards a white planter just ahead of our car. Illuminated by the vehicle's headlights, the planter shone like a beacon in the night. A beacon that screamed to be noticed. And, more importantly, not to be hit.

But that's not what I was really focusing on.

Just to the right of the planter, almost imperceptible in the darkness that surrounded us, was a small object lying prone on top of the stones. It only took me a moment to recognize it for what it was, the red of its hooded head helping me along the way. It was a woodpecker – *the* woodpecker, maybe – lying twisted and mangled in the dirt. Its head was cocked at a weird angle, and its wing – the only one that seemed to be attached – was snapped cleanly in half.

Yet, even though the wing was barely connected, the end of it shot upward as if pointing to something in the night's sky.

I'm not sure how long I stared at it – probably for only a second or two. But it felt much longer – way, way longer, if you know what I mean. And if it wasn't for Lorie's shaky hand touching my sleeve, I definitely would've stayed that way. Lost in the vision.

"Can we go?" she asked, seeming to come back to herself, if only a little. I blinked a couple times before moving my eyes to her.

"Yeah … it's just …" I started then paused to look back toward the planter.

"Just getting my bearings, I suppose," I said, then placed the car in drive.

Within a minute we were on the main road. And within an hour we were back home.

CHAPTER 3

The contorted Woodpecker wasn't the only dead bird I saw that following year. It seemed like every time I went out running, I saw one or two of these oddities along my route. Besides the birds, I also noticed many other dead animals here and there. It got to the point that I couldn't go for a jog without jumping over some animal's corpse. As you'd expect, some of these were just due to nature. Just killed and torn apart by other animals. Normal kills I guess you could say. Others, though – the lion's share – were just in the road or on the sidewalk. All just lying there, lifeless, as if they'd just dropped dead there on the spot. I finally got to the point that I decided to workout exclusively on the treadmill we kept in the spare bedroom.

I'd become tired of seeing all the carnage outside … and all the death.

"Today, four more major animal species have been moved from the endangered list to those extinct," the reporter on the TV announced. “These include the Great Gray Owl, the Brown Bear, the Black-Footed Ferret, and the California Condor. Scientists are baffled as to the decline in these and other North American species, and …”

“Did they say the Brown Bear?” Lorie called from the kitchen, interrupting me from hearing the rest. Not that it mattered. I knew the story. It was – it had been – on every media site. Everywhere they talked about the decline in different populations. But no one seemed to know why.

“Yeah, Babe! And the California Condor!” I yelled back, then stood and joined her in the kitchen.

“Did they say how many species that makes this month?” she asked. She was cutting up vegetables and placing them in a pan.

“Not sure. I think they said fifteen? I didn’t have a chance to check the blogs today. I was too busy and …” I let out a sigh “… it’s too damn depressing.”

We stood there for a moment in silent reflection before I asked the usual question. The question that was on everyone’s mind.

“Did you hear anything on the news today? Any explanation?”

She pursed her lips, then said, “The news saying it was something to do with brain chemistry. You know, like disease.”

I nodded then waited. I could tell she was holding something back.

“And?” I inquired. Hearing my beg for info, she hinted a smile.

“Get this. The latest speculation is string theory.”

“String theory?” I asked, narrowing my eyes.

She nodded. "Something to do with magneto … umm … reception. Yeah, Magnetoreception. You know, what birds use the find their way?"

I shrugged. I knew birds used something, some sort of direction finder in their heads. But had no idea what it was called … until then.

"Yeah. Supposedly some scientists think that there's been a change in how gravity works. Or that maybe the Sun has something to do with it."

"So, basically they're still clueless," I stated. She returned a small shrug.

Shifting her concentration back to the meal, she moved the pan to the stove. The crackle of fried foods started almost immediately. I moved to a chair along the counter and watched as she added spices and various other accoutrements to the sizzle.

We were both silent for a few minutes. Not the awkward kind. More like the contemplative type. I'm sure both of us were thinking about conversations we'd had with others. Anything to divert us from the depressing news. Lorie was the first to break the silence.

"I talked to Dad today."

I smirked. This was nothing new. She talked to her dad almost *every* day. He was a widower, and she was his only child. It made them close. Closer since her mom passed away five years earlier.

"Oh yeah? How's he doing today? How was his weekend?"

Lorie waggled her hand. "So, so. He woke with a cold yesterday … and a bit of a sore throat. I told him he should go see his doctor. But I don't think he will."

"Is it time for a visit?" I asked. We normally visited a couple times a year.

She shook me off. "Nah. He says things are *weird down there.* His words. Says we should just stay put until this whole thing blows over."

I nodded and gave her a couple umm-hmms. I knew he was ornery, especially when it came to his freedoms and him taking care of himself. But he was cool. Ex-military like me. And a good dad. Real good. Better than mine had been. I had no fears he'd be fine.

"Oh, and I forgot!" Lorie blurted, bringing me back to Earth. "I talked to Diane."

Knowing Diane was one of the only friends Lorie had, my interest piqued. "Oh? How's she doing? Is she liking the east side?"

Diane, a work friend she'd kept in contact with after losing her job, used to live on the west side, near us, until a few months prior. When her mom got sick – diagnosed with some sort of heart condition – she'd moved to the east side to be with her. To take care of her fulltime.

Lorie sighed. "Not good. She just lost her mom."

"Oh no! When?" I asked.

"The end of last week," she returned, then paused. I knew I had to inquire.

"What happened? Something to do with her heart?"

Lorie shook her head. "Nope. Diane said she passed in the night. She thinks they'll rule it natural causes."

I widened my eyes as she continued. "The initial coroner's report said no damage to the heart. They're waiting on the test to confirm she passed like the others."

I grimaced knowing what she'd meant. There'd been a lot of deaths due to natural causes since the whole thing started. People just dying in their sleep. They'd just closed their eyes and never woke up. And, supposedly there was a certain protein they'd found in the brain that pointed to this condition.

"She says she's planning on having her cremated. At least that's what she thinks."

I raised my eyebrows. "Oh yeah? Nothing ..."

"Formal," she interrupted, shaking her head. "Diane said she called a couple places and they were all booked. She could wait and have a service in a few weeks, but she doesn't want to. It would just be more time, and well ... what's the point!?"

Lorie turned. Our eyes met. We both had the same look. A stunned look. She finally blinked, then tried a smile.

"Where do you want to eat? Here, or ..."

"Living room is fine," I replied, then rose to join her.

Grabbing the plates from her we walked into the living room. After setting them down in our usual spots, I picked up the remote and flipped to the PS4. Activating the Netflix app, I sat down and dug in while I waited for it to boot.

Moving the vegetables from left to right, then back, I searched for scraps of meat. As if there'd be any. Old habits, you know!? Hard to break. I knew there was no meat. Since the prices went up on beef and pork, we'd gone from eating meat nightly to eating vegetables. On occasion we'd splurge and buy burgers or the rare steak, but those were a delicacy. Between her losing her job and the lack of good meat anywhere to be had, we'd done without.

Oh, sure, we did things like tofu and hummus. And fish was still relatively cheap. But how much of that stuff can one eat. Nah, vegetables were good – and abundant. We got by. We got by just fine.

We watched movies for a bit while we ate, then turned on regular TV. We avoided the news and flipped stations to see what we could see … which wasn't much. Since the decline in the population – maybe about twenty or thirty percent less at that point – TV had become sparse. There were movies still being made, sure. And sitcoms, dramas, and the like were still being produced. But it wasn't like it was just two years earlier. They were dull. So many subjects they couldn't touch on – especially the ones dealing with food shortages, population decline, and any kind of death. Mostly. But how many programs about the cosmos and American History can one watch!? Even for me – a bookworm – I had my limits.

We eventually settled on Friends reruns, then sat back and chilled. It was then that we caught up on the day.

"How was work?" Lorie asked. "Anything new with lockers?"

I shrugged, then gave her the bit of news I'd been avoiding. I reached over to the controller, turned down the volume, then pivoted to her. Her face went from smile to rigid in a split second.

"Oh no …" she started. I cut her off.

"Nothing bad … but …"

"But what?" she asked.

I cleared my throat, then said, "Well, the government decided to cancel production of the museum cases we've been making."

She stared at me just waiting for the other pin to drop. I let it fall.

"Which means there'll be layoffs."

"Fuck," she muttered under her breath.

"Yep," I affirmed under mine, then added. "But for now, it looks like mostly plant people. They said they want to retain their engineering staff … for the time being, that is."

Lorie let out a small sigh of relief. Mine matched hers.

"So, now it's just lockers?" she probed. I nodded.

"Lockers, shelving, work benches, specials; anything we can make, really."

She nodded, then focused back on the TV. I righted the volume and got back to the evening's entertainment … as it was.

The following day started out like any other. I woke, showered, drank a cup of coffee with the wife, grabbed the lunch she'd packed for me, then hit the road.

On my hour-long drive to work, I skipped the novel I'd been listening to and instead turned on some Industrial. Aggrotech – the heavier side of Industrial music. One of my favorites.

That morning's selection included FGFC820, Faderhead, Grendel, and a few others for good measure. Stuff that got my head in the game and got my blood flowing. Not that I required it. Engineering lockers, for those of you that don't know, is – was – rather boring. CNC programming. Figuring out how to fit this type of locker into that type of facility. Is there an easier way to produce this shelf? All boring to most minds. But it's what I did, and I liked my job. Sure, it wasn't figuring vectors or thermodynamics, but it had its own highlights. And, more importantly, it came with a decent paycheck. Seemed like kids graduating from college at that time with a four-year mechanical engineering degree didn't want my type of work. And I was totally fine with that.

When I got to work, I parked in my usual spot, then walked in through the front door straight to my desk. And yeah, I waved to a few coworkers along the way. But besides that, I wanted to get down to it. I hated chitchat.

Sitting down at my desk, I pulled out my laptop from my bag, plugged it into the docking station, then proceeded to boot it up. While I waited, I got up, walked to the cafeteria, snatched a mug from the cabinet and poured myself a cup of disgusting but required java.

"Hey Paul!" came a voice from behind me. It was Phil – the guy that ran production control. Kind of a boring sot, with extreme hygiene issues … but I digress.

"Hey Phil! What's new?" I asked – to be polite.

"Did you hear? Isn't that some shit?" he spouted. I just looked at him. I had no idea what he was talking about.

"About the layoffs! They say they're cutting three-quarters of the production guys!"

I shrugged. "Kind of figured they would. Was just talking to the wife about it last …"

He broke in. "Supposedly they're doing it today … like, right now."

Again, this didn't take me by surprise. It was Friday – end of the pay week – and the company, like most, was generally proactive about hirings and firings when it came to the general working class.

The guys working in the plant. Not that an office position was much different. Companies did what they needed to do to survive.

"Well, that sucks," was all I could think of to reply. Because it did. Especially with the state of the world at that moment.

"Yeah it does!" Phil said, then pointed the coffee cup he was holding at the maker. "Do you … uh …"

Taking the hint, I backed away, waved him in for a landing, then turned and proceeded back to my desk – away from the happenings that were about to take place.

It didn't take long, and the walls were thin.

Within five minutes of Phil's announcement, a general grumbling could be heard throughout the office and plant. The grumbling rose at times becoming shouts and expletives as more and more guys were laid off and began talking amongst themselves. I tried my best to ignore it, but it was impossible.

For the next three hours I heard doors slamming and cars peeling out of the parking lot. And each noise made me jump a bit. I felt horrible for those guys, of which I only personally knew a few. The ones I did know were mostly mid-management, but there were a few of the welders and jig operators I'd talked to from time to time. None of them close enough that I'd call them friends.

Phil on the other hand, being the main production guy, knew most of them by name. He knew not only their wives but their children's names as well. I felt almost as bad for him as I did for them. The whole situation sucked.

It was just after lunch, around 1, when I heard a sound I'd never heard come from the plant. A very distinct sound I remembered from my military days.

At first, my brain refused to recognize it. The sounds rang through my head like the earworm of an 80's song. You know what I mean!? The kind of song that, after hearing only a note or two, started running through your mind like a fully charged battery bunny. A song that unlocked distant feelings of the past, although the memories may evade.

And, I gotta say, it wasn't until I heard the first of the screams that my mind put two and two together.

Like being shocked awake from a dream, my eyes went wide, and I shot forward in my chair. Turning toward the shouts, I rose slightly but kept hunched down as I moved to the side of my cubical. Remembering my military training – and every Western I'd watched as a kid – I remained silent as I slowly peeked over the top of my cube. From my vantage point, I couldn't see much. Just a few people quickly moving, running towards the exit.

That was until the door between the plant and office flew open.

The initial thud of the door made me shrink slightly and back away, my eyes still straining to see the cause. The gunshots that followed made me cower from sight, hoping the gunman didn't see me. Praying the gunman didn't notice me.

As the noises moved away, I dared to rise, just enough to see over the cubical wall. About thirty feet away, at the end of the row of cubes, I saw someone in a medium blue button down. The type of shirt worn by the guys in the shop.

As he moved past the cubes, down the corridor – away from me, thankfully – I tried to identify him. But he was someone I didn't know. He was just one of the hundred plus guys that worked there. Just a face in the crowd.

When he was about fifty or sixty feet from me, he raised his rifle – a semi-automatic. He turned until he was facing into one of the half dozen offices along the corridor then fired three rounds. As the gunman turned and proceeded down the hallway, a figure – John from accounting – staggered from his office. His hand was on his head, pressing it, trying to hold it in. Before he made it even two steps from the doorway he crumpled and dropped from sight.

That was the last I ever heard or saw from him.

"Steve!" I heard someone shout from behind me. From the voice I could tell it was Phil.

"Steve, stop! Please stop! You don't need to do this!" Phil yelled as he ran past my cube towards the gunman.

They were the last words he'd ever make.

The gunman – Steve – hearing someone call his name, did a quick one-eighty. Without a flicker of hesitation, he raised the gun to his shoulder and fired two rounds. I'm not sure where the first one went, but the second one found its mark.

There was a wet kerchunk sound the bullet made as it hit Phil square in the forehead. His head suddenly snapped back, then forward. A moment later his brains and blood were spraying in all directions. I watched in slow motion as his body went limp and collapsed like a cloth dropped to the floor.

To this day, I really don't know what saved me. Was it second thoughts by the gunman when he realized whom he'd killed? Or was it something else – some part of the disease infecting the world that caused him to pause? I'm not sure which. All I do know is, as I turned to face Steve, our eyes momentarily locked. In that instant, that fraction of time, I thought for sure I was a dead man. But then, as I waited for the inevitable shot to take off my head, his shoulders drooping slightly. Without a word, he broke eye contact, lowered his rifle, placed the barrel under his chin and fired. Before I could blink, he, like John, staggered. A moment later he was gone.

It took a few seconds to grasp what I'd seen. And it took a couple more before I could react. Sensing that the immediate danger had passed, I left my cube and quickly made my way to Phil's side.

Until that day, I'd never before seen anyone shot. But it, like the milky bird eyes, is something that will forever haunt my vision.

As I leaned down to check Phil's pulse, I mistakenly took in the carnage that the bullet had wrought. The entry wound in the middle of his forehead was maybe only the size of a quarter. The exit wound, however, was bigger than my hand. The entire back of Phil's head was missing, laying in pieces along the walls, windowsills, and corridor.

My stomach suddenly heaved, unconsciously making me close my eyes and take in a deep breath. It was totally the wrong thing to do. The iron smell of his blood mixed with the odor of his vacated bladder and anus instantly overwhelmed me. I don't remember rising. I barely remember throwing up. And everything, and I mean everything after that, became a semiconscious blur.

I remember someone running to my side to check me out and see if I was alright. I think it was a cop, but I really don't know. Whoever it was they handed me off to someone else who helped guide me from the building. Once outside I was passed onto paramedics who checked me out more thoroughly. As they did, someone else – another officer, I think – started questioning me about everything that'd happened. I think I gave them the right information. To this day I'm not sure. About all I remember was being asked if I was okay, and if there was someone they could call. Like an idiot, I shook them off. I simply asked if I could leave. And they let me. I somehow made my way to my car and drove home.

After that … well … after that I don't remember a thing until I woke in my bed near dinnertime. Lorie was there, at my side.

She didn't ask me much, or maybe it was me not wanting to get into details. She simply let me tell her what I needed to, then left me some dinner.

I won't go into what all occurred that night. Not that I think I have to. I will, however, relay this bit of wisdom – what I've gleaned from this and throughout my life.

I think it's weird how the mind works, and what it chooses to remember. It's equally funny, and downright scary at times, what it chooses to forget.

CHAPTER 4

The next day the company called to inform me that the office and plant would be closed until further notice. No news on pay. No news on when they'd reopen. No news on the happenings of the day before.

The person that called wasn't someone I knew. In fact, the person's voice was so monotone, I wondered if they were a person at all. I guessed he was a hire-out from a company where that was their sole job – to call around and give people bad news. I'm sure a lot of bigger companies did this. No personal investment by the person making the call allowed for less information to leak out. Less of the "Nancy, you're friends with the VP, right? What does she know?"

"Hun, what did they say?" Lorie asked the moment I put down the phone. I didn't hold back. I told her the lack of everything.

Her eyes widened. I knew what she was thinking. All I could do was shrug. I knew we'd be alright for a time. Our rent was cheap, and we had a decent amount of money put away. And, of course, we had at least three … no, four credit cards at the time. Each with little to no balance on them. Not to say we acted like we had lots of money coming in. We both knew we'd need to tighten our belts for a while.

The first things to go would be our peripherals – cable, gym memberships, restaurants, bars. Well, not bars. After that though … well … we'd do what needed to be done. If that took taking jobs as dishwashers or dog sitters, we'd do it. We both remembered our college years. We would do whatever it took.

We would most certainly get by.

Lorie looked at me. It was like she was hearing my thoughts. It was then that she added a thought of her own. "Well, there's always Florida."

I tilted my head at her. She had a point.

"You're right. There's nothing holding us here now."

Since we'd gotten together, we'd talked about moving to Florida someday. Her thought was to be closer to her dad. Mine was heat and sunshine. And now … now that was possible. That is, if I was actually out of work.

"But let's not go counting our chickens," I replied dramatically, then lightened. "After all, I might still have a job. I won't know …"

"Unless we stay … got it," she finished. I gave a little nod.

So, Lorie and I waited.

We waited to see if she'd get hired. We waited to see if my office would reopen. We waited to see how long my paycheck and her unemployment would last.

Oh, not saying we didn't keep busy – don't get me wrong. We both had hobbies. I had my music, reading, and working out. She liked to knit, read, and paint. And we had movies and TV programs that kept us entertained at night.

Along with those things, we traveled a bit. Although not to her dad's. He kept shaking us off, if you get the sports analogy. But one weekend we drove to Atlantic City and spent two days on the boardwalk – seeing sights, eating, drinking, having fun, and drinking. Yeah, I know I mentioned it twice. There was a lot of it. A complete boatload.

Another weekend we went to Niagara Falls and toured its wonder. It wasn't our first time there together, but we made it fun as we always did. We went to "Ripley's Believe It or Not!" and a few other spots on the Canadian side. We went on the Maid of the Mist. We even went to the Butterfly Conservatory. Oh sure, I didn't want to. I'm not really into flying bugs. But it was interesting. Well, the parts we could see, that is. As it happened, the mammals weren't the only creatures affected by whatever was going on in the world. Butterflies – and a butt load of other species – were also on the decline. When we got there, there were maybe only a hundred or so butterflies left. We didn't see many. For me, the trip there was really depressing. It just reminded me of all the other bad things happening in the world.

Speaking of which, it turned out my work shooting wasn't the first, nor the last that season. A lot of other companies experienced the same. People getting laid off then shooting up the place. It seemed, as society's population continued its decline, so did its attitude.

There were two distinct reactions to all the death and deterioration in the world: apathy or anger. It was like people just chose to give up, or they chose to riot.

Okay, to say "give up" might be a little harsh. I'm not sure. All I know is that a lot of people just stopped doing ... well ... everything! They stopped going to work. They stopped having kids. They stopped shopping and exercising, and generally going out. It was as if the world had been suddenly placed on pause. Well, for ninety percent of people, that is.

There were others that went ... to put it mildly ... they went bonkers. As the world unwound to a crawl, there was a percentage of people that didn't take it lying down. These people – these Crazies, as they were starting to be called in the media – did the opposite. It was like all of their ambitions, all of their rage, all of their hate and anger at what was going on doubled or tripled in size.

These Crazies caused riots throughout the world. Breaking into stores. Blowing up buildings and government facilities. Killing police. Killing innocent bystanders. Doing whatever their lack of self-control told them to do. If that meant firing an automatic weapon into a crowd or setting a building on fire, they did it. To hell with the consequences. They just wanted to burn the whole thing down.

Oh sure, just like the people that gave up, the Crazies also burned out and died after a while. As their condition got worse, they started hating the daylight. Most wore shades – you know, sunglasses – even at night, and would only go out after sundown to do raids. But, like everyone else, eventually these people also curled up and went to sleep.

The sleep we were all destined to take unless a cure could be found.

It was sometime late summer when we finally got the call. I walked into the living room just as Lorie answered her cell.

"Yes, this is she," she replied, then paused. She nodded her head a couple times, and I heard some um-hmms, then she picked up a piece of paper and wrote something down. After, she said, "Sure, sure. I'll call them right away. Thank you!"

As soon as she hung up, she looked at me. There was fear in her eyes, and a bit of a tear. I started to ask what was wrong. She shook her head, then looked back at the paper and started punching the virtual keys on her cell. I stood frozen. Waiting.

"Yes, this is Lorie Davidson. I understand you have my dad, Bill Richards, at your facility?"

Interest piqued, I moved slightly to get her attention. Without looking at me she held up a single finger. Her 'wait until I have a chance' digit. I knew it too well.

"Uh-huh. Yeah. Well. Okay," she replied to whomever, then paused and picked up the paper again. She wrote down a few things. I strained to see what they were. I couldn't make out jack shit.

I righted when she said, "But you say he's alright, and has been released?"

Obviously, my eyebrows raised. I tried to ask, but that damned digit shot up again.

"Yeah. Uh-huh. Well, okay. Thank you!" she replied then hung up and put down her cell.

This time I didn't wait. I was tired of the mystery. "What's up? Something wrong with Dad?"

Without speaking, she rose off the couch, walked over, and hugged me. I heard sniffles. She was on the verge of tears.

"Is it your dad?" I whispered. I felt her nod. I hugged her tight.

"Is he okay?" I asked, loosening my grip. She backed away far enough to face me. Her eyes were wet. I was about to offer my shirt up so she could dry them. I didn't have a chance. She buried her face in my shoulder and dried her eyes one at a time. She eventually backed away again.

"Yeah ... he will be. He had a ... a problem. With his heart. They said he'll be alright. They have him in a step-down unit."

"Was it a heart attack?" I asked. She shook her head.

"Was it ..."

"They said his heart stopped," she replied, gulping back a tear on the words "heart" and "stopped." My own heart misfired hearing the distraught sound in her voice.

I latched onto her shoulders. Steadying her. Steadying myself.

"But he's okay? For sure?" I asked. She nodded – not as strongly as the first time.

"They ... umm ..." she paused. "They put him on some meds to help the irregularity they were hearing. They said it's the best they can do for now."

"Best they can do?" I asked, narrowing my eyes. "What does that even mean? The best they can do?"

"They said that the condition might be due to the umm ... the chemical thing."

I scrunched my mouth, moving it to bite the inside of my cheek. It was something I did when I was in contemplation mode.

I knew what she was talking about, though. You probably do too. It was what was ever going on in the world. The chemicals in his brain were off, and that was their best way of fixing it at the moment.

"The doctor … well physician's assistant I talked to … said they might have to put in a pacemaker. But they have a shortage right now."

"A shortage?" I repeated. She nodded.

"She said there's a shortage due to widespread failures."

"Failures? What, bad batches?" I queried. She shrugged.

"Dunno. All she said was there's a huge line for them right now. But with his age and all … she said all they can do is give him pills and make sure he keeps active."

I thought about this for a moment. That's all it took. She didn't have to say another word.

"So, when do you want to leave?"

Lorie looked at me, surprised.

I narrowed my eyes at her. "Like you'd actually have to ask. There is literally nothing holding us here. And you should be with him. We should be with him. He needs us right now."

She nodded, and tears started welling again. Lorie pushed away from me and headed to the end table – and the tissues. I silently watched as she dabbed at her eyes.

Silent, because I was already making plans.

"When *can* we leave?" she asked. I motioned for her to join me in the kitchen. I talked as we walked.

"We could leave tonight, but it'd probably be best if we wait until morning."

She nodded. I made a beeline for the fridge – and the beer. I grabbed one for both of us, then popped one and handed it to her. She didn't want to take it at first.

"For your nerves," I insisted. She quickly acquiesced.

We clinked bottles, then moved back towards the living room. Once seated, we put together a quick plan of action. When we were done, something occurred to me.

"By the way, who was the first call?"

"What's that?" she asked, confused.

"The first phone call. Who did you talk to before the hospital?"

"Oh!" she blurted, getting it. "That was Joan, Dad's neighbor. She called to let me know where they took him. She said she figured …"

"He wouldn't call on his own," I finished for her. I wanted to substitute "He" with "The stubborn bastard," but didn't.

When we'd finished our beers, we got up and started working our plan. The prep work, anyway. We would get a good night's sleep tonight, then … then we would hit the road early.

CHAPTER 5

We woke just after dawn. We both drank a cup of coffee as we started our last day in our first dwelling together.

It took us about a half hour to load the car. We packed it with everything we could think of. Clothes for an extended stay. Toiletries. Bottles of water and a cooler for food. Hot dogs, cheese, and the like. We also seized our computers and every charging cord known to man and shoved them into backpacks. Obviously, we didn't know how soon we'd be back.

After packing all that, we packed some blankets and pillows. When all those were loaded, we went back through the apartment and looked for last-minute items. That's when an idea occurred to me. We'd totally missed something.

Grabbing an accent pillow from the couch, I unzipped its back and tore out the stuffing.

"What are you doing?" Lorie asked, looking at me like I was mad. Mad as a Hatter, I knew. I just held up a finger to silence her, then gestured for her to follow me.

Walking into the bedroom, I opened the top drawer of my dresser, pulled out one of my two jewelry cases and placed it on top. I opened it up, perused its contents, then closed it. After surveying the pillow I'd brought with me for size, I stuffed the jewelry box into it. Placing the pillow down, I picked up the second case then turned to look at Lorie. She was already into the plan and her dresser.

After perusing and stuffing the second case into the pillow, I closed the drawer then walked across the room to join Lorie. She had two piles sitting on top of her dresser.

"We can take those," she stated, pointing at the pile to her left.

"These … these can stay," she stated reluctantly about the pile to her right.

Without another word, I loaded up the pillow. It was almost the perfect size. When we were finished, I laid it on the bed, bottom up, then walked to the bathroom and grabbed a couple towels. These I packed all around our valuables. When I was done, the pillow felt hard, but normal. Normal enough so that if someone broke into our car, they'd only think it was what it appeared to be. At least that's what I hoped.

Feeling set, Lorie and I walked to the doorway of our bedroom headed for the foyer and apartment door. When I reached the doorway, I stopped suddenly, turned, and headed back to my closet. Opening the bi-folding doors, I reached up to the top shelf and pulled down the last thing I thought we'd need.

"Why are you taking that?" Lorie asked, nodding towards the small plastic lockbox I was holding. I looked down at it, then back at her. I felt a little ashamed.

"Well … I … umm," I stuttered, searching for the best answer. Nothing came to mind immediately besides the original reason I'd purchased it. For protection. Home protection.

But Lorie hated guns. And she hated that I – we – owned one.

And, just so you know, I've never been one of those end-of-the-world nuts. You know the type; you see them in movies all the time. The guy who builds a bunker in his backyard. The kind of a bunker with steel walls and a vault door like you'd see in a bank. The kind of bunker one builds in case a nuclear bomb is ever dropped. A fall-out shelter. A place stocked with enough food, water, and ammo to survive a year or three. Then, after it's finished, he has drills with his family, teaching them the ins and outs of the place.

No, I've never been that type of guy. But I am the type of guy that always needs to be prepared.

To give you a little background on me, I was in the military, as I mentioned. Basic four-year stint. Oh, sure, I was a clerk/typist. But clerks are run through Basic just like the next guy. We were taught how to fight, we were taught how to evade, and we were taught how to shoot a variety of weapons.

My favorite was the M-16, but I was just as proficient with a 9mm. And after I got out of the military – some years after, that is – I'd bought a 9. Just for protection – after Lorie and I started living together. And, no, not protection *from* her. Although she *could* be scary at times.

Like I hinted, Lorie didn't like it around – the sight of it – so I kept it in a locked box in the back of the closet. I only took it out every now and then if I thought it needed cleaning.

It took me a minute to think of an excuse. When it came to me I almost smiled.

"Remember … your dad?"

She narrowed her eyes at me.

I cleared my throat. "He wanted to look at it last time he was here. Figured I'd take it to show him."

Okay, just so you know, I went this route for two reasons. One, her dad was ex-military. And two, he also owned guns. A shotgun and an AR-15 – the civilian version of the military M-16. If it was okay for him to own, why not me!? I'd made that point when I bought the 9mm. But, apparently, that didn't matter. What was good for the goose wasn't always good for the gander. Me being said bird, in case you wondered.

My stolid eyes didn't do the trick. She gave me a look. A disappointed look. A look that told me the jig was up. I caved almost instantly.

"Alright! I'm bringing it as a *just in case*, okay!? Strange shit is going on out there. I think we need to be prepared."

I waited for a rebuttal. For the "you know how I feel about guns" spiel. But none came. Lorie simply straightened, gave me a nod, then turned and walked out the door. I followed right after her.

It was just before 11 a.m. when I hopped behind the wheel, and we said our goodbyes to Cleveland.

Eleven was much later than I wanted, but you know how things go. You think you'll get up by five and make it out the door at eight. But, after cleaning, throwing out trash, and debating what you'll take, it's just before noon. Regardless though, before lunch we were finally Florida bound.

From Cleveland to Fort Myers was about a nineteen-hour drive. That is if you only stopped for food and gas. That included no sleep, which was our intent. Oh sure, we'd take turns at driving. Let one drive while the other rested. But that was it. We figured the quicker we got there, the better off we'd be.

And that's kind of how it went. Sort of.

There were two major considerations we hadn't figured in due to the fact that, well, we didn't know about them. Those were who and what was still open for business.

Now, if you remember the days before all this stuff went on – that stuff being all the major closings due to the plummet in the population – you'll remember how it was to take a trip across the country. Particularly through the Midwest and southern states. It pretty much went like this: city, nothing, nothing, nothing, city. Rinse, dry, and repeat. Of course, this didn't include the lovely orange barrels every few miles. But it was what it was.

Having made the trip before, we thought we knew what to expect. Down I-77 South through Cleveland, Akron, and Canton. See nothing for a while until we hit New Philadelphia, then it was back to nothing. Eventually you'd come to Cambridge, then again, nothing, nothing, and more nothing until you hit the West Virginia border. Along the way we'd see small rest areas or exits advertising gas and food. Places to stop if we needed a break.

That being said, the first thing we did – to avoid an early stop – was to fill the tank. The second – and more important in my book – was to select the proper music for the drive. After all, if I was going to stay awake for the next nineteen hours, I needed some decent tunes.

Being the driver, it was my pick. That's how we rolled – some pun intended.

Still sitting at the pump, I quickly scrolled through my options. I had several, and I mean several, playlists to choose from.

In case I didn't mention, I had a veritable plethora of music stored on both my iPhone and ProBook. Somewhere in the neighborhood of six thousand tracks, give or take a few. These tracks ranged from classical to rock to industrial to metal. Well, everything really. I even had some country along with some opera and comedy … oh, and a few show tunes. I mean, who doesn't like to hear *I Am the Very Model of a Modern Major General* every now and then!? If you haven't heard it, it's a must in my opinion.

Anyway, I had hundreds of these songs arranged into several Playlists, and it didn't take me long to choose. I ended up selecting Playlist "Medium-2" to start the drive.

"Medium-2" contained about four plus hours of rock mixed with a little metal and industrial. The best of the 90's and 2000's rock, with a few 80's and newer tracks to break up the monotony. And one special tune to really start us out.

As soon as The Ramones *Blitzkrieg Bop* started, I put the car in drive, smiled at Lorie, then hit the road. It took about the length of the song to make it to I-77. Yeah, we lived that close.

We drove south along our usual route, stopping about two hours out for a quick pee-break, then drove for another two hours.

Nothing seemed out of the ordinary, really. Except for maybe the utter lack of traffic and an overabundance of abandoned cars along the shoulders of the road.

Nothing, that is, until we crossed over into West Virginia. *That* is the point when things moved onto the bizarre.

“Hey, check that out,” Lorie said, pointing to a billboard just south of Parkersburg. It was an ad for The Church of God in Mineralwells, just south of our location. And no, I didn’t get the name wrong. It’s an actual place. Look at the map on the wall if you have any doubt. Don’t worry, I’ll wait while you do.

You good now? Good! Fantastic!

Anyway, the billboard which once had shown a multi-race androgynous picture of Jesus with his arms spread wide to entice, now sported a host of colorful graffiti. And not just the normal graffiti one would see on a highway or inner-city transit. No, this one displayed a Jesus that now held firing pistols in each hand. Each bullet discharged from these had made contact with their marks. A black man to the left, and an Asian man to his right.

To go along with this display of marksmanship were two bubbles over his head. The first one stated that, in no uncertain terms, no lives mattered. And the other said, and I quote, “Cum to Fucking Jesus Motherfuckers.”

Just like that.

Because I was driving, the rest of the sign was pretty much a blur. All I could make out was a bunch of racial and antisemitic hate speech with a little misogyny thrown in for good measure.

I had no words for the artistry I witnessed. Lorie on the other hand … she had quite a bit.

"What the fuck is wrong with people!?"

I could only shake my head.

"I mean, I'm no bible thumper, but who in the actual fuck ..." She continued ... she was on a roll.

"And how do they let that ... that ..." she said. I just slowly nodded.

"Why hasn't anyone torn that down?" she asked, glaring at me like I had all the answers. I had none. She kept staring so I said the only thing that popped into my mind.

"Well, at least it doesn't say Trump 2020."

She tried to say ... something. I'm not sure what. All that came out was a humph. She looked away as she pivoted in her seat and crossed her arms. I knew I'd stepped over the line. Apparently, she was dead serious about it ... and I'd just shit the bed.

"Do you think we should call someone about it?" I asked in a somber and thoughtful tone. It calmed her a little. Without waiting for a verbal response, I picked up my phone from the center console and dialed 911.

And ... nothing happened.

I waited for the phone to connect to something – an officer, an answering service, voicemail – but nothing came through. Then I realized I wasn't hearing anything at all, so I looked at my phone. It showed zero bars.

"Babe, I've got no service. How's about you?" I asked, waggling my cell. I knew she had a different service provider. It was possible her provider had better reach into the boonies.

Lorie picked up her phone and activated it. She stared in disbelief.

"Shows I'm out of range," she said. I looked over. She was scrolling through her own. Every couple seconds she'd narrow her eyes, then shake her head.

"We must be in a dead zone," I said, almost matter-of-factly.

She pushed back with, "Do you remember any dead zones last time we came through? Any time we've come through here?"

I just shrugged. I knew she was right on all counts. We'd been down that way before. More than a few times. We'd never experienced any outages along this route.

"Maybe the local cell towers are out?" I replied, then looked at her. She returned a puzzled and uneasy gaze. I didn't know how to respond to this except to maybe remind her there were cell towers every couple miles, and our services would probably be restored any second.

I never had a chance to say this, though. I didn't even have a chance to open my mouth.

No sooner did the word "out" leave my mouth came a loud thump towards the back end of the car. Lorie heard it as well. Her face instantly changed from one of worry, to one of straight out fear.

"What was that?" she blurted. I was about to say "I don't know" when I heard a pop sound from somewhere behind.

"Was that a blowout?" Lorie asked, her head looking all around the car.

I felt the steering wheel. There wasn't any jiggling or jerking that would denote we'd lost a tire. Believe me, I'd lost one before on the highway. It was nothing like that.

I turned down the radio to see if maybe there was something wrong with the engine or if there was any perceivable rattling. But nothing felt or sounded out of the ordinary.

Then, like a whisper from someone just over my left shoulder, a noise – familiar and chilling – started to build. It was low at first, barely audible. But eventually the noise became a resounding blare.

I looked in the rear-view mirror. About one-hundred yards back I saw two cars come over a hill. The first was a black sports car. A Charger or Challenger – I'm not sure which. I always get those two confused. I still do to this day.

The second was one I'd notice anywhere. Not from the make or model, but from the flashing and strobing lights. It was a State Police car. It was in close pursuit of the lead vehicle. Both were speeding. So fast, in fact, that I barely had a chance to pull to the right lane before both shot by me. They must have been doing at least a hundred twenty, considering how quickly they approached then shot by.

It was then that the sounds caught up with the speed. Coming from the first car – the perp car – I could have sworn I heard a laughing, almost cackling, emanating from it. It could have been my imagination, though. Or maybe it was the remembrance of some movie I'd watched. It could have been, but I doubt it. Not that it mattered which. The next sound I heard was a familiar one. It was one that sent chills up my spine.

It was the report of a handgun.

The second I heard it time seemed to suddenly slow to a crawl. I watched on as the two vehicles, moving left and right on the highway, sent exchanges of gunfire at each other.

"Paul! Stop!" Lorie screamed, momentarily breaking me from the battle. My eyes darted to meet hers.

"Please stop! Please stop!" she screamed again. I nailed the brakes and swerved toward the shoulder in response. It was lucky thing I did. Another police car shot by us in hot pursuit of the others, only missing us by a few feet.

The moment we stopped, I placed the car in park, then continued my gawp of the chase. Not that I could see a whole lot. The first two cars appeared to be a mile ahead. They were visible, sure, but just barely.

Barely, that is, until I saw the perp car swerve to the right. A moment later I saw a flash. Then an eruption of fire. We both jumped when we heard the inevitable explosion.

"Oh my God!" Lorie cried in horror. Her hand shot to her mouth as if to keep the terror from escaping.

I had no words of my own. Mine had been taken away weeks before. This was all too familiar. The violence of the bar was now on the street before us.

Lorie and I both turned when we heard another police vehicle come from behind. A moment later a fourth and fifth joined the mix.

As we watched the vehicles speed away from us, something suddenly changed in me. Call it a culmination of events. Call it an overload or divine inspiration. I'm not sure really what. All I knew was something shifted in me. A new mindset that told me ...

"We need to get the hell out of here. You good?" I asked, looking toward her seatbelt and mood.

"Shouldn't we ..."

"Wait?" I asked, cutting her off. "No. We need to leave … we need to leave now."

I didn't wait for an argument. I simply looked over my left shoulder, put the car back in drive, and punched the accelerator.

Stone spat from under the car as we fishtailed forward. Eventually all the wheels found asphalt. I kept my foot on the accelerator until the car hit seventy, then I moved it left.

I slowed a little as we passed the scene of the accident, but not much. Damn the consequences if they cared. They didn't, though. They – the police – had other issues to deal with.

"Should we …" Lorie started. I just shook my head. She quieted and sat back. Neither one of us spoke again until we saw the next sign for Charleston, a sign depicting normalcy.

A sign pointing toward humanity.

We were a few miles outside of Charleston – and at the end of my first playlist – when we reached the first opened gas station. They were open, but not fully. At least not as fully as I would've liked.

After popping the door to the tank, I got out and walked towards the back of the car. It wasn't until I rounded the back that I saw the sign. The posted note that all drivers dreaded to see.

The one that reads, "Cash Only Please Pay Inside."

"Well, fuck," I muttered aloud, then took a step back like I'd just seen a lump of shit. The situation certainly smelled.

I looked between the other pumps hoping one of those would take credit. I was out of luck. All the others had the same note attached.

I took in deep calming breath, then let it out while I searched for my wallet. It revealed I had five Twenties, and a few singles. I mentally let out a sigh of relief.

After filling the tank – a whopping $32.37 worth of gas – I closed it up then walked towards the station. An older gentleman – an old white guy with a weary look in his eyes – waved me over towards the pay window. He smiled as I approached. He was the first to speak.

"Well, hello dar, Sah! You are the faust customa I'z seen today!"

I stared at him and the circular speaker between us for a moment. His Southern drawl was thick, and it took me a second or two for the words to hit the translation center of my brain.

"Hi," I awkwardly responded as I slid two of my Twenties under the inch-thick glass. He took them, then opened his cash drawer as he replied.

"So sorry fo da cash only. Our credit caud machines have been down fo da last few days."

"It's no problem," I said. The only response I could think of. The only polite one, that is.

"Where's ya headed?" the gentleman asked. He seemed genuinely concerned.

"South … to Florida," I replied, narrowing my eyes slightly.

He let out a huff and shook his head. "Well why ya wanna head down dat way, Sah?"

It kind of felt like a rude question, but I smiled and answered anyway. "We have family down that way."

He gave a small nod then returned my change. My brain's translation center started working overtime at what came next.

"I wishes ya luck, Sah. My brutha …" brother "… owns anatha …" another "… station down near Chalat …" Charlotte. "He says it ain't much betta …" better "… down in his neck a da …" of the "… woods."

Hearing this, I stared at him, confused. "Is there something going on there? Something I should know about?"

His eyes went wide. "Haven't ya hahd …" heard "… about da Sauge?"

I blinked a few times, trying to reconcile jargon with terminology.

"The … The Surge?" I asked, glaring at him to see if I'd gotten it right. He nodded emphatically.

"Yes, Sah. That's what dey's callin' it on da tee vee. Da Sauge. People's goin' bat shit crazy down heya. All ova da Sauth. And all dem electronics is actin' squarrelly."

I assumed he meant squirrelly. And based on what we'd seen an hour or so before, I had to agree. I knew it wasn't just the South. But that was the first time I'd heard the cause called The Surge.

Wanting to get back on the road – and not wanting to draw out the conversation any longer than required – I offered a polite thanks, wished him good tidings, then headed back to my car. As I passed by the back end of it – you know, to make sure I'd closed the tank door, because, well, I hate to admit it, but I've left it open before – I noticed something strange in the bumper. About midway to the right towards the passenger side was something I'd never noticed before. Leaning down, I inspected the spot. Sure as shit, there, plain as day, was a hole about the size of my ring finger. A hole that cut clean through the bumper.

Lowering to my haunches, I placed my pinky in and around the puncture, trying to figure out what I could have possibly backed into. And it took me a good ten seconds to put two and two together.

The moment that realization hit home a cold chill raced through my entire body. That puncture wasn't formed by something I'd hit. That sucker was caused by something that'd hit me. The bang we'd heard hours before had caused this. I was sure of it. And my face went white as a million thoughts suddenly jumped into my head.

What if the bullet had been a little more north or south? What if it'd hit the gas tank? And what if it was even higher? Would it have hit me or Lorie?

The greatest question of these was obvious. *What the hell was I going to tell Lorie?* I was sure she'd notice the hole eventually. If not that day, it'd be soon.

Fuck, man, my brain screamed. *What the actual fuck should I say?*

Standing, I took a calming breath. Then another. After a small nod, I walked to the driver's side door. I was buffeted with questions the moment I closed the door behind me.

The queries, "What's up? What took so long? And what were you checking out at the back of the car?" smacked me in the face as soon as we were sealed in. I turned to her and our eyes met. She was glaring at me as if I'd just hit on another woman. I felt a smirk coming on … but held it back.

"Their card readers are down. I had to pay cash," I replied with a shrug.

"And the back of the car?" she asked, continuing her glower.

I tried to take a noticeable gulp. I'm not sure she even noticed.

"Well, yeah. About that. I, umm, forgot to mention it, but … a … the other day I backed into something. I didn't notice the damage it made until now."

"What damage? I haven't seen damage," she retorted. I gave another shrug.

"It's not much … a hole. The thing I backed into must've had a bolt sticking out of it. It's barely noticeable, though. Probably why you didn't see it."

She narrowed her eyes, glaring at me. "Thing? What thing?"

"It was … a … tractor kind of thing … being towed by a truck. It was low and hard to see. That's why I must've hit it," I replied, trying to sound truthful.

For a moment she just looked at me in disbelief. I took in another deep breath, put the car in gear then stepped on the gas. She sat back and waited. I didn't say anything else until we were safely back on the highway. When I did, I went back to the original topic.

"By the way, the guy at the gas station back there said his readers were down because of something he was calling The Surge. Says he heard the name on TV or some such."

She repeated my last words to make sure she understood me. She did that a lot, come to think of it. I nodded and was about to ask her to look it up. But there was no need.

"I'm on it," she blurted. I glanced over to see she was on her 'internet restored' phone. I waited patiently – or tried to. I wanted to start the next playlist – the one entitled "Industrial" that held about three hours of EBM, Goth, and Aggrotech hits. At least, the songs I considered hits. A lot of them were driving tunes. You know, pounding. Tunes that kept my blood pumping and heart thumping.

Oops … sorry about that. Now that I rethink that statement, it sounds way corny.

"Yep. Says it right here," Lorie stated. She cleared her throat dramatically before she continued.

"The Shift, or The Surge, as some have come to call it, started several months ago after the Sun quote end quote flipped its magnetic field. Although a seemingly normal occurrence, blah blah blah," she added for effect. "Occurring once every eleven years on average, blah blah blah …" she skipped some more, eventually coming to a "Ah! Here it is. This time, unlike the previous, the sun's magnetic field experienced a surge. Not unlike a solar flare, blah blah blah," she said again. Yeah, the blah, blah, blahs were annoying. I mean, she could've just read the entire piece. I still had the music down. And her voice was lovely. She used to sing in a choir, you know. Used to … but that was a lifetime ago.

Anyway, she went on to read, "Scientists are still baffled as to the cause of the magnetic change."

She paused then, reading ahead a little before continuing. "It says that the field shift and following surge changed the earth's magnetic field."

She paused again, then added, "What most scientists thought was impossible, the shift in the Sun's magnetic field has caused a disruption in the Earth's, leading to widespread brownouts, blackouts, loss of cellular communication, and ..."

Her voice then picked up a more serious tone. "Paul, you might want to hear this."

I looked at her and gave a nod to let her know she had my full attention. Or at least as much attention as I could spare from the road.

"Triggering eradicate behavior in some humans," she said, then skimmed a little before saying, "activating, or stimulating, the adrenal medulla, producing what is commonly known as the Fight or Flight response."

She quieted as she read on. Well, not quieted. She was actually mumbling as she read. Nothing discernable to the ear, though.

A minute later she pressed the power button on her phone and placed it in her lap. I looked over to see she was blankly staring out the window.

"Babe, what's up?" I asked. I waited while she gathered her thoughts. The moment I started to ask again she spoke up.

"It … it says that The Surge is the cause of the decline in animal populations …" she said, then hesitated before she finished. "… and in people. People's hearts … their entire systems … are just … stopping."

That statement hit home. Her dad's heart had stopped in just that way. It didn't take a genius to know what she was thinking. I looked at the speedometer. We were going seventy-nine in a seventy. With very little thought I pumped that shit up to ninety.

CHAPTER 6

We hauled balls through the rest of West Virginia and the Carolinas, only stopping once in Charlotte for a bio break and fill-up. We also stopped in Savannah, Georgia, to top off the tank, then didn't stop again until we hit Tampa. All in all, it took us just under seventeen hours from door to door. A record for us. I guess when you cut out all the sightseeing and food smashing you normally do on vacation, you drop a bunch of time! Who knew!?

It was still dark – around 4 a.m. – when we pulled in her dad's drive. Our entry activating the garage door security light. After putting the car in park, I turned off the engine then looked at Lorie.

"We're heeeere," I said softly, trying to sound like that old TV quote. I don't remember which show it was from. It's probably from a dozen of them.

Lorie, who'd been sleeping since our short break in Savannah, yawned, stretched, then looked at me groggily.

"Already?" she asked – an attempt at humor. I was really too tired to deal with jokes.

"Yeah," I nodded. "Now what?"

It took her a moment for the "ask" to hit home. She finally blinked at me and said, "Now what, what?"

I pointed to the time on the dash. Again, it took a moment for comprehension to rise.

"Oh," she uttered, then paused to stare at the lights on the garage. A moment later she reached down, picked up her purse, stuck her hand in it, searched for a second or two, then withdrew it. In her hand she held a set of keys.

With a nod, we exited the car and walked to her dad's front door. We stood there for a moment while she fumbled looking for the right key. But eventually she found gold. Not that it mattered, though. As she moved forward to place the key in the lock, the door suddenly opened. A split second later there was a muzzle pointed squarely in my face.

"Hi Daddy!" Lorie spouted, as if a gun pointing at her husband was no big deal.

"Pumpkin?" he replied questioningly – and definitely less enthusiastically than his daughter.

After looking between the two of us, he asked, "What are you two doing here?"

Lorie let out a small huff, instantly sounding like a teenage schoolgirl.

"Daddy! I told you we were coming! Remember? I called you yesterday!"

He took in a slow breath then let it out. "Let me rephrase. What are you two doing here … at this hour?"

"I told you we might be early," she stated, but he didn't reply. He also didn't lower the weapon. Instead he kept it trained on my forehead. I think he was trying to be funny. You know, in that creepy father-in-law sort of way.

"Daddy!?" Lorie spouted, rolling her eyes. Her dad *finally* lowered the AR-15. The moment the muzzle was pointed at the ground, she walked over and hugged him. He hugged back, sort of. I swear his burning gaze never left me.

Now, if you're a married man, you may know of what I speak. Her dad and I … umm … respected each other. As in to say, he tolerated me, and I kept things civil.

From the time I'd first been introduced to Mr. William Richards, he'd been … what do you say … standoffish? Maybe not one-hundred percent on Team Paulie. I could tell, sort of, that I was not his first choice for a son-in-law. Oh, I'm sure I was on the list. I was ex-military, I had a college education, and I made a decent wage. But, no matter how good I was or friendly I'd be, I would forever be the guy that was banging his one and only daughter.

So, if you can get that – if you can wrap your head around that thought – you'll know the relationship we had.

When they released one another, Lorie looked at me and asked, "Hun, can you get our things from the car?"

She didn't wait for an answer. The two turned and walked into the house. I silently turned and walked back to the car as tasked.

It took three or four trips to bring everything into the house. Luckily the room I had to move the things to – Lorie's old bedroom – was on the first floor.

When I was finished, I joined the two in the kitchen. Her dad had started making eggs. It looked like there was enough for three – barely.

"All set," I announced as I headed for the counter and the coffee. As I passed her dad, I uttered a fond, "How ya doing, Bill?"

He gave a nod and returned a "Paul."

After grabbing some java, I walked over to the kitchen's center island and took the chair to Lorie's right – the spot without the coffee cup in front of it.

"So, I hear you two want to stay with me a while?" her dad asked. I felt him glare at me out of the corner of his eye. "I thought you guys were good on money?"

"Daddy! We are! But we want to be here with *you*! To take care of you!" Lorie answered, hedging off a potential argument. She was good at that. I remained silent … for the most part.

"Be here with *me*?" he asked, sounding put out. "Why would you want to do that!? I'm doing just fine!"

"You are *not* doing fine!" she replied. "You just got out of the hospital, and you know what the doctor said!"

He let out a huff. "He said I have a heart irregularity. That's all. No cause for alarm."

"He said you might need a pacemaker," she retorted.

"Might!" he reiterated. He let out another huff.

"Might … you're right. But we want to be here just in case they decide you do," she said.

Bill moved the pan of eggs off the stove then scooped some onto two waiting plates. After, he turned to me, gave a nod, and held up the pan.

"Yes, please," I returned.

Bill got another plate from a cabinet near the stove then emptied the rest of the eggs onto it. After placing the pan in the sink, he picked up two of the plates, placing one in front of Lorie and the other where he'd been sitting. He then turned, grabbed the remaining plate and placed it in front of me. We both waited until he sat and started on his own before we took a bite. Out of respect – not because we thought he'd poisoned us. That was still an option, though.

After a couple forkfuls, something dawned on me. "Hey, Hun. If your dad has a heart condition, should we be eating eggs?"

She didn't have a chance to answer.

"They're the heart healthy ones!" Bill stated loudly, holding up a forkful and glaring at me. "Got any other questions?"

I shrugged and looked at Lorie. She looked like someone caught between a rock and a hard place. Because, really, she was.

Bill didn't wait for a response. He shoved the fork into his mouth then went for more. I did the same – and kept my mouth shut pretty much the rest of that day.

And that's how life went for the next few months. Bill making comments about us freeloading off him – although we'd pretty much paid all the bills since day one. Bill staring at me as if I was an alien or devil come to steal his soul – or, more so, his daughter's virtue. And Bill doing everything bad for himself that he could think of.

But I knew that was his way. Just like him telling us the eggs were heart healthy. I knew they weren't the minute he glanced over his shoulder. That, and the look of the eggs themselves. The eggs actually looked good. Not like the heart healthy ones. They generally looked and tasted synthetic to me. Worse than Army eggs. And that's not saying much.

Anyway, getting back to it, as the weeks passed, the world really started going to shit. Sorry if that sounds harsh. Then again, maybe it's not harsh enough. I mean, here we were, sitting back watching the decline – the collapse, really – of society.

By the onset of Winter, the population had dwindled severely. I don't remember exact numbers, but if I had to hazard a guess, I'd say it was down to maybe fifty percent of what it was at its peak. Oh, sure, that still left about four billion people alive in the world. But think about it. In the space of less than a year, around half of the people on the planet were gone. Just gone! And they estimated that number might be down to one billion within another six months.

As it happened to turn out, it was actually way less.

I remember hearing about mass graves being built in some countries. While others … well … others just left people to rot. I remember hearing about a spot in the UK where the whole neighborhood was found dead, and the place was torched, kind of like a huge funeral pyre. I'm sure there were more like that, but news was spotty at best.

I know, I know. I'm probably preaching to the choir about all this. You remember what happened. But to me, it still seems fresh. Especially considering what was soon to follow in the US.

Christmas that year was bleak, but we made the most of it. Although Amazon had pretty much stopped delivering, we were still able to find some stuff online to buy. It helped we were near a few major cities – places within driving distance. Even though a lot of local shops and grocery stores had shut down, there were still a few open. Almost none of those accepted credit cards anymore. The system had become too unreliable … and practically irrelevant.

If you ever had a chance to watch the movie Mad Max, especially the part at the end, I'm sure you'll understand. With the spotty behavior of the internet and electronics, a lot of places were only accepting cash. And some … well … some only accepted bartered items.

I remember the first time I walked into a store that was only using the barter system. Man, it was way strange. It was a small grocery store that I'd been sent to, and I was just trying to pick up some fruit.

After picking up a dozen oranges and apples, I walked up to the counter and laid them down. The man behind the counter gave me a smile and an uptick of his chin.

"Name?" he asked. I didn't think it mattered, but I told him anyway.

The gentleman was holding a clipboard. On it was a list of names. He looked the list up and down, then asked, "Did you say Paul Davidson?"

I nodded. He looked it over again.

"You're not on the list," he stated, looking for recognition. I shrugged.

He placed down the clipboard. "So, whatcha got?"

I thought he was referring to what I'd just set in front of him. I gestured to them.

"Twelve apples and twelve oranges. That's it."

His eyes narrowed a bit and his smile increased.

"No, I mean, whatcha got? To trade, you know," he replied then pointed at his cash register.

I'm sure my jaw dropped when I read it. I'd never seen anything like it in my life. Taped over the register was a sign that said in huge letters:

NO CASH OR CREDIT ACCEPTED!

TRADE ONLY!

Just below it was a smaller sign that read:

IN NEED OF:

CARROTS, TOMATOES, CELERY, ONIONS

OTHER VARIOUS PRODUCE ALSO ACCEPTED

OTHER FORMS OF TRADE NEGOTIABLE

As you can imagine, I was dumbfounded. I read and reread the signs probably four times before I looked back at the man. His look hadn't changed. He was not joking. I couldn't help but call him out on it, though.

"Are you serious?"

He gave a nod. I continued my stare for a moment, then looked down at the packages of fruit. Each was labeled with a price. He noticed my stare.

"Yeah, those are for store credit."

"Store credit?" I asked. He let out a small laugh.

"You're new here, aren't ya?"

I nodded, but I wasn't. I'd shopped there before. In the past. You know, before the shitastic year.

"Ah, well, here's how it works," he said, then paused. A moment later he nodded. "Think about it like a Sears credit card."

He looked at me for acknowledgment. He found it in my eyes.

"When you bring in a trade, we appraise it, then issue store credit. We put the amount with your name on the list," he gestured down to the clipboard.

"As you come in and buy things, we deduct from the amount. When you bring in trade items, we add. Get it?"

I thought about it for a moment, then gave a nod.

"Good," he stated, then asked again, "So, do you have anything to trade?"

"I don't ..." I started, unconsciously searching my pockets for the secret stash of carrots I kept at the bottom. He saw my distress when I realized they weren't there.

"We also accept items that aren't edible."

I met his eyes, not understanding at first. Then I saw where his eyes were focused. They were fixed on the platinum cross I had on a silver chain. I reached for it. He gave a nod.

"It doesn't have to be that, of course," he stated. "Just something like that. You know, something we can use as trade."

I quickly checked my personal inventory. I couldn't think of anything I had that I wanted to give up. I thought about leaving the store and heading to someplace that would accept cash. But those were all out of the way. And gas was starting to become an expensive commodity. I could ride a bike back here if I needed to.

These, and a dozen other thoughts rapidly ran through my brain. I quickly came to a conclusion. I reached up, took off the necklace, weighed it in my hand, then passed it to him.

"How much for this?"

The gentleman weighed it in his hand, same as me, then looked it up and down. I watched numbers run through his head before placing the necklace on the counter between us.

"I'll give you … say … $50 in store credit."

I blinked a time or two, then let out a small cuff. "Fifty dollars? I paid more than one-fifty for it in Mexico!"

This wasn't exactly true. The original price for both the cross and chain *was* $150. But I'd haggled the guy down to $100.

"Okay, I'm willing to go to $75 …" the man said. He saw me lean my head slightly at his quote.

"… and I throw in these," he added, gesturing to the apples and oranges.

I stared at the man for a few seconds, seeing if there was any more wiggle room in his eyes. I saw none was left.

I then thought about the necklace for a moment. Oh, sure, it was a cross. But I had others. Wearing this one was just the latest thing. I saw no reason to hold onto it. And if it saved us money down the road, all the better.

"Okay … deal," I said, giving a quick nod.

"Well alrighty then," the man replied, then asked for my ID along with my father-in-law's address.

When he was finished, I shook the man's hand, picked up the fruits of my labor then headed home. I remember thinking I couldn't wait to tell Lorie and Bill about the experience.

Especially when you realized it was just the start of the world's new normal.

CHAPTER 7

And, with that, I get into the depressing part. The beginning of what would become *my* new normal.

It all started the day Bill passed, which also happened to be the day the lights went out in Fort Myers, Tampa, and pretty much the entire gulf coast. That day was February 13th, 2024.

Lorie and I had been at her dad's house for, oh, about six months. And over that time his condition had gotten steadily worse.

Much like a lot of the population, he himself had declined. He went from being ornery and aggravating, to accepting, to not caring about anything in what seemed like the blink of an eye.

"Dad! Is soup okay?" Lorie yelled from the kitchen. Bill and I had been watching Westerns – his favorite pastime. I looked at him for a response. He didn't move right away.

"Dad, Lorie wants to know if you want soup for lunch," I prodded. Again, nothing came.

"Dad?" Lorie yelled again.

"Dad?" I echoed, then waited.

When there was still no response, I gave him a little nudge. It seemed to do the trick. He finally looked at me like I'd just woke him up from a dream.

"What's that?" he asked, perplexed.

"Lorie wants to know if soup is okay for lunch," I reiterated. But instead of answering, he just stared at me, all glassy eyed. It was as if my words held no weight.

I started to say something again before he finally came up with an answer.

"Soup … yeah, that's okay."

I turned back towards the doorway and Lorie. "He says soup's fine!"

She came around the corner just as I finished my bark.

"Sorry, Babe," I added and smiled.

She gave a nod then looked towards Bill. "Dad, do you want chicken with rice or tomato?"

He didn't answer her though. His head was pivoted back towards the television.

Lorie and I moved in unison. Me to the edge of the couch, her to just in front of her dad. She knelt down, blocking his view of the set as she tried to meet his eyes.

"Daddy, are you okay?" she asked. She placed a hand on his knee to get his attention.

For a moment there was nothing. But, as if suddenly waking from a dream, he blinked then met her eyes and smiled.

"Yeah Sweetie. I'm fine."

Seeing his cognizance, she smiled in return and asked, "Are you hungry? I was going to make some soup."

Again, he didn't answer.

"Would you like chicken with rice? I can make a turkey sandwich to go with it … if you want," she said. He blinked at her, like maybe she'd just started speaking another language.

"Daddy? Chicken with rice?" she asked again and waited for a response.

Instead of answering, he reached for her hand, removed it from his knee, and gestured for her to move back. They both stood. He then reached for her and pulled her into a hug. He followed it up with a kiss on her cheek.

"I think … I think I'm going to lay down for a bit. Can I have a raincheck on the soup?"

"Well … yeah. Sure. If you want. But you really should eat something."

This was a fact. Her dad, over the past few weeks, had lost more than a few pounds. Not enough to be considered a health risk, but enough that we were concerned. He was no longer the man that I was afraid would kick my ass if I said the wrong thing. He was unquestionably a shadow of his former self.

Without another word, Bill turned and walked towards his bedroom. Once he was through the doorway, he turned and smiled – a strange and haunting grin – before he closed his bedroom door.

"That was weird," I commented as I stood to join Lorie. We both stared at the closed door for a moment before she responded.

"Should we take him to see the doctor?"

Turning to her, I was about to answer when suddenly the TV shut off. And not only the TV. I looked around the room and it seemed that every electronic device had suddenly stopped working.

"What the hell?" I asked moving my eyes to my wife. She continued to look around for another second or two before her eyes met mine.

"Do you think it's a brownout?"

I thought about it, pursing my lips. "I doubt it. It's barely Spring and not that hot out. Brownouts usually only happen when they're not producing enough electricity. You know, to keep up with the demand."

She continued to look at me for an answer. I had only speculation to give.

"Maybe they umm ... maybe a problem with the transformer?" I shrugged then made my way to the door.

Walking outside, I went to the end of the driveway then looked right and left and listened. I couldn't hear anything that sounded like there was power. Not a TV. Not a radio. Not even an air conditioner running. It – the entire neighborhood – was eerily silent.

Just then Brad – a guy from a few houses down – peeked out from the side of his house. Seeing me and Lorie, he walked down the street to joined us. I gave him the standard bro-nod as he approached.

"You guys got power?" he asked. We both shook our heads.

"Me neither. It just went out, like, poof."

Brad made a magician's sleight of hand motion in the air. The kind one does as he's tossing magical dust or some such. I raised an eyebrow but didn't say anything. I mean poof ... really!? I remember thinking, *whatever, dude.*

"I was on my cell one minute with my sister in Boston, then, well, nothing," he pulled his phone out of his pocket and looked at it. He then waggled it in front of us. "See! I ain't getting no reception!"

We couldn't, obviously. Not with his waggling, that is.

He followed this up by uttering, "Fucking cheap ass phone," then put the phone back from whence it came.

Wanting to check for myself, I reached for my own. Sure enough, I hit the power button and looked at the upper right-hand corner. "No Service" was displayed clear as day. I looked towards Lorie to make mention, but she was looking at hers. I could see from the look on her face she was seeing the same.

"Strange as shit, am I right!? I've never had bad service here," Brad said, looking for some sort of confirmation. I gave a nod to appease.

"Maybe it *is* a brownout," I said, looking towards Lorie. Usually she would have thrown a comment like that back in my face. Instead she just returned a forlorn gaze.

"Well ... umm ... anyways ... good seeing you guys. Glad to see I'm not the only one left on this street," Brad said, then gave a small nod and turned to leave.

"What do you mean?" I asked. He stopped and turned back.

"Last count only four of the ten houses had residents," he said, gesturing with his head around the small development. "But I haven't seen the Shepards or Kims in days. I think they left."

I looked between the two houses he was talking about. Neither had any indication of change. Both had cars in the driveways. The one house – the Shepards' – even had their garage door wide open.

"Well, I gotta go. Gonna take a ride down the road some … see if maybe I can get any reception closer to town," he stated, then looked at his phone again. "Fucking piece of shit."

I thought about stopping him to ask why he'd bother a drive with gas at a premium, but, you know, people do strange things for even stranger reasons. So, who was I to question? Instead I turned to Lorie. She was staring at the house with the open garage door.

"Babe, you think we should check on the Shepards?"

I joined her stare, then moved my eyes to her. Neither of us knew them very well, which made me wonder why she was so concerned. Was she actually worried? Or was she just being nosey? It could have been either. It could have been both.

I shrugged and said, "I guess. It's not like we have anything better to do."

She nodded, and I took the lead. I walked across the street and made my way to their front door. When Lorie was at my side, I opened the screen door and knocked. We patiently waited for a response. After about ten seconds or so, I gave a second, louder knock. That time I listened for movement. There was nothing from inside. I looked over at Lorie. She motioned for me to do more. You know, like the silent "go ahead!"

So, I did.

After knocking a third time, I called out, "Hello! Anyone home? It's Lorie and Paul … Bill Richard's kids … from across the street!"

When no answer or movement came, I tried a fourth time. First by banging on the door, then by calling out with my hands cupped at the sides of my mouth.

"Hello! Mister and Missus Shepard! Are you home?"

Still there was nothing. I backed away, letting the screen door slam.

"Well, what now?" I asked, raising my eyebrows at Lorie.

"Want to try the garage door?" she asked, pointing over her shoulder with her thumb. I blinked a couple times in disbelief.

"What? Are you serious? Do we even know them well enough to go in?"

She shrugged. "They did leave it open."

I pursed my lips. I knew she had a point.

"Okay … fine," I replied, then turned and walked around to their garage. Lorie followed close behind me, almost pushing me along the way.

We had to sidestep a couple of bikes and more than a few boxes, but eventually made our way to their door. I stopped in my tracks the moment I saw it was cracked open.

I looked back at Lorie, motioning towards it. She saw it and gave an "I don't care" shrug. I just glared back.

To me, going into the garage like that felt way too invasive, and more than a little creepy. I mean, I'd never want anyone in *my* garage if the inside door was open. I don't care if you're a neighbor or not. Stay the fuck out. That's my motto. One of them, anyway. But then, the wife happened. I'm sure you guys know what I mean.

I took in a raspy breath, then moved towards the door. As I reached up to knock, I noticed my hand was shaking. I withdrew it and took a step back.

"What's wrong, Babe?" Lorie asked. I really didn't know.

Was it fear? Because – damn – it sure felt like fear. But I couldn't figure out where it was coming from. There was nothing to be afraid of about knocking on a door, even if it was inside someone else's garage. I mean, what's the worst thing that could've happened? Would old man Shepard step out with a shotgun and blow me away? I highly doubted that. He was near seventy if he was a day. Shooting a shotgun would probably tear his shoulder off. But if it wasn't that, what was it!?

"Babe?" Lorie questioned again. Even her voice made me jump a little.

"Yeah!" I blurted, a little too loud. I corrected myself.

"Yeah, I'm getting to it," I said then moved forward, ignoring the shake and the screaming voice in my head.

Like I'd done outside, I first knocked – on the door frame, this time – and waited for an answer. When none came, I knocked again and called in, "Hello!? Mister and Missus Shepard? Are you home?"

Like before, I listened and waited. There wasn't a single noise to be heard.

"Maybe they're not home," Lorie said, almost questioning. I shook my head.

"Both their cars are here. Someone has to be home," I replied, not that I thought it was true.

"Should we go in?" Lorie asked. I gaped at her, but she had a look of confidence in her eyes. A confidence that told me if I didn't go in, she would.

"Okay, okay," I replied, holding my hand up as a stopgap. "I think it's a bad idea, but I'll check it out. You stay here."

As I turned back and started towards the door, Lorie started to follow. I quickly pivoted and held up my hand again.

"Please …" I barked, a little angry at her move. Somehow, the anger at her eased my fear a little, so I decided to keep it up.

Pounding up the two steps that led to the door, I knocked hard and called out again. When no answer came, I announced, "Okay! I hope someone's home because I'm coming in!"

Pushing the door open, I peered into the house. There were no lights on, like the rest of the neighborhood. There was also no movement.

Biting my lip, I took a step in, then two. Before I knew it, I was down the hall.

I called out again, "Hey! Anyone home?"

But there was no answer. Only a strange silence that seemed to steal its way into me. Through my shoes, through my hands, through the middle of my back and up my neck. I don't know what kept me going. I seriously wanted to run. But instead I moved forward through their kitchen towards the living room.

That's when I smelled it. The smell of something off. An odor like the kind you get from an attic when something … something has …

"Oh fuck!" I yelled. I couldn't help myself. It just came out like the sick does from a heaving stomach.

I quickly reversed, trying to find my way back – my way out. But it was dark. Too dark to see reliably. I wanted to hit myself for not activating ...

"My phone!" my brain suddenly screamed, or maybe I did. Not that it mattered. I reached into my back pocket and withdrew it. The moment I turned it toward my face the screen alit. The abrupt brightness stung my eyes. I quickly found the light button and pressed it. *It worked, thank God!* was all I could think. My heart slowed for a moment as I pointed the light in the direction of the way out. My path to freedom. My channel to salvation.

As I made my way back through the kitchen, the light glinted off something. Something metallic, or maybe something reflective. And part of me told myself to not worry about it – that I should just make my way out and everything would be fine.

But me, being me – oh stupid, stupid me – I just had to see what that glint was. And it's a choice I'll always regret.

Instead of walking towards the hallway, I made my way around the kitchen counter and found her. Mrs. Shepard. She was lying there, on the floor, motionless.

At first, I thought about leaving; to continue the plan I'd discarded only moments before. But another part of me – a darker part, maybe – wanted to see her up close. Although I'll never for sure know why.

As I approached her the odor became worse, almost overpowering. I could tell she'd been dead for a while. For a few days, at least.

I moved my light up and down her, to see if there was an accident. To see if maybe there was a clue as to why she'd come to be like that. I couldn't see anything. No blood. No contusions. Nothing. Only one thing stood out. One thing that I'd seen before.

Her head was turned as if she was looking at the ceiling; her glossed over, milky eyes, staring into the nothingness above.

That was all I could take. I don't even know how I kept it all in. I simply made my way out of the kitchen, through the hall, and back through the garage door.

"You okay, Babe?" Lorie asked the moment I emerged. She picked it up instantly, even though she didn't know what that 'it' was.

Instead of answering, I waved for her to follow. She was reluctant at first, but eventually complied. When we were safely outside, I summed up the only things I knew. Those being that both Mister and Missus Shepard were dead, and that they had been for days.

"What … what do you want to do?" she asked. I could only think of one thing. And my answer came out in a stutter.

"Wa-wa-with the phones out, wa-one of us … a … one of us na-na-needs to drive into town … and … and needs to alert the police. They'll na-need to send someone to a … umm … to take care of things here."

Lorie thought for a moment, then said, "I think we both need to go. You're in no condition to drive yourself. And … well … you saw what was inside."

I looked at her, realizing, "Your da-dad? What about your dad?"

She looked towards his house then back at me. "We won't be gone long. He'll be alright for a bit."

I reluctantly agreed to this, although I probably shouldn't have. But what could I do!? He was her dad, and, at that moment, she knew what was best.

Long story short, we drove – well, she drove us – to the nearest police station. It was only ten minutes away. I should say an eerie ten minutes away. Nothing had power. No traffic lights. No stores. Nothing. Nothing except our vehicle and the one we passed along the way.

When we got to the station there was only one person working. He was younger officer, who – due to circumstances as they were – was the only one on duty at that time.

We reported what we knew, and he courteously wrote it all down. He then informed us that he'd have someone check on the house as soon as they could. Apparently, the Shepards weren't the only ones that'd been found dead recently. He had a whole list of people and houses he let us glance at. He then told us it might be days before someone got there to deal with the situation. By his tone, I knew what he meant though.

What he was really saying was, "If at all."

When we got back, Lorie helped me into the house. Not that I needed much help. By then my nerves had mostly calmed. But her steadying touch certainly helped. Once inside, she had me take a seat in the living room while she went in to check on her dad.

I don't know how long it took me to hear her sobbing. It sounded so faint and far away at first. The second I heard it though, I shot up and practically ran to be by her side.

I didn't need to ask what was wrong. Somehow, I already knew. Much like the Shepards, and many others that year, Bill had simply laid down and gone to sleep. The kind of sleep he'd never wake up from.

We stayed there for a bit – me holding her, her holding her dad's hand and cupping his face – until I was able to urge her away. I knew it was my turn to take care of her.

Lorie and I both knew Bill had prearranged the disposition of his body, so my first step was to leave Lorie for a bit and head to Landes Funeral Homes. They were the ones that'd been hired – and paid quite well, mind you – to come pick up his body. They'd also been hired to hold two evening wakes, provide flowers and all the trimmings, and bury him at Sunset Memorial next to Lorie's mom. Unfortunately, like many other businesses that year, the overdemand and lack of supplies had thrown a wrench into the premade plans.

"So, what can you do?" I asked, more than a little irritated. A very nervous gentleman named Marcus laid out the details – as they were.

"Well, we can certainly pick up your father-in-law," he uttered, then cleared his throat. "We just can't ... umm ... provide a few of the ... umm ... other services he purchased."

"Such as?" I asked rather loudly. The man, hearing my tone, practically jumped out of his skin.

"Your ... umm ... father-in-law will have ... umm ... he'll have to be cremated," he stated.

"Have to be cremated!? Why's that?" I barked. Again, the sound of my voice made him jump back, almost like I'd taken a swing at him.

"It's umm ... State law. Because of all the recent ... err ... passings, the board of health and human services requires all bodies be cremated."

I let out a deep breath. I did it loud enough for Marcus to hear my frustration. I knew Lorie wasn't going to be happy, and that was going to make me very unhappy. I had to share the wealth, as they say.

"Well, that blows!" I stated, then drew in another breath. "What's the timetable?"

The man shuffled some papers, then said, "We can pick him up this Thursday."

I looked at my watch. Thursday was four days away.

"Four days!? Four fucking days!?" I barked.

"Yes sir," he replied, his voice breaking in the middle. "That's the soonest we'll have a crew here to help. I had to call my brother-in-law to help. He doesn't live around here, so ..."

"You know what!" I shouted. "I don't care what you need to do! Get someone over there and get them there now! I'll help you if you need it. But I just need his body out of there. Like pronto!"

After some more nervous shuffling, he agreed to take me up on my offer. I'm sure he didn't see the same generosity from others.

It took a few hours before he showed. There was another guy with him, so I didn't have to do much, as it turned out.

While they loaded the body, Lorie and I picked out a suit and some personal effects. These were handed to the guys, knowing they'd take care of the rest.

The funeral, if you could call it that, took place the next day. Bill's ashes were laid to rest next to his wife's remains, so there's that. The only people in attendance were Lorie and me, and Marcus, of course. We couldn't even get a preacher to show. That being the case, Marcus, Lorie and I said what we could.

Oh, and I tried to hit up Brad to see if he was available, but he was nowhere to be found. I guessed with all the death around him he'd decided to skip town. That's what I would have done if I were in his shoes.

Life – the new normal, without her dad – was strange. After talking with Lorie about moving back to Cleveland, it was decided that we should stay put. We figured that once everything blew over and returned to normal, we'd reevaluate. Plus, there was no way we were returning to Cleveland in its current state. It, like Fort Myers, had no power or was spotty at best. Oh sure, we'd do alright during the summer. But when Winter hit there was no telling what would happen.

On the bright side, we were able to locate a small generator that provided some power. Enough to run some essential household items like the refrigerator, freezer, TV, and electric stove. For the rest we boiled water and cooked outside. And we grilled every chance we got.

Occasionally we'd even make trips into town. Sometimes on bikes, sometimes in the car. There we could still pick up some supplies. For the rest, we scavenged houses when and where we could.

Okay, so, I know it sounds gross, and maybe weird to you. But assuming you went through the same, you probably did it as well. It wasn't the greatest thing I'd done in my life, because it felt a lot like stealing. Then, again, it wasn't the worst – so there's that.

When you think about it, that's what survival really is. Doing whatever needs to be done to live. And even though there were times that I just wanted to curl up and die, I didn't. I had Lorie to think of. And I knew I'd do whatever I needed to, to make her happy. Not that I could. Oh sure, there were spirts of happiness. But, the death of her father hit Lorie hard. As days passed, she grew increasingly sad, wishing her father was still around.

"Paul, can we go to the beach today?" she'd ask, almost every day. It didn't matter to her if it was raining, or cold, or windy out. She just loved being at the beach. And, in particular, one place along it. The spot wasn't too far from her dad's, which made it easy to get to on bikes. She used to go there with her dad when she was younger, and as she grew older, she went there whenever she was depressed or wanted to get away from it all.

She used to consider it her happy place, her happiest place on Earth.

As it happened, it was only a few weeks into Spring that there came a time in our lives that will forever be etched into my memory. It was a time when we both knew we should probably leave Florida and with it, her family.

The only problem was Lorie.

"But I really don't want to leave my dad," she'd said that night as we readied for bed. I understood, of course. But I also knew it just wasn't practical.

"Babe, our supplies are running low. The generator only has a day or so left before it's empty, and I haven't been able to find more supplies locally."

"Yeah, I know," she sleepily replied.

"And we've only got maybe enough gas to make it to Orlando. It's probably the only place left with power in the state."

"I know, I get that. But ..." she yawned, then paused. She then looked at me with a blank stare, as if she suddenly forgot where we were or what the conversation was. I almost said something. Almost. But what did I know!? What did I ever know!? Before I had the words to even attempt a reply, a smile slowly alit her face.

"I'm tired. You ready?" she asked, gesturing to the bed. I gave a nod and we both climbed in. After turning out the propane lantern, I closed my eyes and waited for the dreamworld to take me.

"Hey Babe," Lorie said, pulling back momentarily from the edge. "Do you remember when we went to the boardwalk?"

"Yeah," I replied weakly. "It seems like just yesterday."

"Yeah," she agreed, then took a long pause before saying, "It really was nice, wasn't it?"

"It really was," I replied, then slipped a little more.

"If we go anyplace, that's where we should go, don't you think?" she said.

"What's that?" I asked, drifting in and out.

"If we leave and go anyplace, that's where we should go," she said again. I barely remember giving her the simple "uh-huh" as I nuzzled near her ear.

She took my hand and pulled me forward – into her – until we became one. She then put my hand to her face and kissed it. The most sweet and gentle kiss I'd ever felt.

Less than a minute she was fast asleep. A minute after that I was as well.

CHAPTER 8

The boardwalk was packed. Summer packed. Not quite as busy as the last time Lorie and I were there. The previous Fourth of July. A very hot, smoldering, Independence Day. It was no wonder, though. It was a beautiful day.

It was maybe around 2 or 3 o'clock in the afternoon. It was a little overcast, so it was hard to tell where the sun was in its progress towards the horizon. I only guessed the time by the noises and smells around me. It was like the boardwalk had been open for a bit, but the evening crowd hadn't arrived.

As we strolled, I held onto Lorie's hand. More for her protection than anything else. Not that I didn't like holding hands. Far from it, actually. It was just that it was a warm day, and the skin-on-skin contact made for a very sweaty connection. Nice. Loving. But ultra-sweaty.

"What would you like to do first?" I asked, leaning in so she could hear me over the din of rides and attractions.

"Dunno," she replied, giving a shrug. I felt the tug against our connection even without looking at her.

We walked on for a bit longer, looking from booth to booth before I posed the same question.

"What would you like to do?"

"How about the star shoot-em-up thingy?" she asked, pointing to an attraction to our left. Without a word I steered us to it, front and center. No one was there except for the vendor.

"One or two?" the vendor – the carny – asked. I held up two fingers in a backward peace sign.

"That'll be two dollars," he relayed, grabbing two BB guns from the rack. These he placed in front of us then collected my bills.

"You know what to do?" the carney asked, nodding towards a sign. A sign I'd seen at least a dozen times. Shoot out the red star, it said. It had to be completely gone to win a prize.

After giving the carney a nod, I turned to Lorie, picked up her rifle, and held it prone in front of her.

"You first, my dear."

She smiled. The kind of smile that always warmed my heart. Warmed me to my core.

Lorie took the rifle from my waiting arms, crouched down, took aim, and shot. BBs came out in a rapid succession. The first few went wide, but then she got the hang of it. Within twenty seconds the shooting ceased. After placing the gun down, she righted herself.

"Nice shooting!" the carney relayed, then walked back and pulled the target from the clip. He reviewed it for a moment before turning to us and rendering his verdict.

"I'm sorry, miss," he said, placing the target in front of her. He pointed to a spot at the top of the star. "There's still a little left."

Turning, he walked back towards the back of his stand, picked up another target, then mounted it. He turned and gestured towards me. "I hope your gentleman friend fares better!"

When the carney was safely back on his perch – a wooden stool to the left of the booth – I picked up my rifle, stooped down, and took aim.

"You got this!" Lorie stated, leaning in to give me a kiss on my cheek.

I turned my head towards her, gave a smile, then once again set my sights.

I took a deep, calming breath, let it out, then pulled in another. Holding it, I depressed the trigger.

As before, a stream of pellets exploded from the rifle. I tried to make the first shot fast so that only a few left. The few that would be my tracer rounds for the volley that would follow.

Unlike Lorie's attempt, my first few hit close to dead center of the star, telling me the sight – and the barrel – were accurate. Accurate enough, at least.

I spent the next few seconds – seconds that came and went in a heartbeat – carving and honing, trying to make sure every bit of red was obliterated. When I was finished, I took a cleansing breath, set down the rifle, then rose and waited for the judge to rise and speak.

The carney did as we expected. He walked over, grabbed the target, inspected it, then turned and walked towards us.

"Well," he started, slapping down the target. He held his hand on top of it for a moment keeping us in suspense. Removing his hand, he passed his judgment.

"Folks, it looks like ... we have a winner!" he announced loud enough for the surrounding booths to hear. Reaching up he pulled a cord. Bells and whistles started whirling and ringing from the top of the kiosk.

"You did it, Babe! You did it!" Lorie exclaimed, practically knocking me down as she leapt into my arms and proceeded to smother me with kisses.

"What would you like, buddy? Anything on the top row."

Placing her down, I turned my attention to the vendor. He had a stick in his hand and was pointing towards the top shelf that lined his little booth.

There were a menagerie of stuffed animals and assorted items to choose from. There were giraffes, lions, and monkeys. There were toy squirt guns and games. There were balls of every shape, color, and size. Too much to take in at one glance, let alone pick on a whim.

"What do you think, Babe?" I asked, trying my best to think of what she'd like. After all, I'd won this item for *her.* Everything I'd ever won was for her.

At first, when she didn't respond, I assumed she was as perplexed as I was, and she was perusing her options. After what felt like a minute, an impatient look from the carney made me ask again.

"The world is your oyster, Babe? What would you like?"

When no retort came, I turned to question her. Or at least I tried to. To my side was only emptiness. She was no longer standing there.

"Babe? Where'd you go?" I asked loudly, leaning slightly away from the booth to look down the boardwalk. I peered in both directions. There were several people walking to and fro. None of them were her.

"Lorie! Where are you?" I called out, louder than before. I waited a moment for a response. When none came, I pivoted to the carney.

"Did you see where she went?"

His stare was blank, as if I'd said nothing. As if he never heard my query. Ignoring his lack of reaction, I turned back towards the boardwalk.

Cupping my hands around my mouth I shouted, "*Lorie! Lorie!*" hoping someone – anyone – would turn and be her. But no one did. Not one single person acknowledged me. The only replies returned were the bells and yells coming from the games and a general cacophony from the crowd.

"You might want to try the boat docks?" I heard the carney say, breaking me from the panic that was starting to loom. I turned back to him and met his eyes.

"What was that?" I asked. He nodded and pointed.

"The boat docks. Down at the end of the pier. You can't miss 'em," he said as he continued to point down the long stretch to my right.

I stared at him for a moment, searching, trying to figure out where this logic was coming from. Did he see her walk that way and not say anything? Was he just guessing? I needed to know more.

As I tried to speak – tried to question him – my mouth suddenly grew dry. It was as if the heat of the day had inexplicably made me mute, choking off any utterance.

I stood there for a moment, staring at the carney with incomprehension, before I started to sense a strange pull in the back of my mind. A sensation that told me my asking would come to nothing, and that I needed to leave. That I needed to reach the end of the docks like he'd instructed.

Without grabbing a prize, I turned and started walking. A walk that turned into a jog, then into a run. I quickly hustled by people, passing strangers on my left and right. It was a miracle that I didn't hit anyone as I ran. For some odd reason, I felt light on my feet, as if I could sprint like that all day – or for at least as long as it took me to find my love.

As I approached the end of the boardwalk, the people cleared, enabling me to see a white railing with nothing but blue behind it. When I neared, I slowed my run to a walk, advancing sluggishly towards the rail.

I was about a foot or two away when I finally saw her – my Lorie – standing on the docks twenty feet below. She was facing away from me, staring off into the vast sea in front of her.

"Lorie!" I called out, hoping she'd turn.

"Lorie!" I shouted again. She ignored my plea. It was as if my words were getting lost in the wind.

As I started to shout a third time, Lorie – still oblivious to my presence – began walking towards a boat at the end of the dock.

Seeing this, I quickly turned, searching for a way to get down to her. But from what I could see there was nothing. There seemed to be no break – no exit – from the chest high wood rail that lined the entire boardwalk.

Desperate and heart racing, I turned back to the dock. "Lorie! Lorie! Where are you going?"

There was still no reply – no acknowledgment from her.

When she reached the end of the dock, she turned and walked up the gangplank onto the schooner. A boat that looked eerily like her Uncle Ricco's. I knew it couldn't be though. She'd said her Uncle no longer owned the boat. Unless she was mistaken. Or she lied.

"Lorie! Lorie!" I screamed and frantically waved. Finally, she turned and met my eyes. I smiled. I couldn't help it.

Without saying a word, she slowly raised her arm … and waved goodbye.

"Wait!" I yelled. As I did Lorie pivoted toward the boat's bow, her back to me.

"Wait!" I shrieked. The moorings of the boat were cast away, tossed by unseen hands.

I leaned over the rail and looked down. It was about a fifteen-foot drop to the deck below. I could make it easily, I knew that. If I hurried, I could catch the boat before it went out to the endless sea.

Climbing upward, I threw both my legs over the railing. After taking a deep breath, I paused while I gathered my will, then pushed off. The sensation of falling – forever falling – sprinted through my mind. My heart pounded in my chest as I waited for the inevitable impact with the deck below.

An impact … that never came.

CHAPTER 9

I shot awake with fear. Fear like I'd never felt before. I knew almost instantly that what I'd experienced was only a dream. But knowing that fact didn't help. Although awake, my heart continued racing, and my entire body was drenched with sweat.

I took a few deep breaths, in and out, in and out, calming myself. Telling myself it was only a dream. Reminding myself that strange things happen in dreams and I should just relax. Rest and just let sleep envelop me again.

And that seemed to do the trick.

Closing my eyes, I laid back with every intention of falling back asleep once more. I wanted the dream world to take me again. To let it hold me and caress me, to blanket me maybe forever.

I reached a hand for Lorie, for the calm and ease I always felt when we touched. I knew if I did, she would unconsciously take my hand and the moment would be perfect.

But, as I moved my arm towards her, expecting to contact flesh, I felt nothing but bedding. Cold, silken emptiness.

Sitting up, I turned to where she'd been just minutes or maybe hours before. But she wasn't there. I then tried peering around the room. But the room was still pitch black. And the dark that surrounded me felt odd. It felt like it was trying to smother me – suffocate me. So much so it made my heart leap in my chest and suddenly start to race. Everything felt wrong. The entire room, the entire house, everything around me felt unexpectedly and inexplicably wrong.

Reaching for the nightstand, I groped for the flashlight I'd left there the night before. Snatching it from the table, I lifted it, turned it on, and quickly scanned my surroundings. It only took a few seconds to confirm that Lorie was no longer in the room.

"Babe? You in here?" I uttered into the darkness, hoping I was wrong. I waited for a reply, but nothing was returned.

"Lorie? You awake? Where are you?" I asked, louder than before. Loud enough that if she was in the hall, she'd hear me. Again, I waited. And again, there was no response.

I pointed the light at the windup clock. It read 5:30 am. Too early for the sun. Too late for the moon. Way too early to be awake.

Then it hit me. Maybe she was in the bathroom with the door closed. Maybe she just didn't hear me. But something told me not to trust my thoughts. Something felt off. The dream, I guessed. But I needed to be sure.

Crawling from our bed, I found my pants and shoes – not easy to do in the dark – then put them on. Rising, I left the bedroom.

Once in the hall, I stopped and listened. The only sounds were those coming from the bugs outside and the creaks and groans from within. But no human sounds. No people sounds if you know what I mean.

I continued my trek down the hall, eventually reaching the bathroom. The door was wide open. I shined the light in. There was no trace of Lorie.

Next, I made my way downstairs to the kitchen. Morning light was just starting to come in through the shades. I could tell right away Lorie wasn't there either.

I scanned the kitchen for any sign of her. Like, maybe she'd made coffee and gone outside to see the sunrise. But, no. There was nothing. No smells except the lingering hint of what we'd eaten for dinner the night before.

"Lorie?" I called out, then started walking the house.

Retracing my steps, I made my way back upstairs to each of the bedrooms and the bathroom. But nothing – no hint she'd recently been in any of them.

Next, I went back downstairs and searched the living room, dining room, kitchen, and laundry room. Again, there was no sign of her.

Lastly, I tried the garage. It was empty. Well, empty of her.

Walking through it, I opened the door that led to the drive. What I saw there hit me like a two-ton weight. One of the cars – her dad's – was nowhere to be seen.

"What the f …" I started but cut myself off. You know how you do. When something so inexplicable hits you that it makes you dumb. Void of speech, that is. That's how I felt at that moment. Dumb. Dumb as a doorknob.

I had no idea how I could've slept so soundly that I didn't feel her get out of bed. Not only that, but I'd also slept so deeply that I'd missed her starting up the car and driving off. Was it all the work from the days before? Or maybe the alcohol from the previous evening? I didn't have a clue. I didn't have any idea what would possess her to leave. I had no idea where she would go if she did.

That's when the bolt of lightning hit me. A veritable lightbulb shining over my head. I knew instantly where she'd gone. And I hoped I didn't know why.

With barely a thought I ran inside, grabbed my keys and a shirt, then hopped in my car. The drive didn't take long. No one was on the road at that point. Not that there would've been with The Surge and all. And it didn't take long to get there. The highway was congested with abandoned cars and trash, which made for slow going. But the back roads were fine. As usual I used as many as I could along the way.

Just like the times before, I pulled through the open gates of the park and drove back towards the beach. As I made the left turn into the lot my headlights glinted off car glass. An automobile parked off towards the back. It was her dad's Nissan.

Pulling in next to it, I got out and gave it a quick once over. Lorie wasn't in it. And from the feel of the hood it'd been a while since she was.

I followed the path up the sand dune – a path I could easily traverse in the dark having been there at least a dozen times of late. Not that I had to, though. The sun was floating just above the water. Hovering like a large orange beach ball left adrift in a gigantic pool.

Cresting the hill, I didn't see Lorie right away. I knew I wouldn't, though. That wasn't her spot. So, I continued my walk, making my way the couple hundred yards to where I knew she'd be.

I don't remember exactly when I started crying. Was it when I first saw her dad's car or when I crested the dune? Was it the first glimpse of her cold and lifeless body, or was it when I started reading the short note she'd left for me? I don't know exactly, but I do remember the flood of tears. They made the note hard to read – hard to comprehend. They made the letter seem like something out of a dream … all billowy white.

The note went something like this:

Paul,

I don't see the point in it all anymore. And I'm so tired.

I miss how it was. And I miss my dad.

I wish I was as strong as you.

Please stay as strong as you are. For me, if for no other reason.

I will always love you.

Lorie

After reading and rereading the note, I sat there next to her body for a bit as my world cracked in half. The thousand thoughts running through my head forced my body to go limp. I couldn't move. I could hardly breathe.

Looking back on it, I realized that – at that moment – it would have been so easy to just give up. I could have easily laid down next to her, closed my eyes, and waited for the long sleep to envelop me.

After all, what did I have left? My wife was gone, all my family was gone. Everything I'd known, everything I'd loved, had slowly been taken away from me over the previous eighteen months.

But then, something funny happened.

As I sat there feeling low – probably the lowest I'd ever felt in my life – a sudden burst of wind came along. Carried in it was the scent of saltwater. The moment I smelled it, I turned to meet it. I fully intended to let it carry me away to where all the others had gone.

That is until a handful of sand brushed up by this same salty wind rose and smacked me squarely in the face.

You know that feeling. We've all had it. That "what the fuck, Life!?" feeling when the absurd turns into the absolutely ridiculous. The moment you think life couldn't possibly get any worse – and then it does.

For me – as with others, I'm sure – those times make me break into a fit of laughter. A moment when I can do nothing but sit back and chortle at the unbelievable. Like when you're running from your car to an overhang to avoid getting wet in a downpour, only to have a gutter suddenly spill a gallon of cold water right on top of you.

Then there's the other times. Other times when the utterly bizarre makes me hopping fucking mad. Mad at life. Mad at the situation. Mad at the entire world.

And when that happened – the "getting sand thrown in my face" – it turned into the latter.

The sudden feeling of sand in my eyes, mouth, and nose triggered something in me. A feeling that didn't make me forget about Lorie's note so much as it made me mad that she'd taken the time to write it.

Within the space of time it took for me to start coughing, her note suddenly became one with the sand. It became something different than the loving notion she'd intended it to be. No, far from it, in fact.

In my mind, her note instantly became a literal slap in my face.

Standing, spitting, and wiping sand filled snot from my nose, I stood over her – what used to be her – and just stared. *How could she do this to me!?* I thought. *How could she leave me like this!? This wasn't an act of love! How can you tell someone you love them ... and then ... and then ... just leave them!? How could you leave me alone!?*

"*God damn you!*" I yelled at the emptiness in front of me.

"*God damn you for leaving me!*" I screamed.

I then moved forward and glared at her frozen body.

"*Did you ever love me, you selfish, selfish ...*"

I stopped right there, though. I wanted to call her names – every name in the book. I wanted to get into a fight with her. I wanted reasons from her. And I wanted to argue those reasons. I wanted answers. Answers I knew I could never get now.

I looked towards the sky and started screaming aloud. A scream that made me hoarse and eventually turned into a cough.

Losing my balance on the uneven sand, I fell backward onto my ass. The sudden impact momentarily knocked the wind out of me. It knocked a portion of the anger out of me as well. The jolt also let me realize something I hadn't thought of until right then.

That thought was, *I should have seen it coming.*

I knew how depressed she'd been about her dad – and about the world, in general. And I knew she could be very emotional about things. The way she'd always berated herself when she was angry. The way she always broke into tears when she thought about a dead animal or a beautiful flower. All those things – all those feelings – were ingrained in her. They were part of her. And I should have remembered that.

I was the practical one – the "strong" one – after all.

I was the one that always had the final say in where we ate and drank. I was the one that always came to the sensible solution. *Stick and Move, Stick and Move*, the military had taught me. *If you stay stationary too long you could die. Make up your mind quickly and don't cry about the outcome. There's a solution to every problem. Even the wrong answers are answers and are choices you have to live with.*

With all this in mind, I suddenly felt like the world had chosen a new path for me. After all, I was the one who thought about coming here to be with her dad. I was the one who mapped it out and figured out what we needed to bring and what music we should play.

I had always been the practical one – the responsible one. And I knew, I knew, that I was responsible for this.

After that realization hit, I sat there for a moment, waiting for my breath to return. When it did, I knew what I had to do.

Stick and Move, buddy. Always Stick and Fucking Move.

Rising to my feet once more, I looked at the note still clutched in my hand.

"God damn you … God damn me," I said to the note, then dropped it. The wind grabbed it and instantly carried it away to a place I'd never know.

Turning, I walked back down to my car, got in it and drove back to her dad's. There I picked up everything I'd thought I'd need, including clothes and a shovel. After driving back to the spot – her spot – I proceeded to bury her. I figured no one would care, considering the state of things. If and when things got better in the world, I could always retrieve her body for a proper burial.

If ... there were so many ifs in the new normal.

When I was finished, I tossed the shovel, said a final goodbye, then hit the road. After considering my options, and the things we'd talked about, I didn't bother returning to her dad's. I simply plugged in my iPhone, turned on some Industrial, then made my way to the main road.

I figured if I had any luck my next stop would be the great city of Orlando.

CHAPTER 10

Why Orlando you may ask? It's simple, really. Power. Power … and people.

Oh, sure, I knew I was taking a chance by heading to a major city. Anyone I saw along the way might be one of the Crazies I heard about on the radio and TV. But what else could I do!? I knew if I stayed where I was, I was a dead man for sure. I'd end up turning into one of those vegetables. The ones that withered and died on the vine. And I wasn't about to do that. No, sir. No matter how upset I was about Lorie. I knew I needed to move on. She told me to, in fact. And I knew I needed to go someplace where there was guaranteed excitement. A place where people would go for possibly the same reasons as me.

And I thought that place would be Orlando.

Yet, when I got there, the place was just … weird. Yeah, I guess that's the best way to describe it. It held a weirdness that made me leave there almost immediately, bound for Disney instead. Which, as it turned out, was actually a good thing.

Because that's where I met a guy named JC.

No, no. I know what you're thinking. Paulie went crazy and became a Jesus freak. But no, you'd be wrong. It just so happens that, when I got there, the first person I ran into was a guy named Jeremy Christian Bambic. JC to his friends, or so he told me *repeatedly.*

But I'm getting ahead of myself, aren't I? Fuck! Okay, let me back up a bit.

After having buried ... you know, Lorie ... I left Fort Myers and traveled north towards Tampa. With all the abandoned cars, trash, and stuff, US-41 was slow-going. But when I hit I-75, I was able to pick up my pace somewhat. Top speed, maybe 40 miles per hour.

By the time I hit the area just east of Tampa it started getting dark, so I pulled over for the night. Why you may ask? Mainly no lighting. All the lights - and I mean *all* the lights - were out. If you've ever traveled down a country road in the middle of the night, you know what I mean. Not only is it scary being the only one on the road in the dark, but it was dangerous as hell with all the crap strewn about. I had no intention of letting my trip end in some weird traffic accident with a rogue tire or an extension ladder.

Why an extension ladder, you ask? Because that actually happened. Earlier that day I barely missed hitting one that was lying in the middle of the road. It seemed to come out of nowhere. Totally scared the shit out of me. And it was a miracle I didn't wind up in a ditch or skewered by that thing.

Anyway, when things started to get too dark to drive, I pulled over, shut off all my lights, and sweated the night away to some

Filament 38 and Combichrist. Who, you ask? They're Industrial bands. You should listen to them if you have a chance.

Besides getting out of the car to relieve myself once or twice, I stayed in that spot until early the next morning. Then when the sun was far enough up in the sky to see, I started up the SUV and continued my trek onward. I took I-4 east until I neared the Orlando area, reaching it just before noon.

On the bright side, there *were* people … if you could call them that. Did you ever see that scene in the movie *Knowing*, towards the end, where Nick Cage is driving through all the people aimlessly wandering around and trying to stop him as he went by? Well, take that, remove ninety-nine percent of the people, and make those left a mix of people either running for their lives or chasing those running away. Now you get the picture.

In fact, there were these three guys that … well … that tried to rob me. And one of them, he umm … he … umm …

Sorry.

Long story short, it got weird as fuck, and it left me shaking. To coin a phrase from the 1980's pair O.C. and Stiggs, "It was incredible … we hauled ass."

Not quite sure why that popped into my head, considering that was a more cheerful phrase, but there you go. And if you don't get the reference, it's your loss. They were an unbelievably funny team in National Lampoon magazine, back in the day.

Shit, I'm doing it again, aren't I!? I'm losing my train of thought. Okay, enough with the movie references. Time to get back on track.

After a run-in with a few people – people on the cusp of becoming "Crazies" – I left the main part of the city and headed south. It was getting later in the day and I knew I needed to be far enough away from those humans as … well … as humanly possible.

Finding my way back to I-4, I took it south until I saw the main signs for Disney World. Then … well … then I pulled off the road and reviewed my options.

Was going into Disney World the right thing to do? Was I going to get there and discover all Hell had broken loose? Was I going to discover what I was searching for – reasonable people like me and, more importantly, power? I didn't know and … well … I was running out of gas. I needed to make a decision, and I needed to make one fast.

So, what did I do? I literally flipped a coin.

I thought, *heads I continue into Disney World, tails I say fuck it and head east towards Daytona Beach and Jacksonville.*

Why Jacksonville you might ask? Well I figured why the fuck not. Nina Blackwood, one of the only DJs left on SiriusXM radio, said that Jacksonville was still alive and kicking. Yeah, XM was still working at that point. Crazy, right!? Not only was I still getting real time news reports – news like what cities were decent and what ones should be avoided – but she was also still spinning some hellacious tunes. Spinning all the way from SiriusXM's studios in the Los Angeles area – at least that's what she'd said. She was always encouraging people to come visit her there.

Well, the coin came up heads, as you probably inferred. So, after making sure my 9mm was loaded, I donned its handy dandy shoulder holster, strapped that sucker on, then started the car and headed towards the Magic Kingdom.

Before entering, I decided to do one thing first. I wanted to check out the neighborhoods nearest the Kingdom. Why? Well, I'm not quite sure. Maybe it was a sixth sense of things? Or maybe it was to get an initial lay of the land? But, now that I think about it, it was probably because I had a high school buddy that'd moved down there a few years before everything went to shit, and I wanted to see if I could find him. I had no idea his address or the exact neighborhood he was in. But I'd always been kind of jealous he'd moved there, and I wanted to see how the other half lived, as they say. I mean, he posted on Facebook all the time that he could see fireworks from his friggin' back yard! And, like, every night! How cool would that be, I ask!? I even imagined they had their toilets rimmed with little gold Mickeys. I bet you did too.

By the way, they don't. At least not the ones I saw.

Anyway, the first place I found was called Blue Heron Estates. I chose that one because of the name – blue heron. It reminded me of the times Lorie and I went to Hinkley Lake south of Cleveland and watched the blue herons while kayaking. You know, before all the birds died out.

Well, I drove around for a bit, in and out and all around. It was a maze, really. All the little side streets in the development were easy to traverse. Also, they were very easy to get lost in.

After driving around for, say, two hours or so the sun finally started to set. Which was a good thing it did. My heart almost jumped out of my chest when I first noticed it. Power. The streetlights actually had power. Not all of them, it seemed. Some streets didn't turn on. But others ... others were illuminated bright as day.

Finding a street that still had lights, I pulled over to the side, shut off the car, got out, and waited, hoping to see signs of life. I figured someone *must* have heard me driving around. It's not like my car was electric! It made a decent amount of noise. But, as I sat there, gun ready just in case, no one came out to meet me. Not one soul on the street bothered to make an appearance.

At least, not at first.

"Hey! Hey man! How ya doin'?" came a voice from behind. Shocked and thrown off by what'd happened in Orlando, I quickly turned, fumbling to grab my gun from its holster.

"Whoa, man!" the guy said, stopping his approach and raising his hands. "I'm cool, man! I'm cool!"

"Who … who are you?" I blurted, the gun noticeably shaking in my grip.

"My name's Jeremy … but you can call me JC if you want. I'm seriously good with whatever, though. If you can't choose, just make it JC. But I really don't care either way. It's just so … so good to see another person, ya know!?"

Hearing his blunt, almost too jovial of a response, I asked the first thing that came to mind. "You aren't one of the Crazies, are you?"

JC let out a huge laugh. "What, me? No, man."

Then he said something that convinced me of that fact. Under his breath he said, "Jeez man, I know the sun set, but would I even be talking to you right now if I was?"

"What's that?" I called back, a better, more solid grip than before. You know, aiming center mass.

"Nothing, man! Nothin' at all! I was just … well," he looked between his two outstretched arms. "Do you mind if I lower my arms? I swear I'm not packin'.

I motioned with my gun. "Turn around. Let me see."

JC did as asked. He did a complete turn, showing me all sides. When we were back face to face, he slowly reached down with one hand and lifted his shirt, then turned from side to side. I didn't even have to ask.

Re-raising his arm, he gave me a look. "We cool now, man?"

I nodded, then re-holstered my 9, but I kept my hand rested on it just in case. Seeing my gesture, he dropped his arms and slowly approached.

"Wow, man! It's so cool to see ya! I wasn't sure I'd ever meet someone normal again. You know, someone that didn't try to kill me."

"Oh yeah? You get many Crazies around here?" I asked. He gave a halfhearted shrug.

"A few. Not many. They usually come in, pillage a house or two, then leave. But not a lot. Pretty sure the lights in this neighborhood scare them off."

I gestured to one of the streetlamps. "Speaking of which, how are these even on?"

He returned a smile. One of pride. "You like that, huh!? Yeah. I tapped into the main grid at Disney. They have some generators there that are still running. Not sure how long they'll last. But until they do, full power, baby!"

His tone – his accent – made me laugh. I wasn't sure if he was some kind of Junglist or where he came from. It sounded almost northern, but with a "I've smoked weed all my life" twist. I figured that was due to him being excited about seeing me. But I really had no idea at that point.

I let out a small chuckle. "That's awesome! And thanks! I was hoping I'd find a place that still had power."

"Yeah, no problem, man! I was an electrician for Disney before all this. Didn't take much to wrangle," he said, then pointed over his shoulder to a house down the street with a fence surrounding it. "I've been staying over there in one of the fancy spreads. I'm not originally from around here. But I decided to relocate, housing being what it is nowadays. Know what I mean!?"

I gave him a nod of acknowledgment.

"I know you don't know me, but you're welcome to squat at my place … if you'd like. It'd be nice to talk with someone, you know. Nowadays all I have talking to me is the damn TV," he said, then let out a weak laugh.

I wasn't quite sure what he meant by that, but I got the gist. He was bored to the point of being stir crazy. He wanted a friend. And I guess, at that point, I needed one too.

"That'd be cool," I replied. JC blinked a couple times, then practically jumped with joy.

"That's awesome!" he howled, then took a step back. "Grab your stuff and follow me. I'm sure your car will be safe out here."

JC turned and walked back towards his, well, *the* house. Quickly figuring he was on the up and up, I grabbed what I thought I need for one night then caught up with him.

As I approached the fence surrounding the house, I saw signs on it stating, "Electric Fence – High Voltage."

I motioned to it. "High voltage, huh!? How did you …"

JC started laughing, practically cackling. The dude was definitely stir crazy.

"Oh that!" he said. "Well, ya see. Umm. That ain't true."

I glared at him. "Ain't … what?"

He nodded. "Not true … like, a lie. I picked those signs up at Disney. We use them all over the park. I put them around the perimeter. It keeps people out … or at least has to this point."

"So, it's not …" I started. He cut me off.

"Electrified? Nah. Not at all. You know what it would take to electrify it?"

I shook my head. To me it sounded simple. At least it was in the movies.

"Let's just say more trouble than it's worth," he said.

I gave a slight nod and shrug, then followed him through the gate. Once safely through, he closed and locked it with a chain.

"There. Good 'til mornin'," he stated, then waved for me to follow. We walked up the short drive then up a few steps until we were under a covered patio. There he held the door open for me and waved me in. The moment I broke the threshold I was buffeted with air conditioning. It was absolutely delightful. Something I hadn't felt in weeks.

"Welcome to my humble abode," he stated, performing a sweeping gesture with his arm.

"Thank you … I appreciate the hospitality," I replied.

Once the door was closed, I followed him to one of the bedrooms on the main floor.

"You can cop a squat here. My room is across the hall," he pointed, then glared at me with his head cocked to the side. "By the way, do you like pizza?"

I peered at him astonished. “Is there a soul on the planet that doesn’t?”

“Dunno. Thought it best to ask,” he shrugged. “I have some pepperoni and mushroom … frozen … that I can cook for us. It’s no Giovanni’s, but, then again, what is!?”

It was then that I caught the accent, or at least part of it. Chicago. He was referring to a Chicago pizza place. Lorie and I’d been there a couple times. Great deep dish. The thought instantly made me wonder if it was still around.

“Good!” he said, breaking me from my thoughts. “I’ll start the oven. It won’t take long.”

Before I could say thanks, he pointed to the bathroom. “Feel free to take a shower. The pressure in there is amazing. Therapeutic, even.”

“Wait! You still have running water?” I blurted, not believing my ears. He nodded.

“Yep! Gotta thank Uncle Walt for that one. Well, for choosing this spot, anyway. There’s a lot of small lakes around here. Good water sources. This place will always have water. At least as long as the lights stay on.”

Before I could say another word, JC was gone around a corner. I thought it was strange. Then, again, so was he. I chalked it up to the stir-crazy thing. I guessed it’d be hard to work on your politeness skills if you didn’t have anyone around.

Taking him up on his offer, I made my way to the bathroom to drop trow. Once inside, I made sure to lock the door and block it from being opened. I was sure JC wasn’t one of the Crazies, but it still didn’t mean he wasn’t a creeper. I made sure I was on my toes. That was for damn sure.

Once I was fully showered – and he was right about the water pressure, by the way – I dressed in clean-ish clothes and followed JC's sounds out towards the kitchen. I'd made sure I kept my 9mm with me though. Tucked it in the small of my back, TV detective style.

The dining room had been set to include a candle on the table. Talk about wining and dining. I took a standing position on the tables opposite side, away from the noises. I didn't have to wait long for JC to make an appearance.

"Hey, man. All gussied, I see," he said, then paused and stared at me. "You know, in all the excitement, I didn't catch your name."

"Sorry. It's Paul," I stated and stuck out a hand. He quickly hurried over to meet it.

"Good to meet you, man! And glad you accepted my hospitality!"

"The pleasure's all mine," I said, then gestured to the kitchen. "Anything I can help with?"

He shook his head. "Nope. All set. Was just about to put the meal on the table. Take a seat."

Before I could ask another question, he was gone again. The dude was definitely quick on his feet. With a shrug, I chose the seat closest to me. A minute later JC walked out of the kitchen with a large pizza in one hand and a bottle of wine in the other. These he placed in the center of the table then took a seat to my right.

"Guests first. Dig in!" he stated, then picked up the bottle of wine. After opening it, he hovered it over my glass.

"Please," I uttered as I moved a couple slices of pizza to my plate. After a decent size pour for both of us, he grabbed two slices for himself. I waited until he was set before I made a move for food or wine. It was only polite. Plus, I was waiting to see if he said grace or anything.

Lucky for me, he didn't.

Picking up his glass of wine, he held it out. "Cheers! Here's to new friends!"

"To new friends," I echoed, then we clinked glasses. We both took a sip, then dug in.

I quickly engulfed my first two pieces, barely tasting either, then gestured the question of more.

"Help yourself, man! There's more where that came from."

I thanked him, then grabbed two more slices. As I sat back to eat, I asked a question that'd been gnawing at me.

"JC, if you don't mind me asking … how did you know I wasn't one of the Crazies? Seems you really took a chance bringing me in here."

He let out a laugh. "No, not really. To be honest, I did watch you for a bit from my second story window. I had a rifle fixed on you as you drove through. And you did drive by here at least twice before you stopped. When you finally did, you just stood outside your car. No crazy movements. No breaking and entering. Nothing. So, I figured you were safe."

At that, I held up my glass to him and we clinked. I couldn't beat that kind of logic.

When we finished dinner, we moved the leftovers to the kitchen along with the dishes. These we placed into a dishwasher, which he ran. I swear my jaw dropped, not having seen one run in what seemed like forever.

After, the two of us seized another bottle of wine and moved into the living room – and the big screen. There – and I shit you not – mounted on the wall, sat a 105" flat screen. It was bigger than any TV I'd ever seen. I totally understood why he moved in there. The place was phenomenal.

"So, there's a satellite dish, but there's limited programming. A few movie stations seem to be on auto. We can search those … or there's always DVDs."

JC pointed to the wall. Mounted in the wall were shelves filled with DVDs, CDs, and what I assumed were laser discs. I hadn't seen an LD in years, so it was only a guess.

"Thoughts?" he asked. I shrugged. He shrugged in kind.

After motioning to sit, JC picked up a controller, turned on the TV, then did some scrolling. He eventually found an old baseball game. 2016 Cubs vs. Indians. Game seven. It finally hit me why he'd given me a smirk during dinner when I'd told him I was from Cleveland.

"Hope you don't mind," he said, motioning to the screen. "It's the only time my Cubbies won in the last hundred years."

I laughed. "Nah, I'm good. You are the host, after all."

At that he gave a nod of acquiescence then hit play.

We watched for a while, maybe through the third inning, before JC spoke again. His tone more serious than before.

"So, you've felt it, right? That fear?"

I slowly shook my head. I didn't understand what he was on about. At least not at first.

"They say that ... that fear is what changes ya," he continued.

I narrowed my eyes at him. I had no idea where he was going with it.

"I heard it from a friend of mine before all the shit went down. He said it was some sort of medical experiment gone wrong."

I could only shrug. "I have no idea ..."

"Come on man, you know," he interrupted, turning to look at me. He hit the pause button, halting the show in the middle of a double play.

"You know ... that surge thing. My buddy said it was all a plot. Some Deep State shit. You know what I'm talkin' about?"

I raised an eyebrow.

"Yeah, yeah. I know. It was all debunked afterward that Sun thing was made public. But, when all the shit first hit the fan, that's what he said caused it."

JC paused only long enough to take a sip of wine before he continued.

"Anyways, that abdula oblamgata thing ..." don't blame me, that's what he called it. "... in your brain caused a severe fight or flight response. And after it was triggered you either went crazy, or you crawled into a hole and died."

I looked at him in disbelief. I'd heard some wild shit in my time, but this ... this was definitely near the top of the list.

He took another sip, deeper that time, then asked, "So, did you feel it?"

I just stared at him, not getting it.

"Come on, man," he pleaded. "You must remember a point where you felt scared. Like, so scared you wanted to just shit your pants or run for your life? Or maybe even curl up and die?"

He went silent and watched me. His eyes wide and questioning. You know how people do. Like that third-grade teacher asking what nine times nine was when you were barely comfortable with your fives. I felt compelled to answer, so I thought about the ask.

When was there a time when I felt that scared? I thought to myself. *When was there a time I felt scared enough to run … or die?*

Then I remembered the dream. The dream of Lorie leaving me. How haunting it felt. How real. And how I'd woken up and just wanted to … to …

But Lorie was missing. Her sudden disappearance made my heart leap.

"You *do* know what I'm talking about, don't you!?" JC asked. I pursed my lips and gave a small nod.

"Yeah … I … I guess?"

"Well that's what I'm talking about," he barked, pounding his fist once on a side table for effect. "I remember feeling it … oh … probably six months ago. A sudden fear that made me want to run. Made me want to crawl into a ditch and die."

I gave a nod and motioned for him to continue.

"But, as I sat there, arms crossed over my knees, rocking back and forth, thinking I should just roll over and breathe my last, suddenly … well … suddenly the feeling went away. It was like touching a cold wind blowing across a field. One moment it was there, cooling your fingertips and the back of your hand. The next it was gone as if it had better things to do."

Now, I didn't know about all that. But I knew how this … this 'The Surge' had made me feel. If it truly was The Surge I'd felt. I told him as much.

"Well, that's what it sounds like to me," he said. "Sounds like something clicked in you, and if it weren't for your missus … what's her name?"

"Lorie," I replied.

"Yeah, Lorie. See, if it wasn't for her going missing, you might have just curled up and died, my friend," JC stated, then paused for a moment before continuing.

"You see, what I've found … oh, say, over the last few months … is if you keep your ticker going … pumped up and active … then The Surge never has a chance to get ya."

I narrowed my eyes at him. He held up a finger then explained.

"So, one of the things I do is, every night before I go to bed, I set my alarm. Something loud. And for no more than six hours at a stretch. As soon as I hear that damn thing go off, I reach over, grab a couple caffeine pills and I down em with an energy drink. I'm partial to Monster."

I held up my own finger to get a word in, but he rolled right over me.

"I know what you're thinkin'. All that caffeine every day can take a toll? Yeah, well, maybe you're right. But I make sure to add in regular exercise … cardio … to keep my heart healthy. And that's what's key, my friend. Keep the heart tickin'. Just keep the old heart a-tickin'."

When he was finished, he sat back and finally let me speak.

"And that's it? Keep your heart ticking with caffeine and exercise?"

He smirked and added. "Well, I make sure I keep active, too. This is an amusement park, you know. There is literally a boat load of stuff to do around here."

My eyes went wide thinking about these so-called revelations. And I guessed I couldn't argue the facts. He was alive and somewhat sane. So, I thought, why argue!?

And, for the next two months, I followed his lead. We kept active eighteen hours a day and did everything and anything you can possibly … Imagineer.

See what I did there!? Imagineer? You know, Disney? It's okay if you didn't get it. You're still welcome.

CHAPTER 11

I guess, before I tell you about what happened next, I should give you the lowdown on my new friend, Mr. Jeremy Bambic.

As I mentioned, Jeremy – JC to his friends and, well, pretty much everyone, I guess – was born and raised in the great city of Chicago. Home of the Bears, the Bulls, the White Sox, and his beloved Cubbies.

Lindsey, JC's mom, was originally from … umm … I forget where exactly where. It was someplace in southern Illinois if I remember correctly. A place where being seventeen, pregnant, and unwed was akin to being a convict. Because of this, she'd left home and relocated to Chicago shortly before he was born.

JC was hatched on May the Fourth. I know, right!? Star Wars day. Surprises me that he wasn't more of a Star Wars fan. He did like Star Trek, but only the original series.

But I digress.

Lindsey, shortly after her move, met the love of her life, Brenda. The two moved in together when JC was around six months old. So, yeah, he was raised by two moms. I hope that doesn't offend you but, personally, I don't care. The moment he told me I thought it was cool. I can only imagine the shit I could've gotten away with if I had two moms. Not that my dad was super strict. In fact, he could be a pushover when it came to making me …

Well, shit. There I go again. Sorry. Once again, back to JC.

After his two moms got together, the three moved to the north side of Chicago, around the Franklin Park area. Great place, if you ask me. Very eclectic. Cool restaurants. And after getting to know JC, I'd say he fit right in.

Anyway, skip to the end of high school.

JC, being less than a stellar student, dropped out in his junior year. But, for what he lacked in scholarly skills, he totally made up for with his hands-on abilities. Brenda, who was a union electrician, got him into an apprenticeship where, by the time he hit twenty-five, he'd earned his Mastership. Within a year he owned his own union shop working on sites all across the Chicago area.

Enter the love of *his* life, a lady named Linda. Linda, like JC, was bright and motivated. As intelligent as she was, Linda graduated high school at the age of sixteen and earned her master's in electrical engineering by the time she was twenty-one.

JC and Linda met one night at a mutual friend's birthday party, and that's all she wrote. Six months later they were married. And less than two months after that they were pregnant. Pregnant with twins, in fact. A boy and a girl they named Frank and Fred – Fred being short for Frederica.

When Linda got the offer at Disney World, a job she'd applied for as a pipedream, she was over-the-top happy. Since she was little, she'd wanted to be an Imagineer – what Disney called their Engineering and Design group. Growing up she'd fantasized about designing new rides and attractions based on all the Disney works she loved.

Getting the job was her dream come true. A dream JC was more than happy to help with.

So, leaving his mothers, he dissolved his company and moved with Linda and the kids to Orlando. Within a month they established themselves in the area, and a month after that he landed his own job in the Magic Kingdom.

Life was grand … for a while, at least. They both worked at Disney. The kids were healthy and happy. And they'd even picked out a small little house in one of the developments. One with a white picket fence and a small upright pool in the back yard. They were so happy that they even talked about having another child – or maybe two.

Then, wouldn't you know it, fate struck. A fate now known to the world as The Surge.

JC never knew why he was the one to survive. He was older than Linda and had a tougher upbringing. And the kids … well … the kids were healthy and happy, like I'd said. There should've been no reason for him to survive when they hadn't. But, within the space of only a few months, all three were gone, and he was alone.

What kept JC going you might ask? I certainly did. I think it had to do with faith. Linda was raised Catholic, and he'd converted to it for the wedding. That was about all I knew. He was super vague about it. And I felt like I shouldn't pry.

So, why am I telling you all this? I guess it's because I wanted to relay his mindset, and how I came to respect the man. And, in return, why he came to respect *me*.

Because that's what it's really all about. People. The "whys" and "hows" of surviving. And, more so … staying sane and alive.

CHAPTER 12

Getting back to it, from day one – or thereabouts – until about two months after JC and I'd met, I'd been fully onboard with his "energy overload" idea. His routine – our routine – kind of went like this ...

At precisely 5 a.m. my alarm would sound – usually playing some sort of thrash metal. Occasionally I'd throw in some Big Band or P!nk to mix it up, but that's a whole other story. I mentioned my tastes in music varied, right!? Well, there ya go.

Before I could see straight, I'd reach over to the bedside table, find the two caffeine pills I'd left there the night before, and down them with a Rockstar. Why Rockstar? Mostly because I liked the flavor. I also felt drinking them instead of the Monsters JC liked was kind of like sharing the wealth, if you know what I mean.

After taking my pills, I'd get up and do some sit-ups, some push-ups, and some jumping jacks. Doing these so soon after waking kind of made me feel like I was back in Basic. Now that I come to think about it, maybe they had something there.

Eh, who knows.

By 5:30 I was in the shower – cold but not too cold – then I'd get dressed in a jogging suit, throw on my shoulder holster, then meet JC at the front door by 5:45.

It was the same thing every morning.

"You ready?" he asked as he was doing stretches.

"As ready as you are," I'd reply, doing my own.

JC would start the little timer on his wristwatch, and we'd run out the door. I'd normally jog in place as he unlocked the front gate. Then again as he relocked it. Then we hit the road for a three-mile jog. When we got back, usually thirty minutes later, we both took showers, then met in the kitchen to eat breakfast and discuss what we planned on doing that day. It was usually something exciting, but not always.

On normal days, we'd throw on our armaments – me, my 9mm, him, his rifle – and we'd head into Disney. There were literally over a hundred attractions there. And if you include all the cool Star Wars stuff, it was enough entertainment to last a lifetime.

On a few occasions we ran into a normal person or Cusp Crazies – what we called the people that seemed normal but weren't quite right in the head. The normal ones usually ran away from us. Some of the Cusp Crazies though, we had to shoot at to chase them off. Always towards them, but never at them. We had a strict non-kill policy. A strict non-kill policy we kept our entire time there.

The few normal people that didn't run away we tried to convert – as in, we tried to get them to follow along with us. You know, snap out of it and do what we were doing. But it was a no-go most of the time. Sure, they might stay with us a week or so, but after that they'd generally run off … or we found them dead.

There was this one girl …

Man, this is hard …

There was one girl, Tanya, that stayed with us for a short time. She was young – say, maybe eighteen although she wouldn't tell us her true age – with long blonde hair and glasses. She was beautiful, you know. Fantasy librarian type, I'd guess you'd say. She'd traveled there from Miami with her family for about the same reasons I did. But she lost them to The Surge about a month after they'd arrived. And by lost them, I mean she found them one day … all dead.

After finding her, we convinced her to come stay with us. And we actually got her to break out of her shell – for a bit, anyway. We thought she might stay, you know, normal. But after a while, she stopped wanting to come on runs with us. Stopped wanting to visit Disney. Two days after our last "ask" we found her in the upstairs bedroom. You know … like she'd found her family.

The way she looked, though, just lying there. Peaceful. She reminded me of Lorie.

She just … she, umm …

That's … that's about all I want to say about that.

Moving on, I should mention that sometimes the things we did were work related. You know, electromechanical stuff. Not only did we need to keep the lights on and the water running, but if there were attractions we wanted to ride, there were a certain number of things we needed to work on or fix before we could. Being his guest, I volunteered to help wherever I could. I've always been decent with my hands and could fix most things … if I had direction. And I'm sure he appreciated the help. Not everything could be fixed by one person. I certainly came in handy.

By now you're probably asking yourself why I mentioned the two-month mark. I mean, if we could live out our lives playing Han Solo and Chewy – I won't say who was who – for the rest of our lives, why change? It was simple, really.

"Well, we are fucked," JC stated one day, throwing his wrench behind him as he walked towards me. I thought I knew what he meant. We'd talked about it a couple times in the recent past.

"Generator?" I asked. He nodded then wiped sweat from his brow.

"Yep. We maybe have a day or two tops … if we're lucky. After that, the whole park is going dark."

Knowing what I knew, I hazard a guess. "Main coil? Or …"

He shook his head. "Diode array. It's on its last leg. And we don't have a replacement."

I knew he knew all the details. All the ins and outs of the circuits and generators. But, just to make sure he hadn't missed something, I decided to ask.

"If the storehouse is out, can't we rob them from another unit?"

He shook his head again. "Nope. I replaced Main Generator Two with One's array about a week ago."

I thought for a minute. "Any way we can rob one from somewhere else? Like, maybe one of the rides?"

He shook his head.

"Or, what about a nearby plant?" I asked. He continued his shake.

"What about an electronics store … or maybe a warehouse?"

He stopped and just peered at the floor. "The diodes are specially made … in China. There's no way any of the stores or plants anyplace around here would have one. Best guess would be maybe Disney Cali might have one. But that's it. A two-hundred dollar part two-thousand miles away."

We were both silent for a minute or two, contemplating what it all meant. We'd talked about it before. That is, what we'd do if the place went to shit.

"Well then, when do we leave?" I asked.

He drew in a heavy breath. "Load up tomorrow … head out the day after?"

I gave a nod, and we got to work.

It didn't take long to pack. We knew what to take. We'd talked about it. Planned it. You know, like taking a trip for fun. We both hoped for the former, but deep down both knew it'd probably be the latter.

We found a van – not too big, not too small – to travel in and packed it with all the things on our mental lists. You know, bedding, food, and the like. We thought about finding a Winnebago – there were plenty to be had in the Disney parking lot – but figured it would be too easy a target if we were set upon by Crazies. Nope, better to travel small, with just the essentials we'd need.

Main Generator Two failed just as we were finishing. It was like it was predestined. The power went out, we looked at each other, then left through the front door. There was only one thing we hadn't decided on.

"Where to?" JC asked, his hand poised over the ignition.

To be fair, we discussed it and narrowed it down to two places. Either we'd head north along the east coast towards New York, Washington, and Boston – not in that order, obviously – or we head west towards LA. Its merits were New Orleans, Houston, Dallas, Las Vegas, and ... well ... LA. If we made it that far.

With no definite answer, I just returned his gaze and shrugged.

"Flip a coin?" I asked. He gave a nod.

I unbuckled my seatbelt and reached into my jeans for a coin. As I did, JC turned the key and the engine roared to life.

Before I had a chance to retrieve a coin, SiriusXM started blaring – and I mean blaring – through the van's speakers. I'd forgotten that the day before I'd been listening to some 80's rock – Billy Idol, Depeche Mode and the like – so I'd turned it up.

To fix my lapse in etiquette, I quickly reached over and turned it down. The moment I touched the volume knob a familiar voice came on the air

"And that was Siouxsie and the Banshees with Spellbound. One of my personal favorites. I got to meet Siouxsie a few times back in the day. The first time was just after that song hit the top one-hundred. She was a marvelous lady. Just another casualty of the old Surge. Speaking of which ..."

JC reached for the station knob to turn something else on – he disliked most 80's music – but suddenly stopped. We both looked at each other. You know, a shared epiphany. He smiled, then shrugged. I matched his shrug then sat back.

Sure, why not LA, I thought. It obviously still had power, and at least one sane person. And that sane person *had* been inviting anyone and all to come see her.

So, after exiting the maze, we drove north for a bit, then west towards the gulf ... and Nina.

Our intention was to stick to back roads and avoid the highways. We'd heard from Ms. Blackwood and one of the news stations still broadcasting that most of them were overrun by gangs of Crazies. I trusted the report based on some of the things we'd witnessed in the previous month.

We thought our west coast travel plan was solid. We'd head to Panama City first – along the coast, a day trip if all went well – then find a secluded spot to rest up overnight. From there we figured we could make it to New Orleans in less than a day. And with any luck we'd find ... something.

Normal people, power, whatever.

Solid plan, am I right!? Well, as it happened, not so much. We did make it to Panama City. But that's when the plan went straight into the toilet.

We were driving through San Blas – close to Panama City – when we saw a problem.

"Dude! Dude! Stop here!" I barked. JC practically slammed on the brakes.

Once the van had come to a complete stop, he looked over at me. "What? What do you see?"

I continued to look through the binoculars for a moment before I lowered them and answered. "Crazies … a group of them blocking the bridge ahead."

"How many," he asked, opening and closing his hand – the "give me, give me" sign that he wanted the field glasses. As I handed them over, I described what I saw.

"Maybe a dozen of them if I had to guess. Sitting just before the bridge. They're milling around. Looks like they're just waking up."

JC uttered a "fuck" under his breath. I shared his sentiments.

"It'll take us about an hour to backtrack," I said gazing behind us.

He lowered the binoculars. "Shit. It'll be dark by then."

We sat silent for a moment before I spoke. "What if we just shut it down right here and held up for the night? In the morning, after they go to sleep, we can either find a way through or backtrack and go around."

"What about patrols? What if this bunch scavenge at night and they find us?" he asked.

"We can take turns sleeping?" I offered. "If any come near us, we bolt."

I could see he didn't like the plan.

"What if," he started, then took another look through the binos. "What if we just barrel through … like, right now?"

"I'm not sure that's a good idea, we'd probably …" I started. He interrupted; an excited smile lighting up his face as he turned to me.

"Dude, they're just waking up. I bet we can make it through the gauntlet before they have a chance to react!"

I just glared at him, astonished. “And what then? What if they come after us?”

“I’m guessing they wouldn’t … at least not for long. If they don’t give up right away, they’d definitely give up at sunup,” he replied. I continued my glare.

“That’s like ten hours from now. Ten hours of night driving on roads we don’t know. Add to that the fact that we don’t have ten hours’ worth of gas in the tank.”

“I’m sure it wouldn’t be long. No way they’d travel that far to snag us,” he said.

I shrugged. “Do you really want to take that chance?”

He didn’t even think before speaking. “Yes … I think it’s worth it.”

“What does it gain us? A few hours maybe? I asked. “Dude, we are in no rush.”

“I know, I know, but still …” he started. It was my turn to cut him off.

“No! We need to sit here and wait it out. I’m not taking the risk!”

I could see JC wanted to argue the point, but my look was resilient. He stared at me for a bit before letting out a huge huff.

“Fine. We sit,” he shrugged. I didn’t try to grin, but I know I did – at least a little.

Finding a somewhat secluded spot, we backed up the vehicle just off the road. Satisfied with our position – and with the ability to make a run for it if needed – JC shut down the van. After making sure the inside lights were off and couldn’t be activated if a door was opened, we locked them then drew our lots.

"You want first?" he asked, referring to the previously agreed upon four-hour watches.

"Sure … unless you'd rather."

"Nope, all good," he stated, shaking me off. He stood – you know, as best you could in a van, and moved to the back. I stayed in the passenger seat, hunkered down so as not to be noticed by any casual passersby.

I felt the van move back and forth a little as JC got comfortable. When all movement stopped, I turned a bit to verify he was set. Satisfied, I turned back towards the front and watched for movement in the night.

As I sat there, I thought about a variety of things, but mostly about the road ahead. You know, not knowing what else we'd run into or if this whole "travel across the country" thing was even a good idea. I mean, I thought it was – at the time. But I wondered if maybe we were just grabbing at straws? Scratching at the dirt to find bits of seed? I didn't know. I only knew that it felt like the right thing to do then.

My other main train of thought was about JC and his wanting to barrel through a crowd of people. It seemed … well … irrational to me. I knew, from the discussions we'd had over the weeks prior, that he didn't think the Crazies should be considered humans anymore. Oh sure, they were at one time, he'd said. But he was convinced that The Surge had changed them – damaged them – in irreversible ways.

"Their brains are broken now," he'd said. "And they're now no better than rabid dogs. Dogs that should be put down … and out of their misery."

I'd never seen him do this – you know – put one out of his or her misery. But he had talked about it. He'd talked about it a lot.

Obviously, I didn't share his opinion. I did think the Crazies were off and highly dangerous. But in my estimation, it was just an effect from The Surge. I was sure – convinced, even – that if the powers that be could find a cure for The Surge, or it went away, that the Crazies could and would return to normal. Only time would tell, of course.

Time that I hoped we all still had.

As I sat there deep in thought, there was a slight jarring from the back. I turned to see JC lying there, eyes wide open, staring at the ceiling. I didn't think anything of it … at first. But then he spoke, his tone sounding unusual somber. I should have known something was off.

"Did you ever bird watch?" he asked.

"What's that?" I asked peering at him. He didn't meet my eyes. He just continued his stare at and past the roof above him.

"Did you … you know … ever bird watch?" he repeated. I thought about his ask for a moment before replying.

"What do you mean? Like, sitting in a chair with binoculars?"

He gave me a nod.

I thought about it, then shook my head. "Can't say that I have."

JC let out a small but noticeable breath – a breath that sounded a lot like longing.

"I used to, you know," he replied. "I used to sit for hours on my front deck … you know, in the morning as the sun rose … and I just … watched."

He reached over to a canteen, popped it, and took a long drink before continuing.

"I used to love watching the starlings as they zipped and zoomed across the sky. I watched hawks and blue jays and, damn, even pigeons as they moved through the neighborhood scrounging for food. I watched ..."

"Cardinals and Robins," I broke in. He finally turned and met my gaze.

"What's that?"

I gave him a smile. "I used to love seeing cardinals and robins. There was this place the wife and I used to go on the east side of Cleveland. Very scenic. I loved watching the Cardinals and Robins. The males, you know!? The colorful ones. They just seemed so ... so ..."

"Cool," he added, giving me a slow nod.

I moved my finger to my nose and tapped it. He hit the nail on the head.

"Yeah. Cool. Like Fonzie cool," I replied. "Like, those were the ones that could walk into a joint and pick up any girl in the place."

He let out a small huff. "I know, right!? Or they'd be total ass-holes. The kind of friends you don't want to invite to a party because they were too full of themselves."

I chortled and added, "Pompous dicks."

"Pompous strutting dicks," he agreed. "All up in your face like hey, I'm here. And this just became *my* party!"

"And you better have some good beer! Or I'm fucking leaving!" I replied, then started to laugh.

Instead of joining me, JC's smile left his face. After taking in a long, slow breath, he turned his head and started looking at the ceiling once more. It was a moment before he spoke again.

"Damn, I miss good beer. It's all skunked now, you know. All skunked, just like …"

The world, I thought – but didn't say aloud. I didn't have to. We were both thinking it. Some things just go without saying, you know!?

We were both silent for a bit as we reminisced about good beer, parties, and life. Before he drifted off, JC spoke once more.

"Sorry man. I didn't mean to be a Debbie Downer."

I shook my head. "Nah, you weren't. What you said … needed to be said."

JC took in then let out a long breath. "Yeah. I guess. If you say so."

I watched him for a moment to see if he was going to turn and talk more. He didn't. Instead, he just closed his eyes. I watched as the tension left his body and he started to drift.

"Well, sleep easy, man," I quietly said, then turned back to continue my watch.

My watch was boring. The group of Crazies never even came close. My guess was they'd already scavenged the area around us. But you never knew. They were chaotic. We'd seen it before. One moment they'd be focused on trying to get into a locker or a car, the next they'd drop everything they were doing to run off after something. It was kind of like watching a club of ravers – or maybe preschoolers. They seemed to have all the energy, but none of the rationale or wisdom that came with adulthood.

So, yeah, I watched on … but it was mind-numbing. I ended up playing a lot of solitaire on my phone while I waited out my watch.

When 1 a.m. rolled around, I woke JC to let him know it was his turn. As he'd done many times before, he picked up an energy drink, cracked the seal, then drank the thing in practically one gulp. Once he was set, we traded places. He moved to the passenger seat while I crawled underneath the warm covers he'd left. It didn't take long to fall asleep. My brain was drained, and I was tired as fuck.

It was just before sunup when I heard the first of several gunshots. They were so distant – and I was so exhausted – I almost didn't recognize them for what they were. The moment I did though, I shot awake, grabbed my pistol, and made my way to the front of the van.

Peering out the windows I looked around – left, right, up and down – but saw nothing. It took another couple of shots for me to comprehend where the noises were coming from. They were coming from the approximate location of the Crazies' camp near the bridge, just northwest of our position.

The next and probably most important thing I realized was JC was nowhere to be found.

Cracking the door, I listened to see if I could hear him. I figured maybe he was crouched near the outside of the van. Unfortunately, I was wrong. The only sounds I heard near me were the creaking of the van and trees – you know, the normal things you hear at night. That, and yelling coming from the distant camp.

Although unsure it was the right thing to do, I decided to leave the relative safety of the van to have a look around. I thought maybe JC had gone off to see what was causing the commotion, or maybe just to take a piss. I knew I had to take one myself, which was probably why that thought had come to mind.

Grabbing the binoculars off the dash, I quietly opened the door and climbed out. Making my way towards the noises, I crept through some trees until I reached a small ridge that stood between me and the Crazies' camp. Stooping down, I raised the binos just enough to look over the crest of the hill. What I saw there was … well … kind of an unbelievable sight. There, about three-quarters of a mile away, the Crazies' camp appeared to be on fire.

About half the camp, from what I could see, was running around semi-aimlessly screaming, trying to put out the fires. But that was only half. The other portion seemed to be a melee of people pointing north or firing their weapons in that general direction.

This only lasted a minute or so, though. After a yell from one of the people in the shooting crowd – their leader, I assumed – things were swiftly gathered and loaded into different cars. These cars were then quickly boarded by everyone in the camp. In less than a minute the entire hoard drove off over the bridge in hot pursuit of whatever they'd been shooting at.

It wasn't until a good minute or so after all the activity died down that I decided it was safe to move. Venturing back the way I'd come, I passed through the trees and walked back to the van.

Feeling it was relatively safe, I called out to JC, hoping he was in the area. But after calling out about a dozen times, no reply was returned. Although it was still mostly dark, I started searching the entire area. But as the sun started to rise, I finally gave up. I knew that JC was no longer around.

Stunned as to what to do next, I stood outside the van for a bit in hopes that maybe he'd come around a corner and state, "Sorry, man. I had to take a wicked dump. What was all the commotion?"

But that moment never came.

As realization started to set in, I decided to try a last-ditch effort. I thought that maybe if I started the van and revved it a bit, that maybe JC would hear the engine and come running. So, opening the van's driver's side door, I got in and reached for the keys.

Unfortunately, they were no longer there.

"What the fuck!?" I muttered to myself, then looked to the floor thinking that maybe they'd just fallen out of the ignition. But, after a quick search, I could see that wasn't the case.

I sat there for a moment trying to figure out if JC had wandered off with them. But, knowing him as I did, I knew he'd never do that to me. I also knew he must have put them someplace … someplace near.

I started visually searching the cab. Looking up I finally found them. JC had placed them above in the driver's visor. Why, I had no idea. At least not at first.

As I reached up and lower the visor, the keys dropped into my hand. Along with them, a scrap of paper fell. It was a short note from JC. It simply read:

Paul, don't hate me, but I need to do this.

I found an IROQ, my dream car, in a nearby driveway.

My plan is to hit the Crazies' camp just before sunup.

Might draw them away. Might not.

You can take the van. Take it wherever the wind leads you. I plan on doing the same.

Whatever you do, remember this one thing:

Drive To Survive, my friend.

All my best.

JC

After reading the note, I flipped it over hoping for more. There wasn't anything. Flipping it back I reread it one more time then let it slip to the floor.

My mind was a jumble of things. First and foremost was, *You son of a bitch! You crazy son of a bitch! You left me to fend for myself! What the fuck, man!? What the actual fuck!?!*

Obviously, I was upset. Shit, I was hurt to my core! I knew we'd only known each other a short time, but I'd felt that we were in it together. Yet here he was abandoning me, casting me out alone, into the wind.

It – being left by myself like that – felt just like … you know … Lorie. It felt exactly like what Lorie had done to me a few months before. He, much like her, had made a selfish decision. A decision that left me going my own way. A decision that'd left me alone. And I hated her for that. I hated both of them for that.

But, as I sat there in the van waiting for, I don't know what, I thought about the two – my wife, and someone I considered to be a best friend. They'd both done what they thought was best for them without any thought of me.

Yet, as I considered this, I couldn't help but think: Had they really been that selfish?

Lorie knew I wanted to move on – to find a place that was living, and where we could survive the madness taking place in the world. I was emphatic about it, and she knew it. As far as she was concerned, I had literally painted her into a corner. I was making her leave the place where she felt the safest to take a chance on another. Neither was a great option in her mind, so she chose the least scary to her. She chose to follow her father's path.

She chose to let The Surge take her away.

And as far as JC, I always knew he was slightly unhinged. The crazy things we did to keep our blood pumping. His decision to leave to run through the Crazies' camp. All of it was unbalanced. And I'd gone along with all of it until just a few hours before. And to him, maybe that was his tipping point.

Fact is, I just didn't know. The only thing for sure I did know was the one thing that kept driving me onward. The need to not let this be the end.

By the way, cheers JC, wherever you are. I do hope we meet again someday. Either here, or in the great beyond.

CHAPTER 13

Drive to Survive. That's what he'd wrote.

JC's words kind of reminded me about the movie, The Shawshank Redemption. Andy Dufresne's quote – two quotes, actually. The first was in the letter Andy wrote to Red, his best friend in the world: *Remember Red, hope is a good thing, maybe the best of things, and no good thing ever dies.* That one, and: *Get busy living, or get busy dying.* Although, now that I think about it, I don't remember if Andy or Red said that one. Either way, it was a great movie. And it somewhat paralleled what JC had written to me.

"Drive to survive," I said aloud, trying to sound confident. Then, I waited. I waited and watched. I watched for Crazies or Norms. Norms being my new term for humans that weren't crazy. Although, to date, I'd only met a few.

When the coast was clear – around mid-day – I started the car, turned it around and headed away from the bridge. Sure, I was taking a chance heading back the way I'd come. The way we originally rejected. But, hey, I only had a few options.

And, really, what did I have to lose!? Besides the obvious, that is.

So, after working my way back along FL-30, I hit Navarre and FL-87 then headed north. When I hit Highway 90 near East Milton, I headed east until I hit Hwy-184, then took that until I entered Alabama. I then followed AL-112 until close to sundown.

Finding a secluded spot near the town of Douglasville, I shut everything down, prepped my bed, then waited for the new day to arrive.

Okay, I won't go into every twist and turn from there. I know you're like, "Thank God!" Am I right!? I just wanted to prove a point – or maybe just share my struggle. It was slow going, moving only a couple hundred miles at a time, stopping only to find gas and supplies. The whole time also trying not to make too much noise or become noticeable, and also looking for people like me. It was draining. I ran through a lot of energy drinks, and I slept when I could. Mostly I just sat in the dark and waited for the light.

I did see a few Crazies along the way. Typically, individuals. But I avoided them, mostly. Once I scared off a woman who insisted I was her husband Brad or knew where he was. I wasn't sure which. She was way far gone and hard to understand. I totally understood everything when she pulled the knife on me though. That's when I listened to O.C. and Stiggs once more.

Yeah, I hauled ass.

And, by the way, I'll give another shoutout to Nina. As I drove, she helped me keep what little sanity I had left. The news ... the tunes. It felt like I had a constant companion in the car with me the whole while. She was a cohort that knew me and was looking out for me. At least, that's the thought I kept foremost in my mind. A thought that said, *Yes, it would take weeks, maybe even months to get to her, but I would reach her eventually. And all will be right in the world once I did.*

Well, that's what I'd thought, anyway.

It took me a couple days – a few days, actually – to reach New Orleans … the next stop on my world tour. I traveled north away from any cities, then dropped down and followed as close as I could to the coast. Eventually I crossed the border of Louisiana and reached my next destination.

The outskirts of New Orleans – The Big Easy – good ol' N.O.L.A.

By the time I got there over two years had passed since the onset of The Surge. And, as you probably guessed, New Orleans was pretty much a wreck. There was a severe hurricane that had run its way through, crushing most of the city in water. Most of the same areas that'd been underwater during hurricane Katrina in 2005 were flooded again, and – just like the past – most of the people were gone. In fact, as I made my way through the city, I didn't see a soul. I like to think they'd made their way to greener – and less wet – pastures. Well, that's what I hoped.

Instead of doing the same though, I decided to stay a few days. Why, you might ask? Well, hate to say it, but my ass was sore. If you've ever been on a road trip for any extended period of time, you'll know what I mean. My backside aching, and my mind was wibbly wobbly from the constant movement.

Mostly, I needed a mental break. I needed some time to hole up somewhere and get my head straight. And I knew I couldn't do that in a van down by the river. It just didn't feel safe. And I wanted to feel safe … at least for a little while.

That being said, did you get the van reference!? It's okay if you don't. I sure miss TV. I hope it comes back someday.

Anyway, the city at that time of year had some major things going for it.

One, it was warm. Warmish, anyway. Highs in the 60s, lows in the upper 40s. It was like Cleveland in early summer, or late spring. Shorts weather we called it. And that year, because of what had been going on with the sun, it stayed warm in the south.

The second reason I stayed – besides my ass cheek problem – was power. Parts of the city – those not under water – still had current here and there. And as luck would have it, I found a place that did. A little off the beaten path I found a cool hotel that still had power and … get this … supplies! They still had a working fridge and freezer with enough food to last me weeks if I needed. I knew I wouldn't, but, you know, be prepared and all that.

Hey, I was a Cub Scout once … before the world turned to shit.

The only drawback would be … wait for it … Crazies. I hadn't seen any on my initial run through, but that didn't mean they weren't around. And before I setup shop, I had to verify.

So, like I'd done before, I found a place to park where I could view a portion of the city – one that had a quick getaway – then turned off the van and waited. That night I searched with the binoculars for any wavering lights and fires, and listened for any unusual noises – you know, like yelling or screaming.

To my utter relief, there wasn't a hint.

So, when morning came, I drove my van into the city and moved into the Grande Fleur Hotel just outside of the French Quarter. It didn't take long. The most amount of time I spent was looking for a room and trying to find a place for the van. You know, somewhere it wouldn't attract attention. A place I could get to it in a hurry just in case things went bad.

Picking a room was relatively easy. The place was lavish with a bunch of large and small rooms, so I had a huge selection to choose from. Luckily, one of the first ones I looked at totally fit the bill.

It was a small room located on the second floor, not too far from a fire escape, just off the back hall. It had a skylight that opened to the roof – more escape access – and a porthole in the bathroom that looked down on the main walkway into the hotel. Totally weird, yet completely awesome.

And as far as the van, I located it in an alley adjacent to the row of buildings I was in. I had access to it by the alley where the fire escape landed. Perfect for a fast, safe getaway.

The first day there, I swear, I slept like fourteen hours.

I mean, I knew I was exhausted from all the running around, but damn, I had no idea I was that tired until I woke. You know how it feels when you've gotten that much sleep and you still feel exhausted? I'm sure we've all felt that way at one time or another. Well, that was it for me. And after I woke, I stayed in bed listening to music for at least another hour.

When my feet finally hit the floor – somewhere around lunch-time – I washed up best I could with bottled water, then got dressed. Once finished, I strapped my AR to my back and my 9mm to my chest, then left the room and moved to the downstairs to find some grub.

Rummaging through the kitchen I found a bunch of canned food - some spoiled, some not - and cooking paraphernalia. Grabbing some of the still edible things - enough for both lunch and dinner - and a hot plate, I threw these things into a sack, then made my way back to the room to start the feast.

As soon as I was done cooking and eating, fatigue took over once again, and I napped. When I woke a couple hours later, I ate a little more, then listened to some music and played on my internet-less tablet until it got dark. Then feeling the need for sleep once more, I laid back on the bed and didn't wake again until sunrise.

Or, should I say, when I barely woke at sunrise!?

I'm not sure exactly what woke me. It might've been the wind pushing a shutter against a window, or it might've been some obscure creak or groan from the ancient building. I suppose it could have been either. What I really think it was though, was my body telling me something was off and that I needed to rise.

Opening my heavy eyes, I instantly realized my heart felt funny. Like maybe it wasn't beating, or that its beats were off somehow. Shocked awake by the sensation, I shot up in bed, my hand swinging towards my chest. Closing my palm over my heart, I felt as it quickly started racing, adrenalin causing it to go from almost stopped to nearly two-hundred beats a minute.

Swinging my legs off the bed, I hunched forward and tried to calm myself by taking some long slow breaths. It took a good minute or so, but eventually the pounding subsided.

As I sat there just breathing, in and out, in and out, I tried to figure out what'd happened to me. I hadn't felt like that in a while, like maybe months. It took a bit, but I figured it out. And when I did, I almost kicked myself in my ass.

Energy drinks.

I hadn't had an energy drink in almost three days. I'd run out of them while I was on the road, and I'd totally forgotten about stopping for more.

I mean, I'd been drinking Diet Pepsi since I ran out, but it wasn't the same. Not by a long shot. But up until that point I'd only half trusted what JC'd told me about drinking energy drinks to keep up your heart rate.

Obviously, I started feeling that I must've been wrong. What I'd experienced when I woke that morning was proof that his spiel'd been legit. Or at least that's what I thought. I don't know if it was something in the drinks besides the caffeine that kept the heart rate up, or at least surge-proof. JC seemed to think it was.

After he'd relayed this little fact, he'd also confided that he'd tried other avenues as well. But supposedly those avenues, whatever they were, didn't work like the caffeine did. So, with his expertise – and the fact that he was still living and semi-sane – I'd didn't bother trying anything else.

My bad, I guess.

Anyway, feeling like I had the problem solved, I rose from the bed, did some quick calisthenics – push-ups, jumping jacks, knee bends, and the like – then threw on my clothes. After strapping on both my weapons, I left the relative safety of the hotel room, walked down the hall to the fire escape, then made my way down and away from the building.

Traveling down the alley to the van, I gave it a quick once over. I thought about driving it around. You know, to be able to pick up a bunch of drinks. But thinking about the noise I'd make, I opted not to gather the attention.

I walked for a bit through the empty and dead-fish smelling streets until I reached one of the main boulevards – Saint Ann, I think – then followed that for a bit. Filled with all kinds of tourist attractions, I could see that most of the stores – stores that would've carried energy drinks – were already ransacked. But, with my mission in mind, I just kept walking and searching.

It took me about two hours to find a store that had energy drinks. The store I found – a Circle K … shoutout to Bill and Ted … was raided like the others, but it looked like only the shelves and cases had been looted. Looking past the nearly empty shelves to the inside of the cooler, I noticed a small, heavily stretch wrapped, pallet way in the back. It was so heavily stretch wrapped, in fact, that I couldn't quite tell what the contents were. The pallet looked to be stacks of some sort of tall cans, similar to my beloved Rockstars. But beyond that little fact, it – they – were a mystery. So, with weapon in hand, and nothing but time to kill, I decided to investigate.

Entering the cooler by a side entrance, I had to wiggle my way past fallen shelving and over empty stacks of various items to reach the full pallet. Sure, it took some finagling, ducking my head down or twisting my hip and such, but I finally made my way through the cluster to reach the mysterious plastic covered items.

But just as I was about to reach it, my foot suddenly slipped on something – maybe a can – sending me forward. As my body started downward, hitting various metal and plastic containers along the way, I quickly reached out with my free hand to stop my fall. Finding a cloth surface – something that felt similar to a burlap bag – in between a group of pallets, my progress downward was halted mere inches from smacking my head on a wood slat.

I stayed that way for a moment, trying to figure out my balance – trying to figure out what I could put where to right myself – when suddenly the burlap sack gave way. Hearing a snap like a tree limb, I suddenly dropped about four inches, sending my balancing hand into something murky. Murky, and wet.

Finding my balance – trying quickly to get away from the grossness – I jumped up, hitting my head on a metal rack. Stunned slightly, it took me a moment. I reached up to touch the back of my head to make sure it wasn't bleeding but stopped when I realized that my hand was covered in something. A thick, dark liquid that was sticky and smelled to high heaven.

Putting down my 9, I reached for my phone, turned on its light, then shined it on my hand. Sure enough, my hand was covered with a reddish-brown sheen from fingertips to wrist.

In the back of my mind, I knew instantly what it was. But, just like most things you don't want to admit to yourself, the back of my brain didn't want to relay that info to the front. Instead of admitting it to myself, I did the one thing I probably shouldn't have. I twisted my light around and pointed it on the spot where my hand had picked up the goo. And the moment my eyes met the object, fire shot to the back of my throat and my stomach retched.

Lying there, shoved between two pallets, was a human body. A body in the midst of decay.

It was a male – that much I could tell. He had very short hair – the hair that was still attached, that is. And his eyes and tongue were bulging out from a grotesquely emaciated face. In the middle of his chest – a chest still covered by a plaid shirt – was the indent where my hand had gone through. But that indent was slowly going away.

The center was starting to fill with fluid. A thick dark liquid that I could only guess was a mixture of bile … and blood.

When the smell finally hit my nose, I instantly turned away as I tried not to vomit. I was unsuccessful. Finding a spot off to the side, I emptied the contents of my stomach onto the floor at least three times before I even thought about recovering.

Momentarily ignoring my stomach, I snatched a cloth from one of the shelves, quickly wiped off my hand, then moved past the body to continue my quest. And, as you'd probably guessed, I was in luck. Tearing back some of the stretch wrapped plastic I saw that the pallet in question was indeed full of energy drinks. My energy drinks. My Rockstars.

Quickly grabbing as many as I could carry, I swiftly made my way out of the cooler, through the store, and back to the outside. As soon as the fresh air hit me, I breathed in deep, trying to get the stink – and the sight – out of my mind.

Walking back towards the hotel, I vowed to myself that I would be back for more before I left the city. I mean, regardless of the body, the pallet of drinks was veritable gold. A precious commodity that I might not find again. I just had to keep telling myself it was more of a need than a want. It was something I needed to survive.

CHAPTER 14

That night, with Rockstar on my nightstand, I slept quite well. That night, and the next. I'd grabbed enough for a few days, which I figured was all I'd need until I hit the road again. In fact, I told myself just that. That once the ones I'd nabbed ran out, I would pack up my stuff, load up my van, then hit the road, grabbing the rest of the pallet on my way out of town.

Unfortunately, that didn't quite happen. I mean, it did … just not in the way I thought it would.

It was about three days later – near the end of my Rockstar stash – that I woke to some noises coming from outside. And actually, to be honest, when the noises started, I didn't wake at first. You'd think, with my body now replenished with energy drink, I would've been on my tiptoes. But I wasn't. The caffeine – or whatever it was in the glorious drink – had me pacified, sleeping like a small tike nestled in his mother's bosom. And if it wasn't for the loud crash that followed the appearance of the noises, I might've slept through the whole thing.

Lucky for me, I didn't.

The crash I heard – the one that woke me – sounded like it was caused by a trash can being knocked over. At least that's what I guessed it was. Hearing it, my eyes shot open and I looked up through the skylight. But it was still dark out. All I could see when I looked up was a dark purplish haze. The kind you see sometimes in the morning, telling you it was way too early to get out of bed.

Feeling that my brain should still be in dreamland, I closed my eyes and tried to pretend it was part of a dream. Or maybe a remnant of my past. And it would've worked, except for the noises that followed.

Hearing a murmur – something that sounded barely human – I closed my eyes and focused on sound. This was not an easy feat for me. My hearing, damaged by years of hard rock and metal, only heard a constant high-pitched ringing at first. The constant buzz that started after a Metallica concert I'd gone to in 2005.

Trying to ignore the drone, I continued to concentrate. Eventually it finally came to me. The noises turned out to be voices. One I could hear distinctly, one not so much.

"I'm sure she ran down here," a deep male voice whispered. It was followed by the mumble I'd heard before.

"It's either this building or the one across the way. Nah, I'm sure it's this one," the male voice said.

This voice, and what would become another, started getting louder as they approached. I knew instantly they were coming from the alleyway just to the right of my second story room. I then heard footsteps on the cobblestones below. I could tell it wasn't just one, or even two guys. It was at least four or five – maybe more. Some blended together and there were echoes, making it hard to tell. And the ringing in my ears didn't help, obviously.

The footsteps continued to get louder for a few moments until they abruptly stopped just to the left of my room, where the side entrance to the hotel sat.

"It's this one. I know it's this one," voice one said.

"How do you know, Brainiac?" another male voice retorted, no longer a whisper.

"Because … look," voice one replied, then paused for a second. "See that? That wasn't like that the last time we came through here!"

My mind instantly whirled, spinning with a thousand questions. Who were these guys? How many were there? Were they Crazies? How often did they come through here? *Why* were they here? Who is this *she* they were looking for? And, more importantly, did they see my van?

These, and a hundred more just like them, spun into a tornado in my mind. They eventually culminated into a single and most important question: Did they know I was in the hotel?

I tried to stay quiet, listening but not reacting. It was difficult to do. My brain was telling me to run and hide. And it took everything I had to stay where I was, and to also not piss the bed. It felt like an eternity but was only mere seconds. Finally, voice two – apparently the leader of the group – spoke up.

"You two, head to the front. You guys, go to the back. Dingus and me will go in this way. The minute you hear me head in, get your asses in there. You got that?"

"Yeah," came at least six voices – maybe ten. The thought that there were so many practically sent me into shock. I easily could have frozen and just stayed that way, but I didn't. Coming up with a quick plan, I waited for a sign before I started to react.

I stayed still while they all moved off. As soon as they were away, I heard the leader, and apparently a guy named Dingus, move into the doorway of the side entrance. The moment there were no more footsteps in the alley, I quietly rose from the bed and got dressed.

Okay, here's the thing.

As you probably remember, I'm ex-military, and had been on the move before. What does that mean? Well, I was already used to having my things ready to go mostly all the time. So, it only took me a few moments to get dressed, grab my essentials, and get ready to make my escape. All I needed was that one clue that my route was clear, and I'd be on it in a moment.

I knew once all the guys were inside the hotel downstairs, I'd have a clear shot for the roof. And from there it was only a hop, skip, and a jump down the fire escape to my waiting van. Oh sure, there were other factors to think about. Factors such as the number of guys in their party, if they knew about my van, and the like. But with each of those was a contingency I'd previously planned for. All I needed to do was start my move.

Stick and move, buddy. Simply stick and move, I told myself once again.

Yet, as it turned out, that didn't happen.

As soon as I was ready to bolt, I moved over to the porthole – you know, the one that looked down into the main hotel walkway – to see if all the guys I'd heard were assembled. After quietly opening it, I peered down into the dimly lit corridor and saw a group of three approach from the left, three more from the right, and another couple from porthole south. All-in-all, eight guys. All milling around and chattering but remaining in the center as if waiting for something.

I don't know why I stayed. Maybe it was to listen to their prattle, to see if they were actually Crazies or if they were normal like me. Up to that point it could have gone either way.

My thoughts were confirmed a moment later when I heard a loud crunching sound come from north of the porthole. A cracking sound that was followed by a very high-pitched scream. Next came some breaking noises, followed by a woman screaming.

"Let go of me, you son of a bitch!" the woman yelled. It was then followed by another scream. But it wasn't a scream that contained any fear. It was more of a howl filled with pure anger. A shriek of genuine, unadulterated rage.

"Jesus fucking Christ!" I heard someone yell, then, "Fucking bitch bit me!"

Next, I heard a smacking sound, then another, then … nothing. Nothing but the milling and mumbling I'd heard from the crew below.

Just as I was about to turn and head out – take myself away from the potential danger – I saw three people appear from the direction of the sound. Two men … and a woman being dragged. She wasn't struggling, though. In fact, she looked to be unconscious.

That is, until she wasn't.

Swiftly raising her head from the floor, she looked left, then right, quickly getting her bearings. The moment she seemed to realize the seriousness of her situation, she started kicking, punching, and, of course, squealing her fucking head off.

"You fucking bastards! Get your fucking hands off me! ARRR!" she howled, then increased her flailing. A second later one of her legs got lose from her captor. She wasted no time using it to kick the guy directly in the balls. And it made solid contact. I could almost feel the guy's pain from fifty feet away.

"Fuck!" the guy howled as he dropped to his knees. She then sent him sprawling with another kick. That time to his jaw.

The other guy, seeing her free foot, dropped the other before he could get his. And that was all she needed. Like a flash she was on her feet, sprinting to get away. But it did her no good. Before she could make it two steps, the guy closest to her shoved her hard. She shot back like a rocket into the wall, hitting her head. Dazed by the blow, her knees wobbled, and she slumped like a rag doll to the floor.

"What the actual fuck were you thinking, little girl?" one of the milling guys spat. The others, upon hearing his taunt, broke out into a fit of laughter. Stepping forward from the two closest to my vantage point, the accuser walked over to the girl, shaking his head. When he was within a step, he bent down to address her.

"You really thought you'd get away from us, did you?" he asked, then waited for a response. But she didn't give one. Instead she just looked at him like she was too stunned to answer.

Seeing this, the man let out a small laugh and again started shaking his head. Thinking this was her chance, the girl put on a sudden burst of speed, swinging her leg out to kick the guy. But it was like he knew it was coming. Instead of being caught off guard, the man gave a small jump, easily avoiding the contact. The moment both his feet were firmly back on the ground, he moved forward, latched onto her hair with his left hand, balled a fist with his right and connected … hard.

Even at a distance I could hear the impact, and the groan that followed. Both noises sounded wet, but in different ways. Both made me feel the same, though. Angry and sick to my stomach.

Prostrate by the evident agony, the girl managed to find enough strength to get her hands and feet under her. But as she tried to rise, the man pushed her down once more then kicked her in the stomach. After that blow, I could almost feel the air change. Instead of trying to rise, she just laid there whimpering and crying from pain.

"See boys!" the man said, turning to each in the group. "There's nothing special about this one! She's just as weak as any other woman."

I could hear the girl wince as if she wanted to say something. Instead she just laid there on her side, crying and clutching her stomach. A weeping that called out for help.

Now, had this been happening in my life before The Surge, I would've leapt to her aid … or at least called the cops. But it wasn't. Below me now was a group of Crazies. An assembly that outnumbered me ten to one. And I knew I had no chance. Oh sure, I had military training. But that was no match for ten guys, no matter how many spaghetti westerns or John Wick films I'd seen in my past.

Then again, I was still me, and I knew I had to do something.

So, fighting against every rational thought in my head, I reached over to my side, found a semi heavy tchotchke – you know, a figurine like your grandma used to collect – and picked it up. Raising it above my head, I prepared to smash it, hoping the noise would make a few investigate. I knew, being on the second floor, I'd have some time to get away if I did it right. But my timing had to be spot on. I gave myself a fifty-fifty chance of making it out of there alive.

Yeah, I was totally being optimistic. But I had to do something, right!?

Anyway, just as I was about to smash the bobble, I heard the main Crazy call out to the others.

"So, what do you say boys? How's about we teach this bitch a lesson on who's in charge?"

Turning to her, he reached down to her jeans, flipped her onto her belly, then started yanking them down. Seeing this, I knew it was my last opportunity to help her. My final chance to be heroic.

Unfortunately, that chance never came.

As I turned and lifted my arm to throw the figurine, I heard the woman scream. That was followed by a man's shout.

Pausing mid-throw, I looked back down through the porthole. My eyes went wide at what I saw.

Instead of the rape scene I'd expected to see, something totally different occurred. The woman, no longer prone, was now standing and she was holding a knife. The man who had started undressing her was now lying on the floor in front of her clutching at his throat. Just below him was a puddle of blood which was quickly pooling around him.

As the man laid there bleeding, begging for help from the others, each tried to rush forward to assist. But the woman wasn't having it. As each moved forward to assist him, the woman swung her knife at them, forcing them to stay back.

This only went on for a minute or so, though. The gash in his neck – apparently a deep one – didn't take long to take its toll. Before anyone could make it to his side, the bleeding man slowly stopped moving, and his body went totally limp.

It also didn't take long for the men to realize that the odds were now nine to one. Seeing their boss lying dead in front of them, they immediately dismissed him and started closing on the woman. As they did, for a split second I thought that maybe she had a way out.

I was wrong, of course.

Seeing the one against nine odds, the anger in the woman's eyes suddenly disappeared. And for a moment – just for a moment, though – I thought that maybe she'd drop the knife and let them have their way. But then I saw something alight in her. A glint in her eye that was followed by the glint of the knife. Shifting the blade in her hand, she unexpectedly brought it to her throat then ran it across, inflicting a fatal wound.

Everything seemed to stop for a moment then. Both below me and in my own mind. All ten of us watched as blood suddenly sprang from the woman's carotid artery. Then we all watched on as the life quickly left her body. No more than a heartbeat later she fell dead to the floor next to her intended rapist.

Shocked and horrified by the sight of her suicide, I almost dropped the figurine. Not that I'm sure it would've mattered. The nine guys below were transfixed on the woman and their dead leader.

Then, if things weren't surreal enough, everything went totally sideways.

Two men, I'm not sure which ones, quickly ran forward to their boss' body. Dragging him to the side, the two started stripping him of any loot he might've been carrying. I didn't see what they took. I couldn't. My eyes were fixed on what the others were doing.

As if some strange call was invoked from an entity I couldn't hear, the remaining men moved forward, seized the girl's body, and started stripping it of its clothing. At first, I thought that maybe these guys were doing the same to her as the others were doing to their leader. I was dead wrong, though. As soon as the woman was naked, the biggest of the lot pushed the others aside, dropped his pants, and mounted her lifeless corpse.

Seeing this, I think I threw up in my mouth.

Obviously, I didn't want to – couldn't – see any more. Gently placing down the tchotchke, I picked up my gear and quietly made my way out of the joint.

Lucky for me, the Crazies in the hotel must've been the only ones there. Although it was still dark out, I didn't see any sign of anyone else as I made my way to the van. After hightailing it away from that neighborhood, I stopped at the store with the energy drinks, grabbed what I could, then quickly made my way out of Dodge.

As soon as I was away from the congested part of the city – as soon as I had a chance to relax a little – my mind immediately returned to what I'd witnessed.

I had no doubt that those guys were Crazies and figured the woman was probably one as well. I didn't know why they were chasing her. Was she someone from their tribe that'd done something wrong? Or was she just some random woman they'd run into then chased? I knew, in the long run, these questions didn't matter. I knew what I'd seen was a thousand ways wrong. And there was no getting over that. But that was the way of society, then and now.

And it'd be something I'd have to live with … if I wanted to continue living.

CHAPTER 15

The first thing that came to mind as I saw the "Welcome to New Orleans" sign in my rear-view mirror were the words JC had left me with: Drive to Survive.

Had I kept those simple words in mind, I would've never witnessed the things I'd seen in NOLA. Then again, had I not seen them – experienced them, really – I may not have lasted through the things yet to come.

But I'm getting ahead of myself again, aren't I!? So, let me pick up after I crossed the Mississippi.

It was still winter, and although it'd been mild to that point, there were still storms ahead. And I think I ran into every single one of them.

Following US-90 west, I didn't make it far before I ran into a storm that practically blasted me off the road. In fact, I only made it a little past New Iberia before I had to find shelter. Lucky for me I found a little cabin just outside of town where I was able to hole up until the storm passed … three days later!

As soon as the weather cleared, I was back on the road. I left US-90 and followed LA-14 which took me directly west for a spell before taking me north to I-10. I-10 was the only good place to cross the lakes and rivers between there and the roads leading to Houston.

That time I was able to make it all the way to Beaumont, Texas, before I hit another storm. Only eighty-five miles from Houston, Luckily, that one only laid me up for just over a day.

That night, through the window of my van, I could see the lights of Houston, and couldn't help but get excited. Although Nina and her rock and roll had been keeping me company to that point, I couldn't wait to see if I could find someone like me in a big city.

I mean, big city … am I right!? There just had to be people there like me.

Although it'd only been a few weeks since I'd had human companionship, I found myself longing for it. Which was weird, considering I'd always thought of myself as a loner. Except when I was with Lorie, that is. Together … just us. We were loners together. And everyone else could piss off. At least that's how I always thought.

Anyway, like I was saying. I was only about eighty-five miles away from Houston, and I could see the lights in the distance. But, no matter how excited I was, I knew I needed to wait until the morning before heading there. Not that I'd seen any Crazies on the road. But if there were Norms in the city making those lights, I knew there had to be Crazies as well.

As soon as the sun was up, so was I. I left the side roads and jumped on I-10 to take me into the city. After driving a few miles, I stopped by a car on the side of the road and took the gas that was left in its tank. Then, after I had the van mostly topped off, I hopped in and made my way into Houston.

Or at least I tried.

As I approached the city, the first thing I noticed was a funny smell. Well, funny's not the word for it. It was more of a sickly, farty odor … but kind of off. I thought nothing of it, though. I figured it was just the smell of Houston. After all, I grew up in Cleveland. And anyone who's been to Cleveland, or any other major city – especially the steel producing ones – knows the odor that comes from them. Put simply, they smell like old farts.

More than a few times, back in the day, while passing through the outskirts of Cleveland along I-490, I've looked over at my passenger and said, "Damn, dude! That was rude! Roll the fucking window down!" But then I remembered, *you're passing through Cleveland, Paul. That's just the Cleveland smell.*

Well, that's kind of what I was sensing. But it was slightly different. *Different location?* I thought. Maybe. But I didn't know. At least not at first.

Because of the time of year and the weather, there was a haze in the air. You know, a cloud cover that hung low, just over the tops of the downtown buildings. But it wasn't until I got close that I saw that the haze wasn't really cloud cover at all. The strangeness of it alerted me immediately. It was much darker and thicker. Like the kind you'd see coming out of smokestacks. Again, a lot like Cleveland.

In addition to this, as I got closer, I could see a hint of orange every now and then. But I disregarded it. I just figured it was the morning sun glinting off skyscraper windows. I mean, what did I know!?

It wasn't until I was within, maybe, five miles or so that I put two, and two, and two together. But you've probably already guessed where I was headed with this. I'm sure you've read the headlines.

Houston, my friend, was on fire.

Not all of it, mind you. Just the major parts of downtown.

As I got closer, I could see that every building had some sort of fire inside of it. Or at least smoke coming out of it. It was literally like something you'd see in a sci-fi movie about the end of the world. Which, I guess, was … well, you know … what was really happening.

Seeing this horrific sight made me take pause … and well, pull over and stop the car so I could figure out my next steps.

Houston seemed like a bust. After all, I couldn't just drive through burning streets, no matter how cool and post-apocalyptic it was. If a fire itself didn't get me, the smoke definitely would. No, I had to stay put and figure out my options.

Pulling out one of the handy-dandy maps I'd picked up along the way, I started leafing through it. Up to that point, the satellite navigation was still working, but I knew that it wasn't sophisticated enough to reroute me around a burning Houston.

So, manual routing it was.

Turning to a map of the greater Houston area, I saw that the beltway – the loop that encircled the city – wasn't too far from my current location. In fact, it was just behind me a couple miles. I knew I'd have to backtrack a little, but that was fine. It was a much better option than going straight through hell itself.

Placing the van in drive, I checked my side mirror – force of habit – then moved left on the highway. Looking down the road a piece, I didn't see a break in the median. The median at that point being a concrete strip that separated the eastbound and westbound lanes. Which I considered was no big deal. As I'd driven in, I remembered seeing breaks every few miles or so. All I'd need to do was back up, drive the way direction for a bit, then cut over to the other side.

Seemed like a good plan, am I right!?

Well, after looking around to verify that nothing was in the road – you know, as one does – I placed the van in reverse and lightly touched the gas pedal. The van immediately started backing up. As soon as I felt the rear tires go off the pavement, I stopped, placed the car back in Drive, then stepped on the gas once more.

And that's when I felt it.

I felt a strange lurch like one of my wheels had just dropped into a pothole. Yet it didn't feel quite like that. It was a lurch that rocked and popped up the entire van, as if something had suddenly ... well ... popped up under the car, then immediately sent it downward. Feeling this ... this weirdness ... I took my foot off the gas for a moment to see if the van would continue forward, or if it would remain stopped.

Unfortunately, it did the latter.

Having been stuck in a ditch or two before in my life, I figured this was no big deal. Lowering the shifter to first gear, I stepped on the gas expecting the front to come back up. But it didn't. I tried it a second time, punching it then letting up, punching it then letting up. You know, trying to rock it. But again, I felt nothing. No movement forward ... no movement backward.

Looking in the rearview, I glanced back then tried again. But again, nothing. The van didn't rock, and the wheels – the portions I could see at least – didn't seem to be spinning at all.

I instantly thought to myself, *This ... this is No Bueno.*

With a heavy sigh, I placed the van in park, shut off the engine, picked up my 9, then exited the vehicle. Walking around to its front, I looked under the bumper to see if I could see anything. But nothing jumped out at me. You know, leaking fluids or smoke billowing out. So, I moved around to the back.

As soon as I passed the side door, I saw the problem ... and my jaw dropped.

The back passenger-side wheel was sticking up into the wheel well. And as I leaned down to inspect, I could see why. The entire wheel – the u-joint – was disconnected from the drive train. The one and only driving wheel I had was no longer part of the van.

"Fuck," I said aloud as I inspected the damage and, more so, what I thought it would take to fix it. That being a fucking miracle. After a few seconds of this, I stared up into the sky as I repeated my feelings in a much harsher tone.

A thousand thoughts instantly hit my brain. First and foremost was how screwed I was. The second was the most obvious. My van had all my stuff in it; I couldn't just leave it there. They kind of dwindled from there.

After the initial shock and worry ran their course, I told my brain to start working the problem. It was still early, but I was nowhere near another working vehicle. I needed to get to a car and get moving again. I knew I needed to make my way far beyond the city before any Crazies inside it woke.

Grabbing my binoculars, I quickly searched the areas closest to the van. As luck would have it, there was a neighborhood off to the north that looked promising. And it didn't seem to be that distant. I figured I could probably make it there in fifteen minutes. Then my only problem would be finding transportation … without finding any trouble.

Climbing back into the van, I quickly grabbed the things I'd thought I'd need – my weapons, a warmer jacket, my fully charged iPhone, and a few other items – then locked it up and hit the road. As I'd thought, it didn't take long to get there. It was just before noon when I walked through the gates of the nearest development.

The small suburban community I entered held maybe about thirty or forty houses that zigged and zagged, this way and that, and had a lot of cul-de-sacs. This was typical of the suburbs if you've ever spent time in one. Most of the houses were pretty upscale, telling me I'd stumbled into the "rich" side of town. A little weird that it was so close to the highway, but I guessed it might have been a Texas thing. I mean, who am I to judge!? I grew up on the westside of Cleveland. There was your fancy, and then there was your "not so much." I was just lucky the piece of shit crapped out where it did. A better neighborhood meant a better chance of finding an SUV or, if I was lucky, maybe a full-sized van.

I decided my best approach was to head straight down the middle of the street. Yeah, easier to spot me, but that was the point. It was the middle of the day. Almost zero chance of one of the Crazies being up. I still didn't make a huge amount of noise, just in case.

As I walked, I used the "wall-follower" rule – always taking a right turn as I headed in and around the subdivision. And, as you guessed it, as I passed each house – inspecting driveways for possible cars – that tune from Rush kept … well … rushing into my head.

Pausing in my search, I reached for my iPhone, did some scrolling, then found Rush's Greatest Hits. After placing it on Shuffle, I raised the volume just loud enough to hear, then continued walking. It helped to pass the time, if only marginally.

I was probably six songs into the playlist when I found what I thought I was looking for. A relatively new, jet black, 2021 BMW X7.

Quickly surveying its interior, it appeared to be immaculate – pristine even. The outside was only slightly worse for the wear. A layer of dust and dirt covering the vehicle, showing it hadn't been used in months. If I'd had to hazard a guess, I would've said it was newly purchased before the worst had befallen the family that owned it. Presumably the owners of the house I now stood in front of.

The SUV was locked, so I knew what I had to do. Walking up the driveway, past the attached garage, I climbed the steps onto the small front porch then tried the door. It was locked, of course, but I had a work-around. Smashing one of the small windows to the left of the door, I reached in, found the lock, turned it, then tried the handle. The door swung open easy as pie.

Not being my first rodeo, I seized two pieces of cotton from my jacket pocket then shoved each in a nostril. You probably guessed why. Odds were the interior smelled to high heaven – dead bodies, spoiled food, and whatnot – and I wanted to spare my olfactory center any onslaught if I could.

As I entered the house, I briefly thought about searching the rooms to see what I could find. But remembering the time and my "miles-to-go" situation, I nixed that idea and made a beeline for the kitchen. I was hoping for a pegboard or a bowl with keys. Not finding anything, I moved to the foyer, then down the hall. Seeing a doorway that led to the garage, I followed it, searching the walls with my light as I went. Not having any luck, I decided to try the garage itself before moving back into the house. I started to get depressed thinking that I'd have to look for dead bodies next, searching pockets for keys.

Opening the door to the garage, I shined my light on the wall. Sure enough, there was a pegboard with several sets of keys. Reaching up, I started leafing through them trying to find the ones with the BMW key fob attached. Once I found them, I started to pull them from the hook. I stopped the moment my eyes caught a glimpse of a sight I'd only seen on TV.

A sleek, silver embossed cat, known to most as the leaping Jaguar.

I instantly stayed my hand, not believing my eyes. After blinking a couple times, I let go of the BMW keys and grabbed the other set from the hook, then peered at them as if caught up in a dream.

It took me … oh … about a minute to recover. At least that's what it felt like in my mind, even though in all reality it was only a second or two.

When I finally recovered, I did the obvious. I pressed the top button – the one that usually locked or unlocked all the doors.

Hearing a familiar chirp directly behind me, I practically fell down the steps into the garage as I whirled. The place was pitch black and I couldn't make out anything, so I hit the button again. That time yellow and red lights flashed, and I saw the hint of … a sports car.

Turning my light towards the center of the garage, I could barely make out the form. But being like a kid in a candy store, I knew I had to have more.

Moving between cars, I located the red pulldown attached to the nearest pulley. After releasing the catch, I moved to the door. It took a little bit of effort to get it going, but in the end, I was able to raise it. Following the early afternoon light into the garage, I did another doubletake the moment I saw the image I'd only seen in car magazines.

The flowing form of a cherry red Jaguar F-type.

Obviously, seeing this, I couldn't believe my eyes … even though it was right in front of me. And all thoughts of obtaining an SUV or surviving The Surge left my mind as I beheld one of my dream cars.

Feeling like Ferris Bueller on his day off, I knew instantly what I had to do. Looking towards the imaginary fourth wall to my right, I smiled at it then gave a slow nod. I think I also said "Fuckin' A right!" But that's a whole-nother movie.

Moving towards the vision, I unlocked its doors, threw my weapons and backpack onto the passenger seat, then got behind the wheel to examine it. It had everything, and I mean everything, that I wanted and needed in life. Leather accoutrements, power everything, GPS navigation, and, of course, SiriusXM.

Without another thought I started it up. And without even a consideration of time or location, the car instantly roared to life.

Hearing the engine's purr, I suddenly felt as if I was meant to find this prize. Like this vehicle was specially left there for me as some sort of gift. I'd missed Christmas along the way, I knew that. And this prize … this "best gift ever" certainly made up for it.

Saying "fuck it" to every consideration about my current situation or future, I placed the car in reverse and moved it to the street. After adjusting the mirrors, I drove the Jag out of the development and made my way back to the busted-down van.

The Jag, being the two-door type, couldn't carry much besides me and a few essentials. But at that point, I didn't care. I'd been through a lot, and I knew Santa knew that. What I needed to survive would have to take a backseat for a while.

At least until the universe or the Easter Bunny told me something different.

Backtracking as I'd originally intended, I skirted around Houston, then got back on the I-10. As the sun started to set that night, I was about one-hundred miles out of town, thanks to the speed and maneuverability of my newfound friend.

I continued to drive for a bit longer until my eyes started to drag. Finding a secluded spot just off the highway, I pulled over and shut down the car. After feeling the leather steering wheel in my hands one final time, I leaned back the seat and let rock and roll – and Nina's voice – carry me off to dreamland.

When I woke the next morning, I was a little sore, sure, but I ignored it. After relieving myself – outside the car, obviously – I ate some food and hit the road. My next stop would be … well … closer to my destination.

And with a V-8 under my control, I had a blast getting there.

CHAPTER 16

And now we get to the freaky part. Oh, I know, I know, there's been a lot of freakiness up until now, but this … this was ultra-freaky. But not in the way you're probably thinking.

After I'd made my way out of Houston, I drove down I-10 towards San Antonio. I thought about driving towards Dallas, but after what I'd heard from Nina on XM, I was sure it'd be a shit show.

As I neared San Antonio, I'd been on the road for nearly twelve hours. Twelve very slow-going hours. Hours of having to veer around wrecks and trash – not to mention the occasional corpse here and there.

Driving up the turnpike a ways, I reached a point in the road where I thought it'd be safe to open it up a little. You know, sports car and all. And, as my speed gradually increased, so did the volume on the radio. You know how it is. I was listening to my favorite playlist – my Industrial one. Listening. Screaming at the top of my lungs.

Not paying full attention to the road. Super sloppy of me, I know, but lack of sleep and stress will do that to a body.

Cresting a hill, I should've been looking ahead, just in case someone was up there to the side of the road. It was late in the day. The sun was almost completely down, and I should've known better. But, like an idiot, I wasn't watching. Instead I was zigzagging the car as I barked out the words to the song *Oxyacetylene* by the band Cubanate.

Reaching back for another Rockstar to replace the dead soldier I'd just tossed out the window, I almost missed it. And, I swear, if it wasn't for the glint of some glass from the side of the road, I would have, and I probably would've been as dead as that can I'd thrown out moments before.

The split second my eyes caught the glint, I slammed – and I mean slammed – on the brakes. Which was a good thing. Because no more than one-hundred yards in front of me I saw movement. Someone was just off to the side of the road. I watched as the person moved up and tossed something across both lanes. I could tell what it was right away. I'm not sure what they called it in your neck of the woods. But to me – a Clevelander – I knew what the device was and, more importantly, what it did.

The device lying across the road was a Spike Strip.

The car bucked and jumped as it slowed, but eventually came to a complete stop no more than ten yards from the spikes. Like a rabbit seeing a trap, I quickly glanced around, then jammed the car into reverse. It was of no use, though. Two men suddenly appeared behind me; guns raised. Turning, I saw two more appear to my front and out my passenger's side. Then, as if the flood gates released, a slew of guys all dressed in cyberpunk gear – you know, Road Warrior style – appeared to my left, all sprinting towards my car.

Without anywhere to go, and thinking I was probably already dead meat, I placed the car in park, lowered the driver's window, and placed both hands on the steering wheel.

Something funny happened then. Something that in a million years I would've never expected. From somewhere in the back of the crowd a loud almost ear shattering whistle erupted. You know the kind. When someone sticks their fingers in their mouth and blows hard!? I've never been able to do it myself, so whoever did it was a pro – or at least much better at it than I was.

Anyway, as soon as the ear-piercing sound dissipated, the entire group – down to the last man – suddenly stopped and came to attention.

Keeping my hands on the wheel, I shifted and craned to see if I could see where and, more importantly, who'd just broken the sound barrier. It didn't take long to pick him out. The group of men to my left suddenly parted to reveal a character – and I do mean a character.

The guy – the only one still moving towards my car – was tall, maybe six-foot-three, and skinny. He sported brown and purple hair cut short, a brownish beard neatly trimmed, and – get this – he was dressed fully from head to foot like fucking Aquaman.

Yes … *that* Aquaman. I shit you not.

As far as I could tell, the only difference between the Jason Momoa Aquaman and this dude were muscles – which this guy severely lacked. He also wore a pair of ivory handled six shooters, one strapped low on each hip. Gunslinger style.

Color me impressed.

Before I had a chance to take the guy in – really take him in, that is – he was standing three feet from me, glaring at me. He was also doing something I didn't expect. He was slowly bobbing his head up and down to the music still blaring from my speakers. He stayed that way – staring at me and bobbing – until the chorus broke. The moment it did, he leaned down, raised a hand to his neck, then gave me the universal signal to cut the motor. Returning a small nod, I reached down and hit the stop button. As soon as the motor died, I reached over and turned down the music to a loud roar.

The guy gave me a smile, then as if we were old friends, he said, "Great tune, man! That's Cubanate, right?"

Confused, I blinked at him a couple times before I could respond.

"Ya … yeah. It is …" I barely managed. "How … how did you know that?"

He let out a small laugh. "Eh, my band opened for them a few years back. You know, before humanity took a dump."

He motioned around. It didn't take a brain surgeon to know what he meant.

"Cool guys, Cubanate. I heard they both bought it during The Surge. Kinda sad about that."

I was barely able to nod, but I did. The kind of nod you give a car salesman when he's droning on about a new vehicle.

There was something about this guy and his stature that triggered something. It might have been his comment about opening for Cubanate, or maybe it was his smile. I wasn't quite sure which. But there was definitely something familiar about him, like maybe I'd seen him before.

"So, you're probably wondering why we stopped you?" he asked, all cop-like. I only returned a shrug.

"Well, here's the thing. We're pirates ... sort of. We prey on the traffic passing through our area here. There isn't a lot, but we make do."

I continued my stare, only half listening as he rambled.

"Speaking of which, we'll be taking your car," he stated, then added. "And probably your life. Unless there's some sort of ... you know ... trade you can make for it. Gas, grass, or cash, as they say. You got a lead on any of that stuff?"

The words were coming so fast I didn't know how to respond. Plus, there was that something about him, you know, nagging me – dragging my thoughts away from his rhetoric.

The guy stared at me, as if waiting for something. An answer. The guy was waiting on an answer. He spoke again before I could give one.

"Too bad you didn't come through here yesterday. We weren't here. We'd actually gotten a little too drunk the night before. Well, *they* did. I'm sober. Have been for years now. But I don't hold them back. I let them do whatever the fuck they want. Keeps them happy. Happy wife, happy life, so they say. Although, well, not really."

There was a mumble from the crowd. Someone must have been getting antsy. The guy standing before me turned and that's when everything he was saying and doing finally coalesced. It was the tattoo on his left bicep that triggered it, really. That tat was one I'd seen years back ... at a show. An Industrial show ... in Chicago. The opening bands were ones I'd never seen before. But I couldn't remember their names. At least not at first.

Turning away from the guy, I hit the next button on my radio. Skinny Puppy started playing, but I didn't let it continue. I hit next again, and again, and again until I heard what I was searching for.

Within seconds of the song starting, a loud, almost shrill voice blared from the speakers. A voice telling me how to get thirty extra guys on Contra – a Nintendo game. As soon as I knew I had it, I looked down at the name of the song, and more importantly, the name of the group. It was a group called "The Gothsicles." And the singer – the leader of the band – was none other than ...

"Brian?" I uttered, turning to the guy at my window. Hearing his name, he slowly turned to meet my gaze.

"What was that?" he asked. I continued.

"Brian ... Brian ... umm ... Ga ... Gaupner, isn't it?"

The guy's eyes went wide, and he blinked a few times before answering.

"It's Graupner. Do ... do I know you?"

I shook my head. "A ... a ... no. We've never met. But that's you on the radio, right?"

He listened for a moment, then his face changed. It was as if he'd just awoken from a dream. Hearing his name – hearing his song – had jogged his fading memory. A memory I knew was largely compromised by The Surge.

"Yeah ..." he nodded slowly. First to me, then to the beat.

"Yeah, that's me. Where did you ..."

"Get this?" I interrupted, everything suddenly coming back to me. "I've got a shit ton of music. All kinds of Industrial. Pretty sure I picked up *NESferatu* at the show you did a while back in Chicago. The one where you opened for Assemblage 23."

"No shit!?" he brightened, laughing a little. "Man, come to think of it, that was one great show! That was around 2008 if I remember. First time we opened for that big a crowd. And in Chicago, no less. Dude, that sure was a time."

"I traveled all the way from Cleveland to see it," I continued. "A23 skipped us that year. Only places close to see them were Chicago or Toronto. I picked Chicago. Because … you know … well … Chicago … and deep dish."

"No shit," he repeated then rotated his finger, motioning me to turn up the music. I did as asked. When I had it blaring once again, he turned to the guys behind him.

"Guys! Guys! Remember that band I told you I was in? This is one of my songs!"

The men started looking around at each other, then at Brian. By then he'd moved his hand near his face – you know, like he had a microphone – then started doing karaoke. The man knew what he was doing. He started jumping up and down, pointing to the crowd, and everything else he'd done on stage back in the day. It was a real treat to see.

Damn, I really miss live shows. Don't you!?

Anyway, while Brian went to town, the others watched for a moment, then joined in. They all started cavorting around, dancing and howling, as if they were all part of some sort of Industrial hoedown. And I guess, for all intents and purposes, that's exactly what it was. As the song ended, a very sweaty Brian slowed and turned to me.

"Wow! That was one huge trip down memory lane, man! Do you have any more of my tunes?"

I thought about it, then said, "Sure. I've got them and a couple thousand other songs on here."

I pointed to the thumb drive sticking out of the dash's USB. Without having to be asked, I removed it and handed it to him.

He took it, then stared at it for a bit as if contemplating what to do with it. He turned to his men and started tapping the drive with his finger.

"Hey Brian, I have a player in the back you can have. That's if you need one," I said. He turned back to me.

"It's Brain," he replied in a distant voice. I narrowed my eyes at him.

"My men call me Brain," he stated. "No one calls me Brian … at least not anymore."

"Brain?" I inquired. He was quick to respond.

"Yeah. I came down to Dallas about two years ago to play a show … you know … before all the shit hit the fan. When it did, me and a couple of guys left Dallas and headed out here to escape things. All the looting and killings and such. It didn't take long for them to realize my leadership skills … being the *brains* of it all. That's when they made me their leader," he pointed to all the guys around us.

"I changed my name to suit," he continued. "Not that it was much of a change. Now everyone just calls me Brain. Or *The* Brain. But no one calls me Brian. At least not anymore."

I gave a quick nod. Thoughts of Pinky and The Brain came to mind. Still do to this day.

"Since then, we've picked up about two dozen guys and some ladies. We have a commune about a mile that way," he stated, pointing a thumb to the south.

Right after saying this, his eyes changed. They went from coherency to … something. I'm not sure what. It was as if someone had flipped a switch changing Brian to Brain. It was really weird to see. Even weirder to hear.

Brian, now Brain, suddenly turned to the guys … or should I say, "his concert goers?" He then yelled out, "Hey guys! This dude has a shit ton of music!"

This announcement was followed by a thunderous roar from the crowd.

"There will be singing tonight … and dancing!" he barked, then asked. "What do you say about that!?"

There was another thunderous roar. Hearing it, Brain looked at me and smiled as if to say, "See? See what I've done here!?" And I couldn't let him down. He was looking for approval and I was willing to give it – especially if it meant saving my life. I took my hands off the wheel and started clapping and cheering along with the rest, trying my best to be a fellow groupie.

Brain gave a small nod of approval, then started performing a little jig. Seeing this, his guys started matching his movements. For a second, I thought I was in some strange musical. A dystopian "Music Man," if you get my drift. The man, Brain, was an absolute spellbinder. It was easy to see why he was the one put in charge.

They all pranced around, hooting, and hollering for a bit until Brain suddenly stopped. He started looking at a guy, just down the ridge, that wasn't dancing. He was just standing there looking over at us.

Brain's eyes narrowed on the man and waved for him to approach. When the man was within shouting distance, he motioned for him to stop.

"What's up?" Brain asked, then waited for an answer. It took a moment or two, but the man finally spoke.

"Does … does he have any No Doubt we can listen to?"

Brain glared at the man quizzically. "Does he have any … what?"

The man looked nervous – Rodney Dangerfield style. It took a coaxing wave of Brain's hand for him to speak again.

"I asked if he had … umm … any No Doubt. You know, Gwen Stefani's old band?"

Brain turned to me as if to ask. But before I had a chance to answer, he quickly turned, grabbed his left pistol from its holster, took aim, and shot the man smack dab in the middle of his forehead. It was a clean shot – through and through. The man lurched and wobbled a bit before his knees gave out. He was dead before he hit the ground.

Hearing the shot ring out, the entire place abruptly came to a standstill. There was a moment of silence as the others stared from Brain to lifeless body, back to Brain. Then, as if on cue, the entire group – including Brain – broke into a fit of laughter. And, after a moment, I did as well. Not because I wanted to, but because I felt I had to. I knew with a certainty that if I ever wanted to leave there alive it would've been expected of me.

"Bahahaha!" Brain cackled, his head arching towards the sky. When he was finished, he turned to me. I pretended to beat on the door out of hilarity.

"Ya see, guys!? This is what I'm talking about. This guy gets it. He's alright!" he called out. There was a cacophony of approval cries and shouts that followed. Guys cheering "Yeah, man!" and "Awesome!" along with general ovations.

As if the switch clicked off again, Brain immediately stopped laughing and turned to me.

"What's your name, man?"

"Pa … Pa … Paul," I stuttered, then straightened. "But my friends call me Paulie."

Brain stuck out his hand – the one not holding the pistol – and took mine. We shook for a moment.

"Nice to meet you, Paulie," he stated.

"Nice to meet you too, Brain," I returned.

Brain's face changed again. He suddenly stopped shaking my hand, then pulled me closer until we were within inches of one another.

"By the way, *do* you have any No Doubt?"

I narrowed my eyes at him. I was about to tell him, "Yeah, sure. Her greatest hits were on the thumb drive as well," but I didn't get a chance. Brain instantly broke into a fit of laughter and motioned to the dead guy. I broke into one too. That time not because I thought I was going to die, but because Brain's sudden humorous comment did make me laugh.

Seeing my amusement, Brain let go of my hand, turned, and cleared his throat loud enough for all to hear. The guys behind him all quieted except for a few who whispered around for everyone to hush. They all turned to Brain to see what he'd do next. He turned back to me.

"You know, Paulie, normally I'd kill ya and just take all your stuff … and this sweet ride," he stated, then paused to look up and down the vehicle.

"But not this time," he stated as his eyes returned to me.

There was a word of dissension uttered from the gang. But by the time Brain turned to see who it was, there was nothing but silence. He gave a small nod then turned to me once more.

"Since you've been such a good sport about all this, I'll give you two choices. One … get out of the car and join us. We've got more than enough room and, well, I probably won't kill you. At least not for a while."

He looked at me for acknowledgment. I gave it, then asked, "What's my other option?"

After returning his pistol back to its holster, he placed his hands on his hips. "Or … and here's the big one … give me the player you mentioned and leave. And don't ever come back."

Again, there was a slight murmur from the gang, but it lasted no more than a second or two.

"So, what do ya say, Paulie?" he asked. "Wanna give us a go?"

I thought about it for a moment – or at least pretended to. I didn't want him to think I'd just made up my mind without giving it at least a decent shake, even though I hadn't. When Brain's eyebrow raised – the sign he wanted an answer – I cleared my throat and spoke.

"Well, I do appreciate the offer … and, you know … I *am* tempted. But … well … I was on my way to LA, and …"

Brain stopped me there. "LA you say!? Well, damn! Have you ever been there before?"

I shook my head.

"Well then, say no more! I'd never stop a guy from visiting la-la-land! It's a trip and a half … if you get my drift. I'm sure you'll enjoy the shit out of it."

I wasn't sure what he'd meant by that comment but didn't have a chance to ask. Brain stuck out his hands, palms up. I knew what he wanted. I leaned back, grabbed the player from the back and handed it to him.

After taking it, Brain motioned for a couple of the guys to remove the spike strip from the road. As soon as it was clear, he leaned down and gave me a look. A look that told me it was not Brain, but Brian speaking.

"Well, Paul, best of luck to you out there. I hope you find what you're searching for."

I gave him a return look and nod that spoke volumes – to both of us.

Brian presented a smile, rose, then patted the top of my roof. Without a second's thought, I started up the car, waved to the gang, then hit the accelerator.

As dust kicked up and rubber squealed, Brian took a few steps back and waved. I kept my arm out the window in return until I was at least a mile down the road.

The minute I felt safe – about ten miles from the encounter – I pulled off to the side, got out of the car and collapsed to my knees. I was shaking so bad I couldn't stand, let alone drive. I don't know if it was due to the Flight response I'd held back during the run-in, but I'm sure that was part of it. The only thing I truly knew was I was lucky to be alive.

Then, something hit me as if out of the blue. A single thought that let me stand again and continue my journey.

God was on my side.

Oh, I know, I know. Up until now you've probably thought I was an atheist or at least agnostic. And, I guess, thinking about it, maybe a large part of me leans towards the latter. But as I crouched there, wondering, thinking – internally screaming – a sensation came over me. A feeling of security, of belonging. A sense that maybe I'd been spared for a reason.

I mean, of all people to run into, I ran into a guy I knew – sort of, anyway. A guy that shared my same musical taste.

A taste for the unusual that probably saved my life.

Now, I don't know much about divine intervention, but to me, that was it in a nutshell. Me being saved pointed to me having a purpose to fulfill. And, from that point forward, that's all that mattered to me.

Rising to my feet, I stared into the night's sky, placed my hands together, and said the Lord's Prayer. Since then I've tried to do it every night, or whenever the feeling strikes.

No, I'll never be a holy roller, but from that moment on I decided to give some credit where credit was due.

CHAPTER 17

Have you ever heard the song *99 Red Balloons* by Nena? You know, the song from the Eighties? Okay, yeah, I know. It wasn't called 99 Red Balloons in the UK. There it was called 99 Luftballons. Which, I guess translates to ninety-nine air balloons, and is a lot more bland than saying red balloons in my opinion. Red denoting something wrong … or maybe critical. Like Red Alert or Red Light. Much more ear and eye catching than just saying air, don't you think!?

Speaking of which, eye catching is kind of a funny term, isn't it!? As in *meant to catch one's eye.* Weird and unnatural. Even weirder when I think that's exactly what would've happened to me if I'd been awake when the bomb went off.

You probably know what I'm talking about. They felt its effects throughout the entire western part of the US.

But, in case you don't, I'm talking about the explosion. The one in New Mexico. The one near White Sands, where they did all those atomic tests years ago.

The night before the explosion I'd found a spot just outside El Paso to park. Once settled, I spent about an hour backing up my music onto a new thumb drive just in case I ran into another "Brain" along my route. When I was done, I listened to Nina – *my* Nina – for a bit. With her soothing sounds it wasn't long before I fell into a deep and restful sleep.

Well, much like the guys that broke into the facility north of me, I didn't know what hit me when the bomb went off. At least, I didn't know at first. All I remember is being awoken by the brightest light I'd ever seen in my life. It was followed by a slight rattling of the car, then by a sudden silence all around.

I didn't know what to do at first. You know … when the car died and everything around me seemed to stop. I didn't know if it was just the battery in the car dying, or if it was just a glitch in the Jag. Like, maybe the programming only allowed you to run it for so long before it shut down.

So, not knowing what'd happened, I did what anyone else would do. I pressed the button to restart the car.

The moment I pushed it I knew something was wrong. Mostly because absolutely nothing happened when I did. Seeing this … this nothing, I waited a moment then tried again. When nothing happened a second time, I looked around the car to see if anything was illuminated. You know, like a dummy light, or the dome. But there was literally nothing on.

Next, I tried to unlock the door. That too was a bust. The door just stayed locked. I tried it a couple more times before I gave up and simply pulled forward the catch.

I then tried opening and closing the door, thinking maybe that would reset things. As you can guess, again nothing happened.

After sitting behind the driver's seat for a bit thinking about things and, really, trying to wake up, I got out and checked under the hood. Not that I knew what I was looking for. I wasn't a mechanic – or a nuclear physicist. After peering here and there, I tried jiggling some wires, but nothing seemed loose or damaged. The engine was still pretty immaculate, considering the ride. And nothing was obviously out of place.

It took me a minute or two of scratching my head before I shrugged and closed the hood. Turning, I planted my ass on the side panel as plans and options started coursing through my brain. All thoughts were based on my load, destination, and current position. To add to this equation would be time, knowing I had until maybe 6 p.m. local before the sun would lower and things got weird.

Pulling my phone out to check the time, I pressed the side button, and … nothing happened. Absolutely nothing. I tried again – shaking it for good measure like, yeah, that might help – then tried holding down the power button and volume up button hoping for a reset. But, after trying that a few times it was obvious the thing – my former lifeline – was dead in the water.

Sitting back, totally confused, my brain increased its effort to work the problem. Eventually it worked its way back to the possible causes.

It took a while, but it finally came to me. The flash … the rumble … and the silence. All of them couldn't be a coincidence. I remember thinking it all seemed really sci-fi, like something out of a Michael Crichton novel. A novel where everything goes dark, like after …

"A nuclear explosion," I uttered lightly, then turned, looking north back towards where I thought the flash had come from.

"A nuclear explosion?" I repeated as a question, then thought back to when I was in school.

I remembered reading in physics about EMPs – Electromagnetic Pulses – and their possible effects on, well, everything. Everything electronic, especially powered items, could be frizzled. Everything could be fried, unless protected like certain military vehicles were.

Wanting to confirm my suspicions, I got back in the car and checked out a few of my other electronics. The shaver I'd brought, a battery powered radio I'd picked up for emergencies, and a few other bobbles. All were dead. Cooked. None of them worked … except for my MacBook Pro. For some reason, when I powered that up, it came to life. Everything else though was dead as a doornail.

Pursing my lips, I tapped my fingers on the dash of my dead masterpiece and wondered what I should do. Looking out the window towards the north, my eyes happened upon a sign. A distance marker that called out a turnoff to Fort Bliss only a few miles ahead.

Like a gift from, well, you know, this sign seemed to present itself to me like it was the universe pointing my way. There was an EMP … Military vehicles were supposed to be designed against EMPs … and there was a military post only a few miles away. On top of all that it was still way early in the day. Early enough for a small walk. A journey that'd take me only a few hours.

Yeah, I was totally reading into my situation. But, even so, I grabbed my gear – food, Rockstars, guns, ammo, and a few other items – then said goodbye to my Christmas gift and hit the road headed north.

The trip took me way longer than expected.

It wasn't until I was four or five miles down the road that I saw another sign stating it'd be another fifteen until I reached my destination. With the load I was carrying I knew it would take me hours, and my only hope was to make it there long before the sun went down.

With rest stops it took me about five hours to reach the gates of the post. A post that, from what I could tell, had been abandoned for many, many months.

Looking through the broken windows of the guard shack, I could see a thick layer of dust and dirt had accumulated on, well, everything. Floor, counters, shards of window glass. I could tell no one had been there in quite a while. I didn't know if that was a good or bad thing though. One of the possible good things was no Crazies to deal with. One of the bad, though … no people like me. And, maybe no vehicles. If the fort had truly been abandoned – evacuated – there might not be anything left for me to find.

Trying to move past those thoughts, I walked through the open gates and entered the post. Seeing a sign for the 1st Armored Division, I proceeded in that direction. You know – because "armored." It meant there might be vehicles like tanks and APCs. And, if I was lucky, maybe a working Humvee.

At least that was my hope.

Just so you know, the Humvee was another one of my dream cars. I'd driven them when I was in the military and always liked them. In fact, had I had the money before The Surge, I would've bought one of the civilian versions for myself. Sure, they were big and bulky, and maybe got five miles to the gallon, but there's nothing that says power like that size in a vehicle.

For whatever reason, I feel like you're judging me right now. Please don't. Humvees, like bowties, are cool. And will forever be "the shit" in my book.

Anyway, moving on.

I walked through the area designated for the 1st AD. As I passed billets and offices, I made sure to inspect each. Well, as close as I dared. Sure, they all looked empty. But there was something that just felt creepy about the place. An eerie sensation that ran from the base of my neck straight down my spine. The feeling was … weird. It felt like I was missing something. You know, like there was something hidden within that I wasn't meant to see. It wasn't until I got past the main billets on my way to the motor pool that I caught a glimpse of the thing I'd been missing.

There, hanging out of a third story window, was a drooping hand.

I did a doubletake the moment I realized what it was. A hand attached to an arm, just hanging out an open window, as if someone had fallen asleep while enjoying a nice breeze. I knew this wasn't the case, of course. I knew the body it was attached to was dead. But still …

I looked down at my watch … which was also dead. Realizing that sucker would never come back to life, I removed it from my wrist, tossed it to the ground, then looked towards the sky for the time. It was getting late. If I was gonna make it out of the fort by sundown, I knew I needed to get to the motor pool and get there fast. But, curiosity being what it was, I was drawn to the hand and the body it was attached to. I felt I needed to know what killed the guy. Sure, it was probably The Surge. But something in my mind told me this was different. What that something was I had no idea. But I thought, by searching, maybe I'd find out.

After checking the AR's clip and its chambered round once more, I moved to the closest billets door and opened it. I was instantly buffeted by a smell that I was more than familiar with. It was a smell I'd run into a bunch of times along my journey.

The smell was one of rotting corpses … and death.

Letting the door close, I stepped back then kicked myself for not thinking ahead. Grabbing the handy dandy cotton from my pocket, I rolled a couple healthy sized swabs then shoved one in each nostril. After taking a deep breath, I reopened the door and slowly proceeded in and up the stairs.

As I rounded the corner on the first landing, I found the cause of the smell – or at least one of them. There, laying on the next set of stairs was a soldier, dead eyes fixed upon the ceiling above.

Now, you have to understand, this was nothing new. As you know, seeing a dead body for me had become somewhat mundane. I'd run into, well, a lot of them along my travels. But there was something off about this one, and it took me a few seconds to figure out why.

Most of the other bodies I'd seen – those of the people effected by The Surge – were normally tucked away in their bed or were lying in a corner somewhere, having just fallen asleep before they passed. But this was different. This guy's eyes were wide open, and his face was twisted in horror, telling me he didn't expect what was coming.

Although the sight of his eyes told me I shouldn't, I moved closer to inspect the body. I bent over and did a quick exam, moving it this way and that as much as I could without disturbing it too much.

From what I could tell the guy had been dead for a while. Months, if not a year. And it didn't look like it was from a puncture wound – you know, like a bullet, or a knife. Something that would've been done by an attacker, as you'd expect. In fact, I could see no trace of what'd killed the guy. He was just lying there with his dead, emaciated eyes, staring straight into the heavens.

Righting myself, I suddenly became dizzy, and a little nauseous. At first, I thought it might be the guy's stare. But, as I stood there, I suddenly realized I was having problems breathing. An abrupt lightheaded feeling came over me that left me gasping, begging for air.

Knowing something was off, I held my breath – as much breath as I had left – and quickly made my way out, back down the steps and out through the doors.

As soon as I was outside, I gasped for air. I kept walking for a bit, wheezing, as my lungs searched for oxygen. Finding very little, I dropped to my knees, then puked. The world suddenly started spinning uncontrollably, and a moment later everything went black.

It was a little over six hours later when the world came back to me. It was pitch black out, and I didn't know why I was out in the open staring at the night sky. All I really knew, all I could feel at the time, was I was cold and confused. That, and my throat and lungs hurt. Which, in the long run, was probably a good thing. It meant I was still alive.

After taking in and letting out several deep and cleansing breaths my situation started coming back. Realizing I was potentially a sitting duck lying there in the open, I forced myself to roll onto my stomach, then up on all fours. I used my rifle as a crutch to get me to my knees, then started pointing it in all directions. I searched through the scope and listened, trying to see if any Crazies were near. A full minute went by and I didn't hear a thing, so I forced myself to relax a little.

Rising to my feet, I looked back at the billets and wondered what the hell had just happened to me. Obviously, it was some sort of biologic. I mean, it had to be, right!? It didn't take a genius or a scientist – or both – to tell me that. But what the hell was it actually? What'd made me so sick? And, if it was strong enough to kill the others in the building, why … why was I still alive?

The only thing I could guess was time. In the year between the guy's death and my arrival the chemical's effects may have faded. Weak enough to let me escape, but still strong enough to nearly take me out. Of course, in my current position, I could only speculate.

Part of me wanted to search for answers, but most of me – the saner side of me – knew I needed to continue on with my mission. It was night, and I was out in the open. My first and most important task was to get the hell out of there. Find the ride I most desperately needed and leave that place.

Using as much stealth as I could, I moved towards the motor pool. I did stop every now and then to look in a building. But what I'd seen in the first was pretty much what I saw in the others. Soldiers laying here and there, dead of no apparent reason.

When I reached the first motor pool it was as I'd expected. A lot of the vehicles – tanks and such – were gone. But there was the occasional vehicle here and there, although most of those had been ransacked or just didn't start.

It took some searching, but in the third motor pool I found a Humvee with both a working motor and gas. It took a little prodding to get started, but eventually it did. And within minutes of its engine firing to life, I was back on the road and exiting the base.

On my way out, I stopped at the fort's main office, hoping to find something that'd tell me what happened there. I knew forts normally had a bulletin board out front of their main offices that displayed global communications of import. You know, like military holidays, post rules, and the like. It didn't take much to find what I was looking for. In fact, it took almost no effort at all.

A sheet of paper was tacked to the sign, covering all the others. It was held in place but a huge knife. I assumed this was to make it noticeable. I also assumed this was not placed there by the people previously in charge.

The note simply read:

Blah blah blah used here to stop The Surge.

Enter post at your own risk.

Okay, I said blah blah blah because I can't remember what the chemical actually was. I've never been good at names, and only got a "C" in chemistry. So, please forgive me. I can only guess what they'd used was some sort of nerve agent – something to asphyxiate and quickly kill anyone exposed to it.

It only made sense. There was probably an uprising, and the government, in their infinite wisdom, took care of it like they took care of most things – using a tack hammer when a push of the thumb would do.

Anyway, after reading this, I kicked myself for not swinging by the main office first. I could have easily been killed by rushing into something instead of just following my basic training and more so my common sense. I knew that finding that car, surviving Brain, then seeing the signs along the way had made me feel like I was being protected by God. But that simply wasn't the case. I'd just been lucky up to that point. And I needed to keep that little thought in the forefront of my mind if I wanted to continue to survive.

Most importantly, I had to tell myself to stop believing in higher powers. If I wanted to survive The Surge, I needed to start believing in myself.

CHAPTER 18

Okay … well … I wasn't going to get into this but, relaying what'd happened to me at Fort Bliss – and, more so, what I saw – really, really has me triggered. The faces of the guys I'd seen killed by the chemical agent really left me thinking about things. And, well, I've tried to be honest to this point. You know, about all the things I've seen … and especially about my feelings. So, I guess, I'd be remiss if I didn't share this with you. The most horrible part of it all.

Well, besides losing Lorie, that is.

Earlier I mentioned that, after Lorie died, I'd left the Fort Myers area and drove towards Disney. But I really didn't convey what a mess I was. Honestly, for a while, I think I was in denial. You know, like those Trump followers that just wouldn't admit he lost the election. Hell, he wouldn't admit it himself, so why should they. And because I wouldn't be honest to myself, everything that happened up until I left Orlando was kind of a mixed-up angry blur. But I think – I mean, I know – I'm ready to talk about it now.

So, umm, here goes …

The one thing I've omitted talking about – avoided, really – was that I, ahh … well … I killed a guy in Orlando.

He was the first one … the first one I'd killed to that point. And maybe that's why it weighs so heavy on me, and why I always see his face before I close my eyes at night.

Now, I've never been a violent man, and I've always tried to be decent to others. You can probably tell that from everything I've relayed to you by this point. Because, I've always felt that once you start down a dark path – you know, like Yoda said – it's almost impossible to pull yourself out.

Yeah, I'm paraphrasing. I've never done a good Yoda impression. Like, "The path to follow, you must."

You see what I mean!?

Sorry. Segueing. I'll try not to do that again. At least not until I get the whole thing off my chest.

Oh, and I'm also sorry I haven't said anything about this until now. It's just that, well … I hope you'll understand.

Anyway, like I'd mentioned to you earlier, when the sun rose that morning – the morning after I'd lost Lorie – so did I. Not that I slept well that night. I'd just buried my wife, for God's sake, and I was … in a state. Not a crazy state, mind you. And not a depressed and "wanting to end it all" one either. I was just in a state of … well … being numb. I was numb from all that'd happened. Numb … and not thinking straight.

Had my mind been firing all its cylinders, I would've never gone to Orlando. I mean, I could see things weren't right from miles away. Hardly anything had power and there was smoke here and there. But part of me – the part still in a mental fog – told me to venture forward and find … something. Something normal. Something that would link me to the world again. Anything that would make me feel like I had before she left me. And the deepest part of me told me that I could find it in the nearest populated city. Assuming a populated city still existed.

By then I'd been listening to Nina every chance I could. Not only was she just about the only one broadcasting, but she was still doling out information like what cities still had populations. Which cities had none. And which cities to avoid at all costs. Daytona Beach was one of those. But, from what I remembered, Orlando wasn't on her list. Another reason I barreled straight in with hardly a thought.

Well, sort of anyway.

Like I'd mentioned previously, I'd made my way down I-4 until I was near the heart of the city. As I approached, I saw a few people here and there. Some of them were running around, all crazy-like. Crazies, I'd assumed. While others seemed to be running away or hiding in corners and buildings.

Now, not seeing anyone I considered normal, I didn't plan on stopping. But, as I neared the center of the city, I reached a point on an overpass where there were so many cars on the road that it was nearly impossible to get around. It wasn't quite like a traffic jam – you know, like those you see in apocalyptic movies – where there's hundreds of cars just stranded. No, it was nothing like that. This was more like someone's car had broken down and a dozen others had just stopped and parked. Not impassable, mind you. Just difficult to get around. And it didn't look like it'd been intentionally done.

But, as I came to find out, it totally was.

Slowing to a crawl, I looked right and left to see if I could see a path. And sure enough, there was one. Just to the left. Barely big enough to get the SUV through – and I wouldn't even lose any paint do it.

Or that's the way it appeared.

So, taking my time, I moved forward slowly – inch by inch – until I passed a backward broke-ass van to my left and a Jeep with flat tires to my right. I had to hit the wheel hard left, then went straight fifteen feet, then I did a hard jog to the right. All I had to do then was go straight through and I was out of the congestion.

But the moment I did the last maneuver, I saw a motorcycle in the road blocking my way. I knew the moment I saw the bike it was too big an object to drive over – unless I had a Hummer or a tank, that is. So, after a short "oh fuck, what should I do next" moment, I decided on what I thought was the best option. Caught between several cars with nowhere to go, I elected to get out of the SUV and move the motorbike.

Big, big mistake on my part.

Knowing it'd be better if my hands were free, I checked around my vehicle to see if there any sign of life. Seeing no one – no potential movement or anyone hiding – I got out, placed my 9 on the seat, then hurried over to move the bike.

And this movement on my part was just what the thieves were waiting for.

The moment I had the motorcycle propped up and started pushing it, I heard a noise from behind me. I quickly turned to see the van's doors swing open. Two guys then jumped out of it. Both were armed with rifles.

Dropping the bike, I thought about making a run for it. You know, away from them. But as I turned towards my avenue of escape, I saw a third guy emerge from the side of the highway near the wall. That guy was armed with a pistol.

Pivoting right and left, I thought for a hot minute about fleeing in those directions. But unless I wanted to jump off the side of the bridge and take my chances on the fifty-foot drop, there was no escape going either way.

As if guessing my thoughts at that instant, one of the guys from the van – the smaller of the two – called out to me.

"I wouldn't do that if I were you!" he shouted. "The fall may be hazardous to your health!"

He took another step towards me, then called out, "I've had personal experience with this, man. I've seen it happen."

Even with those words lingering in the air, I was still thinking about it. That is until the one from behind me yelled, "Listen! We don't want to hurt you! We just want your stuff!"

Hearing this, I started to turn towards him, to address him. The guy actually sounded sincere.

"Don't move, asshole!" the short guy shouted, stopping me in my tracks. "And keep your hands where we can see dem!"

I thought about saying something, but kept my mouth shut. Instead I just gave a nod and kept still. Well, as still as anyone could be while practically shitting their pants.

I stayed immobile while the three approached. The two that came out of the van stopped when they reached the side door of my SUV. The taller of the two kept his rifle trained on me while the short guy set down his so he could open it up.

"What's this?" he said, letting out a gleeful little laugh. He sounded like a two-year-old. A moment later his hand emerged from within. It was holding my 9.

"Here! Take this!" he shouted at the bigger man. The man lowered his weapon to take it from him.

I thought for a moment that might be my out. I was wrong. The moment I flinched to run for it, I felt the nose of a six shooter in my back.

"Just stay where you are, mister," the guy said, jabbing me with the pistol a couple times before removing it from my spine.

Making sure to move slowly, I turned to see who was poking me. He was young guy. Just a kid really. Maybe nineteen years old. And there was a certain fear I saw in his eyes. I could tell, just from that look, that this was his first time doing this. You know, robbing someone.

I stood there for a bit, watching the guy – the kid. The barrel of his pistol, although no longer in my back, was trained on my chest, center mass. But the look in his eyes told me something. I thought that maybe, given time, I could talk him out of the heist. That maybe he might listen to reason if I tried.

"Jessie! Check this out!" came a shout from behind. The kid, Jessie, looked towards my SUV. The small guy emerged from the driver's side door holding something. It was my AR-15 – the one that used to be my father-in-law's. The small guy waggled it in the air.

"Hey, man! We finally have a rifle for you!" he said, looking for approval.

"That … that's cool!" the kid said as he moved closer to peer around me.

And the moment he did – the moment he dropped his guard – I saw my chance.

As the kid brought his pistol within a few feet of me, my military training – or probably more so the adrenalin from my fear – kicked in. Reaching out I grabbed his hand and, in turn, the pistol. Twisting his wrist inward, it popped out pretty easily. As soon as I had it in hand, I jumped back and attempted to point it at all three.

"Stand back," I remember screaming. "Stand back or I'll blow a hole in you."

Yeah, not my greatest line, but that's what I actually said. I blame the adrenalin.

"Hey there, buddy! Don't do anything crazy!" the tall guy said.

This was followed quickly by the short guy saying, "Drop the gun, man, or we'll shoot you!"

That was then followed by the short guy saying to the tall one, under his breath, "Shoot the fucker, Larry. Shoot the fucking guy."

Taking my eyes off the kid – mainly because he seemed to be just as scared as I was – I looked toward the guy tagged as "Larry." He did a quick glance between me, the short man, then me again before dropping his rifle. He then held up his hands as if in surrender.

"Fuck this shit," I barely heard him utter before he turned and scuttled away.

Seeing his man retreat, the short guy in my SUV barely skipped a beat. Hopping down, he pointed the AR at me.

"Drop the gun, asshole, or I swear I'll blow your head off!"

"You drop yours or I'll blow yours off!" I smiled in return.

Why did I smile, you ask? Mainly because I knew something he didn't.

A moment later I heard an audible click as the short guy pulled the trigger on the AR-15. A very empty AR-15. You see, to be safe, I kept the rifle empty while I was driving. I only loaded it when I was out and about.

Now, here's the part I dread retelling. The part that haunts me every night.

As soon as I heard the click – as soon as both me and the kid heard the sound – the boy thought he saw his chance. After only a slight pause the kid leaped at me. I'm not sure if he was trying to prove something to his friend, or if maybe he thought he could save the situation somehow. All I know is that a split second later the kid was on top me. And less than a heartbeat later, his fully loaded pistol went off in my hand.

Now, I wasn't aiming at the kid – well, not really. The gun was pointed in his general direction, sure, but not directly at him. But the impact of him hitting me and us both hitting the ground had changed everything. It made me pull the trigger by accident.

And before I knew it the kid was dead.

I laid there for a minute – stunned – not fully comprehending what'd happened. My ears were ringing, and my hands were … well … my hands were suddenly wet.

Before I had a chance to take it all in, I heard a shot go off followed by a ricochet to my left. Doing the only thing I could, I rolled to my right, over the kid, and away from the ricochet. A second later I heard another round hit not far from the first, then another that struck a car. Hearing the impacts, I kept rolling. I rolled until there was cover between me and the shooter.

Without another thought – and gun still in hand – I tried a Dirty Harry. Grabbing the pistol with both hands, I leaned around my cover and fired two quick shots, then recovered. I heard one more shot fired – that one from farther away – then … nothing.

Staying prone, weapon in hand, I took a couple deep breaths to try and calm myself as I waited for something to happen. After a minute, I quickly leaned around my cover, then returned. Not seeing or hearing anything – anything like more shots – I performed the maneuver again, then waited. After a few dozen heartbeats, I slowly – methodically even – craned my head around the cement cover until I saw my SUV's front bumper. Then its front wheel. Then its open door. Legs were no longer sticking from under it. In fact, no legs were seen … anywhere.

I knew instantly the short man had fled.

Seeing him gone, my heart began to slow. That is until I remembered the kid. My heart practically leapt from my chest as I twisted to meet him, gun in hand. It only took a moment for me to realize that there was no need. From the vacant look evident in the kid's eyes, I could see he'd left me too.

I stayed on the ground for, oh, maybe ten minutes, just staring at the kid. Peering into eyes that couldn't peer back. I don't know what made me move from that spot. Physically, that is. Mentally I'm still there, and – like I've mentioned – will probably be there for the rest of my life.

After getting to my feet, I cautiously made sure that the short guy was gone. As soon as I was sure, I moved to the kid's side and flipped him over. My inadvertent shot was a clean one. It had gone straight through his heart. I'm told being shot that way, the victim doesn't suffer.

The only one that's still suffering is me.

Well, that's about it, besides to say that I went back to the SUV to inspect it. It was hardly worse for the wear. And my empty AR-15 was lying on the ground next to it, along with my 9. I can only assume they'd been dropped as the two men ran from the scene.

As for the kid and the motorcycle, both were quickly removed from the road. After washing my hands of the kid's blood, I got back in my car and finished making the maneuvers I'd started less than an hour before. Finding the closest highway, I jumped on it and drove away from the city.

And the rest … well … the rest you already know.

CHAPTER 19

Well, now that I've got that off my chest, it's time to move on. Literally.

Like I mentioned, after I found a working Humvee – painted in Desert Storm colors, of course – I left Fort Bliss. I drove until dawn then stopped and got a few hours of sleep.

Upon waking, I drove a ways until I saw a sign for an Army Navy store. There I found some supplies – food, energy drinks, blankets, and the like – and also stopped for gas.

Keeping to I-10 – because I was now "sans GPS" – I drove the four hundred plus miles to Phoenix. It took me the better part of two days. No big deal, though. The weather was mild. Not too hot. A good thing considering the Humvee I was in didn't have air conditioning. I don't know if this was standard in that type of military vehicle. I only knew that, based on the weather in the south, I'd have to find a different mode of transportation before too long.

When I got to Phoenix, I found that it – much like the other cities along the way – was abandoned. Nary a soul to be seen, as they say. But I searched for a few hours anyway. When it started getting late, I knew it was time to hit the road before any Crazies made an appearance.

Driving about fifty miles away from the city I found a nice little spot and pulled off the road. After eating one of the MREs I'd picked up in the Army Navy store, I put on some tunes and fell fast asleep.

My sleep was restless, filled with visions of soldiers bleeding from their noses and creatures that eerily looked like zombies. I don't know if it was because of the things I'd seen, or if it was the aftereffects of the chemical I'd been exposed to. I just know that even though there was a shit ton of room in the back of the Humvee, I tossed and turned and couldn't get comfortable.

Which, as it turned out, was probably for the best.

It was somewhere around 2 a.m. when I finally decided I couldn't take it anymore. Kicking off my covers, I moved from the back to the driver's seat with the intent to drive for a bit. I thought that maybe the activity would numb my mind enough so I could get some sleep.

As I clicked on my seat belt – no, safety never goes away, even in an apocalypse – and looked towards the road I noticed something in the distance. A light … no, two lights … a few miles straight ahead of me.

Grabbing my new binoculars – yeah, more ill-gotten gain I focused on the location of the lights. I couldn't quite make out everything that was out there, but I could for sure tell it was two huge campfires surrounded by people … evidently dancing, by the way the firelight moved.

It was apparent that it was Crazies staking out the road. Based on what'd happened with Brain's group, I guessed this was going to be a thing now.

I sat behind the wheel, engine off, trying to decide what I should do. I knew I could potentially wait until morning and try to run the barrier – assuming they made one. Or I could try to drive around the barrier – again, assuming I could and there weren't other obstacles waiting for me.

My only other option – the only one that came to mind – was to backtrack the way I'd come and see if I could find a way around.

Grabbing a map and penlight I reviewed the route. If I went east on I-10 back to AZ-303, I could head north onto US-93 north. That would lead me to I-40 west and yadda, yadda, yadda. God, it was a long way – a way that might take me another week. Maybe two. But it was a way I felt confident with. A way I felt I had to pursue.

Well … wait for it … believe it or not, things didn't go as planned … again.

I waited until morning before I moved, and I was able to make it to I-40. Just over two hundred miles that day. Slow going, as always. There was a lot of crap in the road.

Upon waking the next day, I had to stop for gas again but was able to find some Rockstars. So, yay! Bonus!

I started driving down I-40 thinking I could follow it until I hit I-15 and signs for LA. Unfortunately, I was wrong. I only made it thirty miles before I ran into a huge problem. A section of the road – an enormous section – was missing. As in, an earthquake or some such had sucked a wide strip out of it.

Upon reaching it, I did what one does. I stopped the Hummer, got out, and looked to see how deep and wide it was. You know, to see if it was passable. Well, it wasn't. The fissure was at least twenty feet across and five feet deep if it was an inch. And, as I stood at its side, I surveyed the length. I could see the fissure stretched in both directions as far as the eye could see.

After a shrug and more than a few expletives, I walked back to the Humvee, pulled out the map once more, and picked a new route. The new one would take me back to where I-40 and US-68 met. From there I could take US-68 to US-95, then back to I-40, which could take me to I-15 and onto Los Angeles.

When I got to US-68 though, I ran into another problem. As I started to turn onto it, I saw a sign that made me slam on the brakes. Written in huge letters on one of the signs that crossed the highway were the words:

Bridge Out Ahead, Go North.

Well, you can probably guess my state of mind. I wondered if I'd ever fucking make it to LA. It seemed like every route I wanted to take was cut off somehow.

I tried not to feel disheartened, but how could I not!? By that point I just wanted my trip to end. I wanted to stretch my legs and breathe some air that didn't smell like fucking sand. And, had I been anyone else, I may have thought about ending things right then and there. You know, offing myself or just lying down and waiting for The Surge to take me.

But no, that wasn't me. I knew I had to continue my journey, no matter how long it took, or how many obstacles I ran into.

Picking up the map, I again studied my options. Looking between it and the signs, it appeared I only had one direction to go – up US-93 towards Vegas. Once I got there, I could head over to I-15 and take that south straight into Los Angeles.

Again, hoping I didn't run into a blockage. Also adding more time to my travels.

But all the bullshit up to that point made me feel like I wasn't in a hurry. Not really. I would get there eventually. I knew that … or tried to convince myself of that presumptive fact.

Well, I followed that plan.

As I neared Vegas it was starting to get dark. So, finding a spot on Bolder Highway between two derelict cars, I pulled over and parked. After a bio break and another one of the MREs, I climbed into the back of the Hummer, threw the covers over my head and quickly fell asleep.

I woke the next morning to a strange sound coming from outside. It was a sound I hadn't heard since I was a teenager. Or maybe even when I was a preteen. At first, I thought it was a skateboard. But then, when the noise got back to me, I rose and saw the cause.

A young woman – twenty or twenty-one at the oldest – was skating down the street. She was maybe five-foot-naught, and skinny. But not in a bad way. She had cropped red hair that danced as she moved. It was quite elegant. Beautiful, actually. There was an iPod attached to the hip of her skinny jeans, and she had earbuds in her ears. I could tell she was singing as she moved. And she was good. Great at skating, that is. Great compared to me, at least.

I mean, I could skate, sure. Inline skates. But I was never a fan of the side-by-sides like she had on. They just felt awkward to me. I couldn't turn in them like most skaters could. But this girl ... this girl was crisscrossing her legs and spinning on them. And even though she was wearing a Puffer vest and a backpack, she made it look easy. To top it off, she was making moves and tricks I'd only seen on videos.

Obviously my first thought was she was one of the Crazies. I mean, who in their right mind would be skating down the middle of a huge street like this!? But as I thought about it – the time of day, the bright sun in the sky – I could only assume she was a Norm like me. I mean, she did have sunglasses on, but the time of day and sun called for it.

The girl continued her skate as she went by my Hummer. I watched her as she passed by, hidden by blankets and whatnot.

At least, that's what I'd thought.

When she was about a car length back, she suddenly twirled – almost like a ballerina – then paused for a moment, looking my way. Her eyes narrowed for a bit as if seeing something far away.

A second or so later she pushed off, slowly rolling towards me. She stopped when she was close to my rear bumper.

"Is anyone in there?" she asked, examining my Hummer, craning her head this way and that to peer inside.

"I said, is there anyone in there?" she repeated, louder the second time. But then she suddenly stopped her inspection. Her eyes were fixed on a spot next to me. I slowly turned to see what she was focused on. The only thing I could see was a pair of sunglasses hanging from the back of the seat. I guessed maybe the light was catching them, making her glare. But I wasn't sure.

After a minute of this, when no answer came, the girl skated forward to the front of the vehicle, looked at the front tire, then skated toward the back.

"You know, I can tell this car wasn't here yesterday," she stated – barked, really. "So, if anyone is in there, you can come out … I won't bite."

When the last words left her mouth, the tiniest of smiles appeared. It was charming, actually. Charming enough for me to want to reveal my presence.

As I cracked open the side door, the girl rolled back slightly, giving me room to exit. I slowly got out, making sure to keep my hand on my 9. I didn't see any weapons on her, but you never know. She had on the vest and backpack, like I'd said. Better safe than sorry.

"Whoa, big boy!" she said, holding up her hands in surrender. "I come in peace! I come in peace!"

The last part sounded like something from a sci-fi movie. You know, like when the hero meets the alien. The sound of it – her mocking tone, or maybe her body language as the words left her mouth – made me relax a little and drop my guard. Taking my finger off the trigger, I moved my hand to my pocket. I did the same with the other. All casual like.

"That's better," she said, relaxing and dropping her hands. "I promise not to make any quick moves. I swear."

I didn't acknowledge her comment. Well, not at first. I waited until she asked for one.

"So sexy, what do I call you?" she asked, moving her hands to her own pockets.

Her comment – her calling me sexy and all – made me nervous as fuck. It made me think she was up to something … or that maybe she was a hooker. The young look, the tight sexy outfit, her demeanor. Everything made me think … things.

“Well?” she said, rolling her eyes. “Did you want me to pick a name? I guess I could just keep calling you sexy, but …”

Hearing this – seeing her – I probably should’ve just gotten in my Humvee and drove off. But I didn’t. And to this day I’m still not sure if that was a good or bad thing. Instead of doing what would’ve been smart, I gave a small nod and relented.

“Paul … Paul Davidson,” I replied, then asked, “And you?”

“Reilly. Reilly Rivera,” she stated, then skated forward and extended her hand. “It’s a pleasure to meet you.”

Meeting her hand – something I hadn’t done in a while, you know, since the whole COVID thing – I gave it a shake. Her hand was … warm. Sincere, and friendly. I knew it was something we both felt because we lingered on the embrace. Holding onto something, grasping for something I’m sure we both hadn’t felt in a while. That feeling of companionship. A sense of connection lost along with the billions that had died all around us.

When we eventually relinquished each other’s hands, she smiled, and I could have sworn I saw a small blush arise in her cheeks.

“So, Paul. What brings you to Las Vegas?” she asked, backing away a bit.

I shrugged and gave her an honest answer. “I was on my way to L.A. but got … err … sidetracked.”

She gave a look of concern. Well, tried to at least. I could tell that no matter what story I told her, she would be alright with it. She was just happy for the company.

"Sidetracked? So, does that mean you'll be staying for a while?"

I thought about the question for a moment, then shrugged. "Not sure. Are there any others around here? Like, umm …"

"Like, not insane you mean?" she interrupted. I nodded. She paused for a moment then shook her head.

"I haven't seen anybody else … like you and me," she motioned between us. "I've seen a couple dozen of the others around …"

"Crazies, you mean?" I added. She nodded.

"Yeah, Crazies … but they don't live in the city. They don't like it here. Not sure why. Lots of openings … you know, places to stay."

I gave a nod, although I'm not sure why. I didn't understand until I asked her, "Speaking of places to stay, does the city have power anywhere?"

Reilly gave me a wide smile, then twirled on her skates. When she stopped, she met my eyes.

"Does the city have power? Hmm …" she said, moving her hand to her face and tapped her lips with her index finger. "I guess you'll just have to see for yourself! Come on … I'll take you."

Before I could utter another word, she walked around to the passenger side of my Hummer and started pulling at the door. Moving over to the driver's door, I unlocked it then hit the switch for her side. We both climbed in, in unison, then I let her show me what she meant.

Following Bolder to Fremont, it wasn't long before we entered the city. A city full of life. Well, not really life. But it was packed with electricity. Every store, every restaurant, every casino I could see was lit. Some had strobing lights, and some had flashing. All had movement of some sort. And all … all had an abundance of power.

"I know, right!?" she hooted, staring at me.

I didn't realize my jaw was open until we locked eyes. Not that it changed my gaze. I couldn't believe how vibrant Las Vegas was. It was almost like being back at Disney World. But, a little scummier Disney World. But Disney World none the less.

As if she knew what I was thinking, she stated, "Hoover Dam hasn't gone down … or at least that's what I think it is. I don't know how it keeps sending power, but it does as you can see."

Her comment kind of made sense. Hoover Dam – and its generators – weren't that far away. And, with the amount of power the place was sucking in, there had to be multiple avenues of power running to the city. I saw the same thing helping JC at Disney. So, yeah, it felt like it all made sense.

It also explained why there were no Crazies coming into town. With all the lights, they'd avoid downtown like the plague. Same as Disney. It only stood to reason.

"So, what do you think?" she asked. I only had one reply.

"This place is fucking amazing!" I shouted. Seeing the joy in my eyes, Reilly started clapping with glee.

As we reached the corner of Fremont Street and Las Vegas Boulevard – you know, the dead end … assuming you've been there – I looked toward Reilly for directions. She pointed left, and away we went.

We drove up and down a few streets as she showed me the sights. I'd been to Vegas before, but never really had a tour, so everything she showed me seemed new ... and exciting.

As we drove, she gave me her history. A full and unrelenting description of everything that'd taken place in her life.

Born and raised in a town not too far from Vegas, she'd grown up there. She knew all the ins and outs of the place, along with every good restaurant and every affordable attraction.

"Not that most of it matters anymore," she went on to say. "Nothing is the same. After my parent's died, and the lights went out, I moved up here full-time. I actually was in a group of people when this started. But some went crazy and left. Others just, you know, laid down and died. Now it's only me. It's been only me for a couple months now."

She then reached into her back pocket and pulled out a cellphone. "At least I think it's only been a couple months, assuming my phone is still displaying the correct date."

I looked over. The date displayed was February 3rd, 2025. Thinking about it, I believed she was correct. I had no idea how any tech like that worked, or how it would continue to work without human interaction – or even a cell tower. But, I supposed if you kept it running and charged, maybe it would just click on like a wristwatch.

"So, that's about it. I've been bored out of my skull for a few months now. So bored I almost thought about joining the Crazies."

I shook my head. "You don't want to do that. I've seen what they do."

"Oh, I know!" she forcefully nodded. "I was just kidding. I've seen things as well."

She got quiet for a moment, lost in her thoughts.

"I … I try not to stay out late. I was caught out on the street once. And there was this group. A group of Crazies. I hid from them, but I saw them. The way they treat each other. How they treat the weak. I saw them … I saw them …" she said, then trailed off.

I looked at her and could see her eyes were misty, and her bottom lip was lightly quivering. I knew whatever she'd seen must've been bad. Maybe even worse than what I'd seen in New Orleans. It was something that'd left a mark, similar to the one I carried with me from Orlando.

And just like that we were kindred spirits. A survivor's group of two.

"It's okay. You don't have to say anything," I replied. She met my eyes then gave a small nod.

It took a few minutes for Reilly to recover, but when she did, she was back to Chatty Kathy once more. She went on to tell me of all the places she'd stayed since the last of her friends left. She pointed each out as we passed the locale. When we got to the MGM Grand, she motioned for us to pull in.

"This … this was my favorite place to stay. It doesn't have the old-world charm like the Paris or the coolness of the Hard Rock, but it's just … neat!" she exclaimed.

I narrowed my eyes at her when she said this. You know, using the word "neat" to describe a place. I didn't know if that was just a term she used, or whether she thought I was old and would appreciate it. I thought it was the latter, based on her conversational style. I could tell she was trying to get me to like her – playing on my emotions, as it were. But it wasn't like she needed to. She had me from "isn't one of the Crazies" right from the start.

We pulled through the drive of the MGM, coming to a stop right in front. After waiting for Reilly to change out of her skates into some shoes she had in her bag, we exited the Hummer. At her persistence, I followed her as she led me through the front doors and around the lower level.

The place smelled … weird. I know, not a technical term. But it's the only way I can think to describe it. Everything was musty, dusty, and unused. But half the machines were still making noise, which made the place feel alive.

We'd been walking for a good five maybe ten minutes before I finally had to ask, "Reilly, where are we going exactly?"

"Oh! It's not much farther," she assured me, then took my hand.

Like before, it felt warm and sweaty. And her grip was firm.

As she pulled me along, guiding me to and up a set of stairs, I felt excited. You know … aroused. I couldn't help it. I hadn't felt the touch of a woman in over six months … closer to a year, actually. And, besides that, she was cute … and hot … and, well, sexual. As to say, she had a certain sexiness about her. A petite pixyish attitude that made me think of that chick from *The Watch*, or maybe Scarlett Johansson in a few of her roles.

"It's through here," she said, pushing open a door on the second floor. She continued to lead me down a hall until we came to room 237. There she paused and motioned towards the door.

"Do you like?"

I tried to deduce what she meant. Was it *The Shining* reference, or something else like *Ready Player One* … which, I guess, is also a *Shining* reference when I think about it. I didn't need to ask, though. The answer came a moment later.

"You know … like the haunted hotel?" she queried.

"The Shining. Yeah. I got that," I flatly replied.

She let out a small huff and rolled her eyes, apparently put off by my not being more excited about the allusion. She then turned towards the door, but suddenly stopped. Her eyes searched the air as if trying to remember something.

"Oh yeah!" she cried, then dropped her backpack. After rummaging through it, she pulled out a lanyard which was attached to a keycard.

"This should still work," she stated, then tried it on the door. A second later it clicked, allowing us entrance into what I could only describe as a menagerie.

Inside the stateroom was everything a teenage girl – or maybe any girl, for that fact – would want. Toys, games, stuffed animals, makeups, and clothing of all types. Well, girl types. You know what I mean.

"What do you think?" she asked, then galloped – yes, galloped – over to the bed. The bed wasn't the standard type. It had been replaced – modified really. What stood there now was what could only be described as a princess bed. Tall corner posts, upper lattice work, and pink and purple drapes that completely enclosed the bed.

"About which part?" I asked, stepping forward to examine the hoard.

"All of it!" she exclaimed then gestured around as she threw herself onto the bed. "It's like my dream bedroom! I always wanted a room like this growing up! And now … now I can have it! Here you can have anything!"

I stuck out my bottom lip and slowly nodded as I continued surveying her boudoir. Moving closer to her, I reached out and grabbed the drapes to examine them more closely. I wasn't sure if they were Disney or something else. Not that it mattered. I just wanted to look interested in her things. I wanted to look interested in her.

And I guessed it worked.

As I moved from right drape to left, Reilly stuck out her leg, stopping me. As I turned to look down, she stuck out her other leg, trapping me in between.

"Come here," she said softly, moving her legs to enclose me.

Pulling me towards her – into her – she inched down the bed until I was practically on top of her. Reaching up, she finished the job by pulling me into a kiss. It was long … and wet … and, well, wonderful. And, yeah, it felt weird after being faithfully married to Lorie for so long. But this was a young, hot woman wanted me. And I … well … I wanted her.

We made out for a while and then … then we did more than make out. But I'm not going into any details. Sorry in advance. That's not what this story is about.

When we were finished, we laid in the bed for a bit just holding each other. It'd been a while for me, and I could tell it'd been a long while for her. So, we savored the moment – holding, then falling asleep together. We stayed that way until dawn.

I'm going to jump a bit here. I'm not going to go into a whole lot of detail about the time Reilly and I spent getting to know each other. Suffice it to say we spent a couple months roaming the city, visiting casinos, eating at different places – places we could find food – and generally having a great time together.

I will say that, no matter how close Reilly and I got, it would never compare to what I shared with my wife. And I think Reilly knew that without me having to say it. But there was one simple thing that Reilly could feel. I mean, how could she not!? No matter how much time we spent together, I was still in love with someone else.

And it didn't matter if she was gone. Lorie would always be the girl of my dreams.

CHAPTER 20

The casino was hopping. Lively. Filled to capacity with people. Just like the old days. I didn't know where they all came from. Part of me said that maybe The Surge had run its course. But part of me – the optimistically naive side of me – thought that maybe The Surge had all been a dream. I knew it couldn't be, but I wanted it to be.

I needed it to be.

Reilly was at my side like she'd been for months. We were walking hand in hand – sort of. It was always a bother with her, having to be stationary. She was always jumping up and down or running off whenever she saw a new "shiny" thing. And these casinos were filled to the rim with shiny. So, you can see my dilemma.

"Oh! Oh! Paul! Check it out!

I looked to where she was pointing. It was a gaming table – roulette. But it had been converted. There was a dancefloor on top of it now. And on top of that dancefloor was a *very* scantily clad woman. Only two strips of cloth were between her and complete nudity.

"Do you think they'd let me do that!?" Reilly asked, tugging on my arm. Practically ripping it out of its socket.

Before I had a chance to answer, she was off – running down the carpet – following the contour of coloring that lined where you should walk and where you should gamble. Within moments she was out of sight.

Finally leaving my spot, I walked in the direction she'd traveled. Taking my time. Looking left and right between machines and people – lights and buzzers – taking everything in. Like that was even possible.

It wasn't long before I could see Reilly in the distance. The moment our eyes connected, she smiled and started running towards me. When she was five feet away, she leapt into my arms. I caught her and spun her around, her kissing me while we twirled. Eventually, my arms gave out and I deposited her back to the earth.

"This place! This place is wonderful! Don't you think?" she asked, staring up at me.

I gave her a smile, and a halfhearted, "Yes … yes I do."

She returned a small nod, then was off again.

I watched her, and the others, as they moved from machine to machine, table to table, winning and losing. Living their lives like the olden days. Days long past.

But were they!?

I was here. They were here, I thought. I knew it couldn't be, but yet, there we were. Enjoying all the things that made Vegas, Vegas. And I was reveling in it, just like they were. Engrossed in the bells and buzzers and activity all around.

That's probably why I didn't notice the one thing that was off.

It took me a few minutes, probably because of all the movement around me, to notice the one thing that was stationary. The one object off to the side, just inside my peripheral. Propped up against a machine. A machine whining and howling as if trying to be seen.

When I noticed the stationary thing, I turned towards it – focused on it – trying to determine what it was. It was gray in color – in shape. A gray speckled with white, giving it an ashen sheen. That's all I could tell from where I was at.

I continued to stare, just watching the shape, waiting for what … I had no idea. I felt like this went on for minutes, but it may have been seconds. Time seemed so surreal.

Because of the way it was drooping, it took me some time to recognized it for what it really was. When I did, I called out to Reilly so she could see the spectacle.

"Reilly, do you see this?" I shouted and turned, pointing at it as I searched for her. "Someone's passed out on that machine! Do you believe that?"

I searched the crowd for her. She'd been just within sight a moment before. But now she was lost to me again. Somewhere vanished into the hoard.

Turning back towards the unconscious person, I noticed they'd shifted slightly. They were no longer slumped over the machine. Now they were sitting up, blankly staring at it. But that's all they were doing. Just sitting there, glaring at it, like maybe it was going to do a trick.

I continued watching this … this peculiar scene, fixated on it, waiting for … something. I was so engrossed waiting for the character to move, I didn't feel her walk up behind me. I only realized she was there after she'd put her loving arms around me.

"Hey, Babe! Whatcha looking at?" came the familiar voice from the lips behind my ear. Turning, I smiled when I saw the face of my dreams.

"Oh, hey Babe!" I replied, then pulled her closer.

We kissed for only a heartbeat – way too short for my liking. Then, as we released, she gave me a final peck on the cheek. It was her way, really. Her signature of affection. Something I seriously could never get enough of, no matter how much time passed by.

Lorie then pushed away so she could look into my eyes.

"What's up with that guy?" she asked. Up until then I hadn't realized the figure was a man.

"Not sure. One minute the guy's passed out. The next he's just looking … weird."

We both turned towards the man. He was still focused on the machine. But then, maybe feeling our gaze, he slowly pivoted to look at us.

Except, I could see he wasn't really seeing us. His eyes weren't … well … they weren't focused on anything. They weren't focused on anything because … because his eyes appeared to be missing.

I blinked a few times thinking I was seeing it wrong. But, as I squinted and leaned forward to get a closer look, the vacancies became even more apparent. By the look of the empty sockets, and the blood trickling from them, I could only surmise that the eyes had been ripped from his head.

"What's wrong, Babe?" Lorie asked, maybe seeing my distress or fear.

"His eyes," I uttered as I managed to point. "Don't you see it? The man has no eyes."

I turned back to Lorie. It was obvious she wasn't seeing what I was seeing. I did a double take, pivoting between the two. Glaring at each, wondering about both.

With my attention split, I didn't see the man move. Well, at least not at first. One moment he was just standing there, staring at us. The next he was slowly walking forward, approaching me and Lorie.

Seeing this – his advancement in our direction – I wasn't sure what I should to do. Lorie wasn't seeing what I was seeing and, as I tried to move the two of us away, she suddenly wouldn't budge. It almost felt like her feet were affixed to the floor. I tried several more times to move her, but each time I only felt resistance.

"Hun, I think we should go," I posed, keeping my eyes on the man as he got close.

"I still don't understand what you mean, Babe," she replied, still acting perplexed. I ignored this little fact and again prodded for us to leave. But instead of heeding my requests, she just continued to stare at me, dumbfounded.

I then looked around to see if maybe someone else was seeing what I was seeing. More so, if anyone else could see the man with the missing eyes. But suddenly everyone seemed to be gone. The room was now completely empty. That is except for me and Lorie … and the approaching man.

Part of me wanted to run at that point. I wanted to run, to get away and hide. But I knew I couldn't leave her. No matter what was going on. Instead, I moved behind her and started pulling. Yanking on her arm trying to free her feet from the floor.

"Babe, please!" I begged her – pleaded with her – as I pulled.

Finally, just as I was about to give up hope, my wrenching did the job. I felt Lorie shift backward slightly, a sudden movement that made me lose my grip.

Reaching out for her once more, I stopped when Lorie abruptly turned. My hands and hopes slowly dropped the moment I saw it.

Lorie's face had suddenly changed. Her complexion had gone pale, and her eyes – her deep and beautiful orbs – were now no longer the ones I'd fallen in love with. Her eyes were now glazed over, covered with a milky white sheen,

Moving backward, I stared at her in horror, not knowing what to do. She suddenly reached out for me, making me instinctively take a step back. Before I could react any further though, she unexpectedly started to speak.

"What's the matter, Paul?" she asked. "Don't you love me anymore?"

Before I could answer, she took another step towards me. Then another. Then another. As she advanced, I moved back further, away from her, trying to distance myself from this … this thing. The thing that was no longer my Lorie.

"Babe, don't you want to stay with me?" she begged as she gained ground.

"Please, just stay with me!" she implored.

Hearing this … this plea … I wanted to. Part of me wanted to stay with her – to be with her forever. But the saner side of me knew deep down that she was the one that'd chosen to leave. And now … now I had to choose the same.

Turning, I started to run. But I could feel her right behind me. More than that, I could feel the cold coming off of her. I could feel it on the back of my neck. Her freezing pleas were sending chills straight down my spine.

Although I wanted to turn, to be with her, I knew what I had to do. I had to keep running. I had to keep looking for avenues of escape.

Then, from somewhere – the back of my mind, maybe – I heard a voice call out to me. A voice – the voice – that pulled me back and away.

"Oh, Paulie! Paulie! I need you to move! I need you to move … just a little …"

CHAPTER 21

"Paulie … oh, Paulie!" I heard someone say in a sing-songy voice.

"It's time to get up, Paulie!" the voice continued. It was distant. Far off. Like "other side of the mountain" off. I did my best to heed the words. They were pulling me back slowly from the night terror I'd been trapped in.

I felt something then. The sensation of my pants being pulled back and forth, and then down. I forced open my eyes to see what was happening, but the room was dark, and I couldn't see jack shit. The next thing I knew I felt a very warm, very wet hand reach down my pants and wrap itself around my cock.

I tried to sit up, tried to move. I was immediately – and roughly pushed back down.

"Don't move, Baby! Please don't spoil it!" the sultry voice pleaded. It was Reilly. I knew that now. She wanted me … wanted sex. But, after the dream I'd been having, I didn't want to. At least not with her.

Part of me was still in that dreamworld with Lorie – a non-zombiefied Lorie. The Lorie I'd fallen in love with and missed terribly. But there I was with Reilly – wild and sexy Reilly – and not with my wife. Lorie was gone and would never be again. I kept telling myself that every time I had a dream about her. Dream or nightmare, it didn't matter. I just wanted to see her face.

"Damn it, Reilly!" I started, trying to rise again – trying to push her away. I was abruptly shoved back down.

"Stop it!" Reilly replied, this time her voice nowhere near sexy. "I want you inside me! I want to feel you inside me … now!"

I wasn't "feeling it" though. Not after just being with Lorie. I again tried to rise. To resist.

"Reilly … I appreciate the sentiment, but I really need to take a piss, and …"

It was like she wasn't hearing me. Reilly wasn't accepting my "not wanting it." She had only two emotions at that point – glee and anger. And me not wanting to have sex, I was about to experience the latter.

"Fuck you! I don't give a shit what you want! I *want* you! So, stop fucking moving!" she barked. Her legs were now straddled over me, holding me down.

Then I felt her shift slightly. One hand was still on my chest, but the other – her right – moved off somewhere. With the shift in her weight I could have thrown her off me easily. But I didn't. I didn't want to hurt her or, worse, I didn't want to totally piss her off.

"Give me a minute to wake up at least!" I begged. All she did was grunt in return.

I tried to shift backward, to shift out from under her. But her full weight came back onto me. Still straddling me. Still pressing me down. I started to say something, but the moment I did her left hand moved to my mouth to cover it.

"Shhhh ... I don't want to hurt you. Please don't make me hurt you," she begged. And that's when I felt it. The cold steel pressing against my neck. A knife less than an inch from my jugular.

I froze not knowing what else to do. Feeling my "rigidity," Reilly removed her hand from my mouth and shifted it between our legs. Grabbing my member, she slid it inside her then moved her hand back to my mouth. All the while she kept the blade against my neck. Had I moved, I would've been a dead man. I knew that. I knew it and could only follow her needs.

Reilly started rocking back and forth on me, getting into a rhythm – *the* rhythm – the one she liked when she was on top. I tried not to think about the blade against my throat and concentrated on the warmth – on the grip of her vagina gliding up and down my cock.

It only took a minute. I felt her stiffen. I felt the twitch in her legs as she came close to her orgasm.

"Don't cum yet! Don't cum yet!" she begged.

"Oh yeah ... oh yeah ... oh ... oh ... oh ..." she moaned. Then I felt her cum. Her legs gripped onto my sides of mine then I felt the flood of her juices shooting all over my groin and legs.

Lucky for me, a second or so before her orgasm, she'd dropped the blade and removed her hand from my mouth. Had the knife still been at my throat during her moment of ultimate pleasure, I would have been cut for sure. Sliced open like an animal being bled out for Sunday evening dinner. Those would have been the words written on my tombstone. One hell of a way to go, for most. To this day I still don't like to think about the bullet that I barely missed there.

When her shaking subsided, she collapsed next to me on the bed.

"Wow, Baby! That was something else!" she said, reaching for me. She wanted to cuddle then. I, of course, did not.

I didn't reply to her. I simply rose, grabbed my clothes, and moved towards the bathroom.

"Is everything okay?" she asked. Part of me wanted to tell her off. To flip her off. But I didn't. Consequences, you know!?

"Yeah. Everything's good. I just need to take a wicked piss," I instead replied, then walked into the bathroom and closed the door.

Before taking said "wicked piss", I stood at the mirror and looked into it. I was shaking – visibly shaking. I mean, who wouldn't be trembling after that. I'd nearly been killed for the sake of a morning fuck. *Who does that!?* I thought as I stared at my reflection. *Who the actual fuck does that!?!* I internally screamed.

I knew it wasn't me. I knew this … the whole thing wasn't me. Sure, I'd been lonely. And I loved the attention she gave. But, man, all that was a bridge too far. I'd gone someplace where I shouldn't have … and I needed to get the fuck out of that place.

"Sweetie! When you're done, do you want me to blow you?" she called out, jolting me from my thoughts.

"Ya-Yeah … but maybe later!" I managed. I knew what would get her. "But I'm … I'm really hungry right now!"

"Wow! You read my mind!" she replied, then said the words I knew would be coming. "But can you bring something back for me? I'm really, really tired at the moment."

"Yeah, sounds good!" I said as I moved from the sink to the toilet. I sat while I relieved myself. I started breathing in and out, in and out, trying to quiet the shivers. When I was finished, I flushed, washed up, then left my sanctuary. I put on a smile as I met my attacker. Not that I had to. She was fast asleep.

I stared down at her for a bit. Thinking. Wondering. Regretting. Not regretting the relationship. Regretting what I was about to do.

Part of me felt like a total asshole leaving her. I knew she loved me … in her way. But I also knew I had no other choice. I figured it'd be only a few days before she went full on crazy. And, when she did, well, one of us wouldn't survive.

I waited a couple more hours, knowing she wouldn't wake during the morning. She didn't wake until close to sundown most days. She explained it off as her being a party girl. A nighttime girl. She didn't want to admit what was happening to her. And I didn't blame her. I didn't want to admit it to myself.

After I'd waited a bit, I grabbed my gear and left. I traveled around to a few stores picking up things from the area. Supplies. It wasn't hard to find a new SUV. Fuck, they were everywhere and better equipped than the Hummer. The biggest problem was finding one with gas. I knew gas was going to be the big problem from there on out. Gas and clear roads once I hit LA. If what Nina was broadcasting was true, I'd only be able to use backroads into LA. Avenues potentially filled with Crazies. But I figured I'd worry about that when I got there.

Live in the now, I tried to remind myself. *Live in the now, and make it to LA.*

So, I left town with that in mind. I drove southeast towards the city of angels – and the ocean. It was a little more difficult than my trip to Vegas, but not much. It was hotter out, that was for sure. But that's okay, it was a dry heat.

Wait … still not funny after all these years? Oh well. I tried.

It took me nearly three days to reach the outskirts of Los Angeles. And it was rough going. Abandoned cars. Dead animals. Huge cracks caused by – and I'm speculating now – at least one major earthquake and probably a few aftershocks. There was no way to know, really. But, just like the road on my way to Vegas, there was a whole section of road near Barstow that was just gone.

Staring at it, I thought about how amazing it was that this much decay could happen in such a short time. Thank God for that SUV. If it wasn't for that, I would've never made it.

Speaking of which – another segue here. If you've never had a chance to sleep on top of an SUV or car parked in the desert at night, you really should. Assuming SUVs and deserts are still around in the future. There's something completely magical about it. Something centering. The nights I spent staring up at the stars and thinking about everything and nothing at all were some of the best nights in my life. Post Lorie that is. The comfort I felt lying under the heavens was something else. Something I didn't know I was missing in my life until it was smack dab in my face. I'm sorry I didn't spend more time doing it. You know, in my life before The Surge.

Getting back to it, after making my way through the San Bernardino National Forest by way of I-15, I took a right on I-10 and followed that towards LA and N. Sycamore Ave – the latest home of SiriusXM California. This time I stuck to the freeways as much as I could. With all the little side streets – and having seen a bunch of episodes of Cops-LA when it was on the air – I knew better than to risk a run-in with another band of Crazies. Not that I saw any signs of them. I had no idea what the population of the area was at the time. But better safe than sorry, I always say.

When I pulled into the parking lot of SiriusXM, my heart was practically pounding out of my chest. I couldn't wait to meet Nina in person. I just knew she'd be as incredible in person as she was on MTV and on the air.

Since "knowing is half the battle … Go Joe," I made sure I was armed when I left my vehicle. As I walked towards the station entrance, I scoped out the surroundings. Besides random cars in the lot, there appeared to be nothing and no one around.

After making my way to the door, I did what one normally does. I tried opening it. But, apparently, it was locked, so I tried the next best thing. I tried the doorbell. But it appeared to be dead.

Next, I tried knocking on the door. I rapped on it a few times, then waited. After a minute when there was no response, I knocked a few more times then waited again. Having heard no answer, and no other recourse really, I did what I thought was proper. I kicked in the door. It was actually relatively easy to do. It felt like the door was just propped closed. Then, after it gave way, I walked into the facility and started looking around.

The place was eight stories tall, with maybe two hundred offices in all. And I swear, even though I had only the use of the stairs, I visited each and every one. It took me about two to three hours to do, but I did it. I didn't want to leave one stone unturned, if you know what I mean. Not that it mattered, though. Every single one of the offices and studios – including Nina's and Howard Sterns' – was empty and looked like it'd been that way for about a year.

Obviously, I was confused. The whole thing made no sense to me. Nina said at least a few hundred times that she'd been transmitting from this location. And she was still on the air last I'd checked. How was it possible for her to still be transmitting from there if it was vacant!?

After I finished checking the last of the rooms on the top floor, I started making my way back downstairs. I knew it was getting late, and even though I didn't have an answer, I needed to find a place to squat for the night. My first thought was to grab some bedding and a meal, then move to a room in the office building. I needed a room I could easily escape from, but not a place Crazies would look if they caught wind that was there. It didn't take long to find. Once I'd found a room on the second floor that checked all the boxes, I made my way out to my waiting SUV.

I was stopped the moment I exited the building.

"Hey, friend! Don't be alarmed!" came a male voice from my left. It wasn't until later that I'd ruminate on his comment. I mean, someone calling out to you when you're not expecting it. How could I not be alarmed!?

Already having my AR in hand, I pivoted and aimed it in his direction. Or should I say group? There were five people in all. Each had their weapon trained on me. It was a miracle that no one got shot. My only guess was they'd been through this little "meeting of the minds" before and were prepared for my reaction.

Seeing this ... this scene, it only took a fraction of a second to realize I was up shit creek, sans paddle. Doing the only thing I thought logical at the moment, I dropped my rifle from shoulder to side, still keeping it trained on them as a whole.

"Sorry if we startled you," I heard another voice say. That time it was a woman's. A female voice that sounded oddly familiar.

I didn't see her at first. She'd been standing to the side of one of the SUVs new to the lot. I was hoping that maybe, just maybe it was the one person I'd headed there to see. But as the fifty-something woman stepped out from behind the vehicle, my hopes were instantly dashed.

"Barb! Stay put! You know better!" the original male voice said in a hushed but angry tone. The guy side-eyed her, then turned his attention back to me. Raising his rifle, he tightened it to his shoulder and peered at me through its sight.

I saw what was going on. It was obvious. And I certainly didn't want to heighten the situation. So, in order to lower the potential of me being dead, I slowly raised my left hand as I moved the rifle barrel to the ground. The moment I did this, I saw the strain in their faces let up, albeit just slightly.

"I take it you're not one of the affected ones?" the lady – Barb – asked as she continued to disregard her protector's mutterings of disapproval. I remember thinking, *man, that's a funny way of thinking about it ... affected.* Guessed it was better than just saying, *are you one of the Crazies?* Much more PC.

"As far as I know ... no?" I smiled and shrugged. Then I looked towards her group. "And I take it you guys aren't either?"

She shook her head. "No. We've been fortunate enough to be spared."

After saying that, she then crossed the line. Or should I say, line of sight. She moved between me and her protector, blocking a potential shot from him and a few of the others.

I heard him mutter something to Barb, then the others, as she continued walking toward me. I didn't quite hear what he'd said because she was speaking.

"As you probably heard, my name is Barb. And you are?" she motioned to me.

"Paul. Paul Davidson," I replied.

She gave a nod. "Paul, it's nice to meet you."

"Nice to meet you as well, Barb," I said.

After she gave me a once over, she asked, "You're not from around here, are you?"

I shook my head. "Nope. I'm originally from Cleveland. But for the last few months, I've been living on the road. And before that, Fort Myers."

"Uh-huh," she nodded. "And what brings you to LA, Paul?"

I thought about her question for a hot minute before replying. I wondered if I should give her some bullshit excuse, or if I should be on the up and up. Something in her kind eyes and demeanor made me answer the latter.

"Umm … this might sound silly, but … I actually came here looking for Nina Blackwood. Her radio broadcast …"

"Said she was here. I know," she interrupted.

I couldn't help but sound a little gleeful asking, "Then she's with you guys?"

She pursed her lips. "She is, in a way. We still broadcast her radio show from here."

I narrowed my eyes at her. "In a way? You still broadcast it from here? What does that mean?"

Barb paused as if hesitating to say something. Maybe it was because she didn't know how I was going to react. Or maybe it was because she didn't know how to put into words what she was feeling. If I had to guess, I think it was a little bit of both.

I am sure that I could hear sorrow in her voice when she told me, "I'm sorry to say that Nina … Nina passed away. About six months ago."

I know Barb could see the shock in my eyes. I mean, I had just been listening to Nina the day before. The friggin' day before! And now I was being told that she'd been gone for half a year!? Okay, yeah … it was more than just shock. I was pissed. And more than a little hurt.

"I'm sorry if you feel … tricked. It wasn't our intention. I promise you," Barb said. But I did a little anyway. That is, until I thought about it.

I tried to think back to the things Nina'd said. She'd announced the tunes, sure. And little updates here and there. But they left the weather and major news to other people. In fact, hearing Barb's voice is what triggered that thought. If I wasn't mistaken, hers was one of the voices I'd been listening to for the past few months.

Seeing the look in her eyes, I felt I needed to explain myself. So, I did.

"It's not that I feel tricked. Well, not really. I was just really hoping to meet her. Nina. She, umm … she's been there for me while

I was on the road. Or at least that's what I'd thought. She was … she was …"

Barb reached out and took my hand, then did something I didn't expect. She pulled me into a hug. For some reason, this little show of affection hit me hard. Hard as a freight train. A feeling that burrowed into my soul and latched on tight.

Maybe it was because she was an older woman – a motherly type. Or maybe it was because I hadn't had a hug – a real, non-sex related hug – in over a year. Hell, maybe it was because I was exhausted from being on the road. I didn't know. All I did know at that moment was it felt good. Comforting. And I cried. Good lord, I cried a veritable ocean.

The whole time I bawled – which was maybe less than a minute but felt longer – Barb continued to hug me and tell me it was okay. I don't know if my breakdown was something she'd expected – something others had done when she announced Nina's passing – or if maybe she just shared how I felt. Either way, it didn't matter. I needed it. I needed that hug – that closeness – at that moment. I needed it more than anything I'd ever needed in my life.

When I was done, I backed away and reached down to grab a handkerchief from my cargo pants. While I wiped my eyes and nose, Barb kept her hand on my arm the entire time. It was as if she was trying to steady me. Which, when I think about it now, she really was.

Finally feeling like I had my shit together – at least a little – I gave Barb an apologetic smile and said, "I'm … I'm sorry about that. And, umm, thank you."

She didn't reply. She only returned a kindly smile.

"Barb, we need to go. It's getting late," I heard the friendly yet disapproving voice from next to her. With my bawling, I hadn't realized her protector had moved forward to join us.

"Yes, you're right," she replied over her shoulder, then met my eyes. "We need to get back. But you're welcome to come with us ... if you'd like."

I squinted at her. "Come with you? Come with you where?"

She looked back for a moment, checking on her other people to make sure they were on the move before answering.

"We have a village not too far from here. About five miles away. It's a safe place. Up in the hills. Would you like to see it?" she asked, then motioned to one of her vehicles.

I glared at her, hesitant at first to accept the offer. I knew she meant for me to leave my car.

I pointed at my SUV. "Can I follow you there?"

She shook her head. "That's not a good idea, logistically, with the time. If you come with us now, we can pick it up tomorrow if you'd like."

I knew the car carried no sentimental value. I'd only had it a short time. Yet there was something ... discomforting about leaving it. Kind of like being asked to drop your drawers at a doctor's office. Barb saw this ... this reluctance in me.

"I swear, it will be okay here for the night. And I promise we can come back for it at first light."

Although part of me wanted to say no, the trusting part of me – the part that felt comfortable enough to cry on a stranger's shoulder – told me it'd be alright.

"Well, can I at least grab a couple things out of it?" I asked. She nodded.

"Sure thing. Shane can help you," she stated, gesturing to her protector. Without a word he did as asked.

As we walked the twenty or so steps to my car, I felt his eyes on me, looking me up and down. I knew he was looking for anything out of the ordinary just in case they hadn't "vetted" me properly. Opening the door, I let Shane take a look around before I reached inside.

"I just need my pack … and a few essentials," I noted.

"Like what," he asked, craning his head. I showed him my pack and its contents.

"MREs?" he asked. Seeing his interest, I held one out. He let his guard down enough to produce a small smile.

"Damn! I haven't seen one of these in a while!" he stated. I motioned for him to take it.

"I picked them up at Fort Bliss a few months ago. They've life-savers on the road."

Shane turned it back and forth in his hand a couple times. I could tell he was reminiscing. After handing it back to me, he asked, "What else you got in there?"

I pulled out a Rockstar. "Just a few of these."

He took one and gave it a once over. When he was done, he gazed at me and my pack. "So, what? You're telling me you've survived only on military MREs and energy drinks?"

"That's it. Mostly," I shrugged. "There was plenty of food in Vegas … that was my last stop."

Shane's eyes widened. "Vegas? What's going on in Vegas?"

I knew what he was hoping for. He was hoping I'd tell him that there were people there. That there was life there. That everything was normal there. His eyes dropped when mine told him the real story.

"Sorry," I replied. His eyes dropped and he let out a heavy breath.

"We should go," Shane nodded, then turned. After quickly making sure I had everything I thought I needed for the night – music player, thumb drive, and a few candy bars ... hey, don't judge me – I closed and locked the SUV then followed him to meet Barb.

As we were spirited away from the studios, Barb relayed a little about their village, and its history. Not that there was a lot to it. I could've guessed what'd happened. You probably could too.

When all the shit started going down, and the Crazies started appearing, Barb and a few of her friends moved from their houses in the greater Los Angeles area to a camp in Griffith Park, in the hills near Mount Hollywood. You might know the place. It's where the Hollywood sign used to be and where the Griffith Observatory still resides.

Up there they had access to a small lake – if you could call it that – along with some caves and some pretty secluded spots. Spots that would take some time finding, unless you knew what you were looking for.

When things really got bad in society – you know, food riots, murders, and such – the group picked one of these spots and fortified it. They had help from a couple military types like Shane.

Originally, I guess the group had close to two-hundred and fifty people in it at its peak. Enough that you could almost call the place a small town or "Village" – which is what its residence ended up naming it. But now, because of the ongoing Surge, they were down to only just over forty. But they were always on the hunt for more.

"I hate to admit it," Barb said. "You're the first normal person we've seen in weeks."

"At XM?" I asked.

"Anywhere," she replied. "XM is the only place we're monitoring these days, though."

I looked at her questioningly. "What's up with that anyway? Do you stalk this area regularly?"

"Well, I guess you could call it stalking," she laughed, then went on to explain how they'd been able to find me so easily.

Barb, in her previous life before The Surge, had been a sound engineer that'd worked for SiriusXM since their start. When she first came on board, she'd helped them develop their network. So, obviously, doing what she knew, when society collapsed and people started dying, it was her idea to keep XM going.

"The government … what was left of it, at least … was doing nothing. And the XM satellite system was still broadcasting nationwide. So, it only made sense to set up our own place. A place unaffected people could go to … survive. Do you know what I mean?" she asked, glaring at me questioningly. I could only nod in agreement. From the first day I'd heard the invite – well, mostly day one – it'd been my idea to go there. So, I guessed she was right.

"When I came up with the idea, I approached Nina and the other DJs still broadcasting. Most agreed to help. I'm just glad it worked out for you and the others."

She then went on to explain that, after most people had left downtown, her village had set up wi-fi cameras on the front of the XM building and inside, just in case anyone showed. They kept the doors locked and the power off, to make it look like the place was dead. A ruse to keep the Crazies away.

When I asked them how they kept the music playing, transmitting from the XM studio, they told me how it all worked. I guess they had a receiver and transmitter in the basement of the studios – locked away and hidden from schlubs like me. There were a couple satellite dishes on top of the building. One dish was directed toward and received transmissions from their village. The other shot that signal up to the satellite system circling above the earth.

We halted our conversation once in sight of the Village. Or should I say Barb shushed me. She wanted me to watch as the gates opened for us. She acted like we were entering doors to a majestic cathedral. It was like an Aladdin "Open Sesame" moment. It was totally weird. But I supposed I could understand a little. The place was something she'd created from scratch. And whatever she was doing was apparently keeping people alive.

Once inside, the ten-foot-tall gates closed behind us as the vehicles were parked and we exited the SUV. The moment we were outside, Barb wasted no time pulling me into the grand tour.

The place wasn't huge. At least not as big as I'd thought it would be considering the two hundred fifty number she'd bantered. The place – the Village – did stretch back along the road a bit, with gardens, huts, and everything I think you'd need to supply a bunch of people with stuff to live on. But it certainly wasn't big enough to hold as many as she'd said. As if reading my mind, she went on to explain.

"When we first started out this was only a small settlement. Less than a dozen of us came here. But as we grew, we expanded the Village, pushing back along the road like you see," she pointed to the hills that surrounded the twisting road we walked. "When that wasn't enough, we created two additional villages. One closer to where the Hollywood sign used to be, and one near the observatory."

She gestured in both directions, then got quiet for a moment. Musing, I assumed. Then she continued with, "Unfortunately, this is all that remains. Just forty-one of us."

"Forty-two," Shane, who'd been stealthily following us, corrected as we came to a stop.

She gave a nod. "Forty-two … if Mr. Davidson is willing to join us, that is."

I stared at Barb, then Shane, then Barb again. Here I thought it was a given that, now I was here, I'd be staying for the duration. I don't know what made me think that, except that people – normal people – were on short supply. Maybe it was also from me watching too many horror movies as a kid. You know the ones. The movies where people crash land on an island and are told they'll never be allowed to leave. Like *The Island of Doctor Moreau.*

You get the picture.

But, true to her word, Barb was giving me a choice. I could stay, or I could move along. And it's weird but, that was the moment I realized, as we'd been walking along, I'd been looking for avenues of escape. As we passed each hut – each tent – I'd been looking in between them, searching for corners I could duck away to. Places I could shimmy up a tree or bound a fence. Areas of weakness that would allow me to flee.

Chances for flight … so I could survive another day.

"What do you say, Mr. Davidson? Would you be willing to stay with us until the tide changes?" Barb asked. My attention instantly snapped back to her.

Briefly unsure of a response, I continued my stare for a moment as I considered the offer. Eventually, I gave her the answer she was hoping for.

"If you'll have me. Sure, I'd be happy to join you."

Yeah, I know – dumb reply. The whole "If you'll have me." But it's what I said. I wanted her to feel like I was humbled or honored maybe for the invite. Which, I guess, I was … at least a little. It also kept me from saying what was foremost in my mind.

The fact that it wasn't a tide we were experiencing … it was a tidal wave.

CHAPTER 22

Life in the Village was, how do you say it!? Rough? Or maybe just roughing it.

It was kind of like being in the military again. On maneuvers. Just slightly better.

We didn't have running water, per se. We had troughs. Communal troughs that were filled daily by a crew that sanitized the water and made sure it was potable.

You know, I've always liked that word … potable. It's kind of a fun word, isn't it!?

Oh, and we did have a crew of cooks, so there's that. Always a hot meal – which is more than I can say for my military days.

When I received my assignment – my job, for lack of a better word – at least I wasn't assigned to the shit crew. Literally the crew that was responsible for removing shit. Yeah, they had one.

Is this where I say shitty job? #DadJoke.

And no, I'm not sorry for that.

Anyway, based on my military background and my accounting/engineering experience, I was assigned to guard duty and supply. Not bad jobs, really. Kept my 9mm at my side twenty-four hours a day, seven days a week. And it also kept me in the know. Ear to the ground, so they say. I was always involved in excursions outside the Village, looking for supplies and getting a lay of the land.

At points, I almost felt like Daryl from *The Walking Dead.* A more clean-cut version though. No matter how far away from civilization I got, I still liked to be washed and perfumed. No point strolling through an apocalypse if you can't look good doing it, am I right!?

The look – Mad Max Couture, you could say – also helped me in another department. Yep, you guessed it – with the ladies. Actually, one lady in particular. Her name was Helen. Yeah, kind of an old school name, but it fit her. She was … I'm not sure if you'd say a homebody? Or maybe a farmgirl? She just had a down to earth way about her that made her fit into the … the rugged lives we lived, somehow.

And don't get me wrong. When I say farmgirl, you might think ugly or homely. But you'd be wrong. She was anything but that. Think Maryann from Gilligan's Island. She was pretty. And young. And all the single "still interested" guys wanted her. But, for some odd reason, she picked me.

The only problem was … I wasn't interested.

Yeah, yeah. Sorry if I got you going there. I didn't mean to. I'm just relaying the facts. At least the facts as I saw them.

Well, Helen and I did hang out, and we did hook up. No, not like that, though. What I mean by hooked up was we just hung out.

Some kissing was had, sure. But deep in my heart, it didn't mean much to me. I knew *it* – the relationship – wouldn't go anywhere. Mainly for two reasons. One, I didn't want a repeat of Vegas. Not that Helen showed signs of being a Crazy. But I still had that fear. You know, that I'd wake up one day to find my dick missing.

The other reason – and the more important one in my mind – was I was still lost in Lorie's world. The world I'd shared with her for such a short time in the scheme of things. She was and would always be the love of my life. I knew that down deep. And I could tell Helen sensed that about me. Not at first, mind you. But after a while. And I knew she wanted more. Something I couldn't give her no matter how sexy, or sweet, or desirable she was.

After a time, Helen eventually stopped trying to "get with me" as she put it. She ended up hooking up – yes, that kind – with one of the guards. A guy not too different than me. Except bigger. And hairier. But not as cool. I mean he only listened to classical. He looked like a biker, yet he didn't act like one. I always pictured bikers as the types that listened to classical seventies rock, not Mozart. Not that I didn't like Mozart, Chopin, or any of the other pirate shirt wearing pianists. It's just … well … umm …

Shit. Did it again. Got lost in minutia when I should've been telling you about life at the Village. A life I liked living, at least for the few months I was there.

The days around the Village started early. At sunrise, or just slightly after.

On the days I wasn't on night watch, I'd get up, wash up, then head to the communal kitchen. There I'd eat my breakfast while I talked with whomever was working. It was usually Judy. She was the head chef … or chief cook … or nutritionist. One of those. Maybe all. Anyway, she was the one that would update me on what they needed, or what they were missing.

After I got the list – and finished my breakfast, of course – I'd meet up with Sam. I guess you could call him my employee. He ran the storeroom and was the guy everyone went to for supplies. Sam had been injured at some point – a point he didn't like to talk about – and never left the safety of the Village. So, it was up to me to fulfill anything we needed, and any special requests.

Once Sam gave me his list, I'd meet with Jerry – the senior guard – and the other guys of the watch. Jerry would update us all on things that happened the night before and give us our assignments for the day. Usually, for me, that meant just filling the grocery list. There were special days, of course. Days where it rained or was dark enough for Crazies to roam. On those days everyone stayed put as to not attract attention. We kept things quiet, and dark. No visible fires or smoke. Especially at night, regardless of the weather. We took no chances, and it kept us alive.

During the day – normal days, that is – me and whomever else was available would take a vehicle out into the city and try to locate the items on our list. Typically, it was me and a guy named Ron. The two of us would drive around to places we knew – Circle Ks, Walmarts, and the like – to fulfill the list. And, if we had time, we'd also hunt for new places for supplies. Oh, and pick up gas. We always made sure we had enough of that.

When it got late – you know, dinner time – Ron and I would head back to the Village with the items we'd gleaned. We'd help unload whatever from the truck, then we'd be done for the day.

At night, after helping close the place down – making sure all the lights were off and such – I'd walk the perimeter or sit in one of the hidden lookout posts we had stationed around. Then, after being relieved, I'd head to bed. The next day I'd rinse, dry, and repeat.

Sound boring? Well, it was … a good portion of the time. And I was okay with that. But there were the days it wasn't. Days when things didn't always go as planned. They were few and far between like any job, but they still happened.

What are they, you ask? Well, there were a couple times me and Ron got stranded in LA. Once it was because the truck broke down and we couldn't make it back before sunset. We ended up leaving the truck and hiding out in an apartment building. It totally sucked. The place was full of dead people and it smelled to high heaven. But at least it kept the Crazies away. We saw a couple groups that night. Wandering. Roaming the streets and smashing things. Although, I must admit, what they were doing did look fun.

Oh, and there was another time we accidentally found a Crazies' camp in East LA. We were looking for … what … I think it was tools. Specifically, a wood saw and a … a … whatchamacallit it. A hammer. No! A mallet! That's it! One of the guys needed a rubber mallet to fix some doohickey.

Anyway, we were running into a Home Depot to find these things and tripped over a group of five Crazies – three guys and two girls. The place had been clear of people the last time we'd checked, but that time it wasn't. Both of us almost got killed. And if it wasn't for it being a bright California day, they might've gotten us.

But that was really the way of things in LA. Groups of Crazies that roamed the city until they couldn't roam anymore. And us, sitting vigil, waiting – hoping – that the whole thing would blow over.

There was a lady in our group nicknamed the Professor – officially known as Doctor Pamela Byrd. Before the world went to shit, she taught Physics at UCLA. She swore up and down that The Surge was just a phase the Sun was going through, and if we could just hold out for a few more months things would turn around. I think she'd said she heard it from one of her colleagues at the university. Someone that used to work for NASA or the government. Someone in the "know," if you know what I mean. We all prayed she was right. Well, hoped anyway. It helped to keep us going. Helped to keep us sane.

Anyhow, getting back to the Crazies, Ron and I ended up outrunning them because of the sun, but we'd had to ditch the truck and hole up in a warehouse overnight. Again, it was gross. No dead bodies that time, but the place was an old fish storage facility, and it just smelled … bad. Left us smelling bad too. I remember thinking that after we'd picked up a new truck the next day. The stench was so bad – I know … how bad was it!? It was so bad we had to burn our clothes when we got back.

But it was still better than the alternative.

Our main fear was that we'd run into a pack of Crazies too late in the day and they'd follow us back. I mean, the Village had precautions, sure. They'd set up outposts along the main road to block Crazies from making their way up. But that only took us so far. If they were to follow us, or see us making our way back, it could've been bad. The end of everything we'd built. And that was the last thing we wanted to do, no matter what supplies we thought were important.

So, like I was saying, it was nice getting back to a semi-normal life. Not that you could call it "normal" by any stretch of the imagination. But it was better than what I'd been doing. Living for myself … day to day.

And it was certainly better than being alone.

CHAPTER 23

Before I get to … well … the end of my story, I need to tell you a little bit about the two people that became my best friends at the Village. I'd feel remiss if I didn't. And no, I'm not talking about Jack and Diane like the song in the background.

I'm talking about Barb and Shane.

Like the others I've mentioned – the other people that made a difference in my … err … journey – Barb and Shane were about the most important. They kept everything in the Village running and feeling … normal. They brought a slice of humanity into a fiercely inhuman world. So, it's only right that I tell you about their backgrounds and how they came to be at the Village.

So, let me start with Shane.

Shane Samuel John McGregor – yeah, four names … kind of weird – was not born in Scotland, as you might think. No, he was born and raised in a small town in Iowa. Spirit Lake, to be exact.

And when I say small town, I mean small. Population maybe three to four thousand people. That is, in the winter. In the summer the population skyrocketed to more than double that. Why, you may ask!? Fishing. The area around Spirit Lake was a huge touristy spot for over half the year.

Like most Midwest, rural cities, Spirit Lake was very … err … patriotic. Shane's dad served in the US Army in the Seventies, his grandfather fought in World War Two, and his great-grandfather, World War One. His younger brother, cousins, and uncles all served at one time or another.

I'm sure now you get the picture.

So, when it came for Shane's turn, he enlisted as soon as he could – right after high school. No thoughts of first going to college. Just thoughts about following the family tradition. Which he did with honor and distinction.

As a mechanic.

Not that there's anything wrong with that. He was good in high school shop class, and he loved all things mechanical. Probably why we hit it off so well. Mechanic … mechanical engineer. Great minds, and all that.

Shane's intention wasn't to spend his life in the military, though. His thoughts were to see the world. After getting out, he planned to go to school, graduate as a mechanical engineer, get a white-collar job, meet a girl, get hitched, have kids, and grow old. Pretty much in that order.

Sounds, like a beautiful life, no!? Unfortunately, like most dreams, his were laid waste by time and intention.

After starting his life in the military, Shane met a girl. I think her name was Rhonda. He didn't like to talk about it or her too much. Supposedly they dated for a bit, she got pregnant, and they got married. Their child – a boy also named Shane, like his dad – was born eight months later … but died shortly after.

Maybe needless to say, their marriage – like a lot of marriages that go through that kind of pain – ended after their loss. After, Shane resolved to never get married again. I'm not sure why. Also, something he didn't like talking about. But if I had to guess, it had to do with not wanting to go through the same pain ever again.

Anyway, after Shane got out of the military, he returned to Spirit Lake – and a very sick father. Colon cancer, I believe. It wasn't long before the cancer did its damage, leaving Shane with a grieving mother to care for and a family business to run.

I'm not sure how long Shane ran the business. I think it was around ten years. Then The Surge hit, and he lost his mother, younger brother, etcetera, etcetera, etcetera.

Having no business left to run, and no family to run it for, he decided to do the one thing he wanted to do when he was in the military. He decided to travel.

Finding a camper, he drove the country seeing sights he'd always dreamed about. He'd seen Devil's Tower, Yellowstone, and the Grand Teton National Parks in Wyoming. He'd driven by the Great Salt Lake near Salt Lake City. He'd seen the Grand Canyon in Arizona, and even driven by Las Vegas so he could see the Hoover Dam. In fact, if I'd not stopped so many times along my way, I may have run into him there. Not that he would've stopped though. As he puts it, he was just "seeing the sights."

His last stop along his western tour wasn't even going to be Los Angeles. His only reason for stopping was to see Hollywood attractions. He said he wanted to see the Walk of Fame and Grauman's

Chinese Theatre, for whatever reason. And if it wasn't for the happenstance meeting of Barb and her people, he would've kept traveling until he'd seen the entire coast. But, as I mentioned, Barb had a way with people. The same friendly, motherly vibe that did me in. After finding out Shane was ex-military, she'd talked him into staying and that was that. Shane moved into the Village and helped shape it into a thriving community.

At least for a while.

Barb's story is much more simple … if you could call anything she'd experienced easy.

She'd also grown up in the heartland, in a small town near Peoria, Illinois. But, unlike a lot of us, she didn't wait until The Surge to move to LA. She'd actually moved there in the mid-eighties when her "lifestyle" became unacceptable to many in her small town.

Barb, and her then girlfriend Sarah … at least I think her name was Sarah. She'd mentioned several girlfriends as I got to know her. Anyway, she and her girlfriend – whoever it was – moved to LA where being a lesbian was more acceptable. There she lived with various girlfriends over the years and, apparently, held many odd jobs. She'd worked as a waitress, a barista, a part-time actress, and, oh, I don't know, about twenty other things. She was literally a jack of all trades. She knew electrical circuits and wiring. She knew how to stitch a wound as well as blankets. Hell, she knew almost more about mechanical engineering than I did! That's why she was perfect for her job at SiriusXM, and as leader of the Village. She was always running around from here to there fixing things or talking to people. She was a wonder … a true, true, wonder to have around.

Well, as I mentioned before, when the shit – aka The Surge – went down, Barb and a few of her friends started the Village. She mentioned losing a partner named Grace, but really didn't go into any details as to where and when. In fact, I really wish I knew more about her. But you know how it is. You work with people, day in and day out, but never really get to know them. Sure, you find out small details about them as life and time progresses. How they got there, where they'd been. But not how they felt about things. Not deep down at least.

And I feel bad that I didn't ask more about her … about them. Because now … now I'll never know.

CHAPTER 24

Now we come down to it. Why I ended up leaving the Village, and, more so, the end of my story. It came about in early Fall, about six months after I'd joined Barb's community.

Everything had been going well – for me at least. I'd moved up the chain, becoming a "second in command" to Shane, and felt like I was a valued part of life there. Although I really shouldn't pat myself on the back. Part of the reason I'd moved up was because of attrition.

As I'd mentioned, there were about forty people living in the Village when I got there. However, that didn't last long. About once a week – or maybe once every two weeks – we'd end up finding someone dead. Just like all the others, either their hearts had just given out or – in rare cases – they'd decided to end it all.

By early Fall there were only fourteen of us left. Fourteen that included me, Barb, and Shane. Ron had passed about a month before, leaving me to scavenge on my own. And Sam as well, making me chief cook and bottle washer. On rare occasions Shane came out with me, but they were few and far between. He was pretty much a one-man band of his own.

Shane was one of only three guys left to defend the Village. Not that the need arose much. We'd been super, super careful not to lead anyone back. And, except for a pair of Crazies that'd made their way past the barricades a couple months prior, no one else had stumbled on the joint.

Anyway, that day – the day things … err … went wrong – had started out like any other. I got up, washed up, ate, checked on supplies, then set out to fulfill the list. For all intents and purposes, it was a light day. Not much was needed besides a part for the well and some flour. Besides those items, I was on my own to check out things and to run by the XM parking lot to see if there were any changes. After, I was to make my way back. All things I'd done numerous times.

Everything pretty much went as planned. I found the needed part – or something very similar – then went by a warehouse that still had semi-perishables. You know, flour, sugar, and the like. When I was done, I stopped on the road along the way, siphoned some gas to replenish the tank, then drove by Sirius.

Pulling in the lot, nothing seemed off … at least not at first. The number of cars and their locations were still the same, and the main door was still closed, just as it'd been the last time I'd checked. But, as I moved through the lot to turn around, something seemed off to me. I couldn't quite put my finger on it, but there was something different since the last time I'd visited.

Then, like a lightning bolt it suddenly hit me. Circling around the end of the lot, I drove back across the front just to confirm. Sure enough, as I passed the front, I noticed the dumpster that sat alongside the back of building had been slightly moved. The dirt underneath it didn't quite align with the dumpster, and there were tracks on the ground where the dumpster had been shifted forward, then back again.

Stopping the car just past the trash bin, I picked up my two-way radio and pressed its call button. It only took a couple seconds for Shane to pick up the other end.

"Yeah, what's up Hero?" he asked.

Now, just so you know, Hero was a name Shane tagged me with after I'd saved Ron from a fall a few months prior. It's kind of a long story, and a really funny one, but I won't go into it right now. Maybe later. We'll see.

"Hey Hot Shot!" I fired back. Yeah, part of the same story.

"Has anyone else been to XM in the past three days?" I asked.

There was a pause, then, "No. Just you. Why are you asking?"

"Might be nothing, but the dumpster out back was moved," I replied.

There was another pause, then, "Got no idea. Like I said, you're the only one from the Village that's been there recently. And I don't think there's been any activity."

I knew by "activity" he meant seismic. We'd had some quakes of late, but nothing that would explain the move. Only a huge tremor would've shifted the dumpster that much. And the dumpster had been shifted back. An earthquake usually wasn't that … considerate.

"Is there a problem?" Shane asked. To tell the truth though, I didn't know. The only thing I had to go on were the hairs on the back of my neck. They were standing at attention.

"Not sure," I replied, then paused before adding. "I'll check things out and let you know."

I set down the radio and grabbed my 9 off the passenger's seat. After checking the magazine for ammo – as one does – I loaded a round in the chamber, then holstered it. As I started to exit the car, the radio blurted once more.

"Be safe, man."

I paused for a split second and thought about replying. I opted to leave the conversation where it was. He knew the relevant info and my location. If it was nothing, then I'd be back on the comm shortly. If not … well … then they'd know where to find the body.

Holding the 9 straight out in front of me – you know, like they do in *all* the cop movies – I kept it at the ready, just in case. In case of what? I wasn't sure. But there was something – about the scene, about the area – that gnawed at the back of my brain and made me skittish. It wasn't until later that I realized what it was. It was intuition. The same kind of sixth sense, or foreboding, animals had. The kind that made them flee under cars or up trees for no apparent reason. It was the same sense of impending danger that I'd seen in Lorie many, many times. Something I thought I'd never have. Or at least not to that extent.

Ignoring the skittish feeling, I moved to the dumpster. Walking its perimeter – as far as I could go, that is – I inspected it. The top and sides were worn and full of dust, as expected. They matched most everything in the world these days.

But as I came around to the non-visible side – the side you couldn't see from the lot – I noticed something off. As in dirt. There was dirt missing in two spots of the horizontal bar handle that ran from one side of the dumpster to the other. One spot on the left of the handle and one spot on the right. Perfect positions for hands.

Seeing this … this evidence of human intervention, the hair on the back of my neck became stiff as boards. A feat I didn't think was even possible. It was completely obvious that someone had moved the dumpster. Someone had placed a hand on both sides of it and shifted it. Then, for some unknown reason, they'd moved it back, trying to hit its original spot.

I looked down and saw that the thing had two locking and two non-locking casters. Both of the locking casters were unlocked. And, like the handle, both were missing dirt on the spots where a person would have to press the toe of their shoe to unlock it.

Holstering my 9, I held a nervous left hand over one spot while I hovered the right over the other. Why, you may ask? I wasn't one-hundred percent sure. Maybe it was to verify that it could only be done by a human. Not that it wasn't completely apparent. But a voice in the back of my mind wanted me to check. Wanted me to verify. And, thinking about it now, it was probably because of what I knew I had to do next. Curiosity being what it was, I had to move the dumpster. I had to know why it'd been stirred.

In hindsight, it was probably a thought that should've never crossed my mind. I probably should have just let sleeping dogs lie. But no, not me.

Fuck me and my curious brain.

Pushing the dumpster to the side, it was instantly apparent why it'd been shifted. It'd been moved to hide a broken window. A window that led directly into the basement.

As I continued pushing the dumpster away from the building, I saw there was a rope attached to the back of it. A rope that led from a welded plate, through the broken window, dropping off into the building.

Now, this could've been anything … or, should I say, anyone. This could've been a Norm that'd found this place – maybe through one of Nina's satellite broadcasts – and they'd decided to take the indirect route into the building. Not sure why anyone would want to do that, but you never know. Some people are just … well … weird. And they often don't make sense – especially during an apocalypse, as I'd come to find out. And I hoped that that was the case. But it seemed odd to me. Off. Like, why go to the trouble!? Why not just do things the right way!?

But, as I stood there gaping into the building, I felt my hairs again. Those fuckers would not let up! They prickled with every thought about the scene. They screamed to me, "Run away! Run Away!" just like the knights in that Monty Python movie.

But instead of heeding their warnings, I barreled right in.

I moved the dumpster far enough out of the way so I could take a closer look. Then, pulling a flashlight from my vest pocket, I shot light into the opening and panned it around. I shifted it this way and that a few times, but didn't see anything besides walls, a few desks, and a couple switched off computers. So, like an inquisitive cat, I moved through the window and entered the building.

Now, up until that point, I'd never been in the SiriusXM basement. Oh sure, I knew it was there, pretty much from day one. But in all the trips I'd made there, I'd never gone back inside the place. I mean, why would I!? The few Norms we'd picked up in the six months prior were all waiting outside – or we'd waited for them to come out, just as Barb had done with me. So, there was no need to explore the inners of the building. There was no need to inspect the basement and the hidden broadcast equipment. So, maybe part of the reason I headed in was curiosity. Part of me wanted to see what was hidden in the mysterious black box.

And, seriously, I should have fucking known better.

After searching the first room, I quietly opened the room's one and only door, then moved into a hallway. Taking a right, I slowly made my way down a short corridor, then took a left onto another. It didn't take long to find what I was looking for.

Being quiet as I moved – as quiet as that inquisitive cat – I turned my light off and approached the first open door. Once there, I stuck my head around and listened. Sure enough, there were sounds in that room. Breathing sounds. Snoring sounds. Sounds that appeared to be those of sleeping humans.

Now, my first thought in hearing this was, "Hey, I found some Norms! Leap in there and introduce yourself!" But as I listened to the noises, and remembered what time of day it was, I immediately knew that'd be a bad idea. The room had to have Crazies in it. And, not just a few. As I listened to the breathing, farts, and snores, I realized I'd found an absolute community of them. Maybe a dozen. Maybe more.

Instantly the hairs on the back of my neck rose again, sticking out so severely that I swear it made my shirt collar tight. It took everything in me to not shake in fear ... or, really, shriek in terror. Obviously, I knew this was the Flight response talking. My body screamed to run and not look back. But luckily my brain was still working, preventing me from doing just that.

Keeping my wits about me, I slowly backed away from the door and made my way down the hall. I made sure to keep my light off for fear that it might wake them. There was still the tiniest amount of light streaming into the hall from the place I'd entered. That trickle of light helped to guide me back.

As I rounded the corner, I saw movement in front of me. There, just past the door where I'd entered was a man. He was standing in the shadows, squinting. His eyes shooting in my direction.

At first, I wasn't sure what to do. I just returned his gaze, wondering if I should say hi – or say anything at all. I didn't have to think beyond that though. The dialog between us never got started.

Upon seeing me the man started to growl. He literally started to growl at me. A deep throated snarl that sent more than one shiver up my spine. Then, without warning – and totally ignoring the burning light coming through the doorway – he leapt at me, arms outstretched. His clawed hands headed directly for my throat.

Lucky for me, because his eyes were mostly closed from the sunshine streaming in, his aim was slightly off. Instead of hitting me full force, he only glanced off. His size and inertia then carried him forward, only halting when he ran into the opposite wall. I heard a very audible humph as the air left his lungs, then a thud when he hit the floor.

Scared shitless from the encounter – and near pummeling – I didn't wait to see if the guy was hurt. In fact, his wellbeing never even crossed my mind. Without a pause, I ran through the open door, jumped onto a table, then barreled back through the window where I'd entered.

And, wouldn't you know it, I almost made it out.

Unfortunately, before I was fully through, I felt strong fingers latch onto my right boot. Fingers that, with their iron grip, started pulling me backward.

Locking my arms on the windowsill, I reeled in my captive foot the best I could, then did a horse-kick. The shove against my opponent – and the decisive crack that followed – gave me the sudden thrust I needed to release his hold. Once my body was completely out of the building, I scramble to my feet, then turned back and prepared for the impending attack.

But, to my complete and utter shock, none was to be found. I'd obviously landed a said "good one" because my pursuer was no longer hot on my tail.

As soon as I realized I didn't need to defend myself, I turned and beat feet. Bolting to my car, I stopped for nothing. And the last thing I heard before I slammed my door shut was the attacker giving another resounding, yet wet sounding growl. Which was followed shortly after by a much louder and angrier scream.

Starting the car, I jammed it into gear, then hit the gas. The tires gave a small chirp as they first fishtailed then found purchase. Which, as it turned out, was a good thing. If it wasn't for that momentary slip, I would've sideswiped a car that was parked between me and the lot's exit. As it was, I barely missed taking off both of our mirrors.

Making a left onto the main road – a left which took me away from the Village –I was about a mile away from XM before I slowed enough to grab my two-way radio. With a very shaky hand, I turned the device on, then put my mouth to it and spoke.

"Sha-Shane … this is … umm … Paul. Ya-ya-ya there?" I mumbled, totally forgetting any radio protocol. When he didn't reply within a split second, I called out again.

"Shane! You there, ma-man? Pick up, pick up, pick up!"

This time, the moment I let go of the button, he was on the other end.

"Paul, this is Shane. What's up?" he replied in a much-needed calming voice. I pressed the button again.

"Shane, this is …" I started, then released the button and dropped the two-way to my lap. It suddenly struck me how nervous and out of control I sounded. Before I continued, I took a couple deep breaths and tried to relax. It felt nearly impossible to do.

"Paul, you there?" Shane asked, then waited. I could hear an urgency in his voice. Knowing he was probably freaking out from my tone and stutter, I finally got back on the horn.

"Shane, this is Paul," I managed in a calmer voice. He responded in kind.

"Talk to me, Paul. What's going on? What did you find?"

I cleared my throat, then said, "Shane … sorry about that. There were … there were squatters … Crazies … at the studio. I had to there leave in a hurry."

Reaching a dead end in the road, I took a right and started heading north. Not quite away from the Village. But I knew if I got too far the two-way wouldn't work.

"You okay, man? You injured?" Shane asked. Before I responded, I pulled the car over and stopped. As if he knew, he waited patiently for me to respond.

"No, I'm fine. One of them leaped at me … but I kicked him. I made it out safe. I'm going to head to one of the safe spots though, just in case."

Usually hearing this, you know, me saying I was going to a safe spot, Shane would get on the horn, ask which place, then wish me well. But this time, instead of that happening, the radio came to life with an equally nervous sounding voice coming from the other end.

"Shane, this is Barb. Na-negative. You need to get back here."

Of course, Barb getting on the line was nothing new. But her ask … her ask seemed strange. I thought about it for a second before I keyed the mic.

"Hey, Barb. Not sure that's a good idea. That's not standard procedure. And it's getting late. Don't want to take any chances. Understood?"

Upon releasing the button, I waited almost a full minute before anyone came back to me. I knew Barb and Shane were probably discussing the situation, and her ask. Hell, if the shoe'd been on the other foot and Shane had been out there, I would have. The request was against everything we'd discussed about keeping the Village safe.

Just as I was about to put the two-way down and start back up with my original plan, it suddenly came to life. And I was floored at what I heard.

"Paul, this is Shane. I agree with Barb. Get your ass back here ASAP."

Hearing that, I literally turned the two-way and stared at it. Like, in doing that, they could see the shocked look on my face. Or, that maybe I could see the reasoning in theirs. Obviously, I couldn't.

So, after staring at it for a few second, I returned it to the side of my head … just as it activated once more.

"Paul, I know what you're thinking, but … two more people died today. Rob and Stella. They both … umm … well, you know," he said, then I heard the hiss of the squelch. A moment later he reactivated his mic. "Like I said, we need you back here ASAP."

Now, I knew I should've argued the point. After all, rules were supposed to be just that. Rules. Rules were made to keep us safe and out of harm's way. And I knew they could live without me for one night. But, as I weighed all the plusses and minuses of my return, I knew what they were thinking. It came down to one simple answer.

They didn't want to lose another person that day.

So, instead of doing the logical thing – the smart thing – I did as they asked.

"On my way," I replied, then hung up and got back on the road.

It took me over an hour of driving through car and trash filled streets to reach the road that led to the Village. Once there, I moved the barricade – a dilapidated car – drove past it, then moved it back into place. I then drove up the winding road towards the Village, making sure I avoided the spike strips and obstacles along the way.

It was almost full-on dark by the time I reached the top. The moment I was close, the main gates were opened, and I drove in. It was so dark out I decided to stop just inside the gates. I didn't want to risk damaging the car or anything else by driving to its normal parking spot.

Before I had a chance to exit the car, I felt my door open, and a friendly voice spoke to me.

"Hey, Hero ... glad you made it back!" Shane said, then did something he hadn't done up to that point. He pulled me into a bro-hug.

I thought about saying something snarky, but opted for a quick, "Good to be back, man!" as I returned his hug.

After grabbing the few items I'd snagged that day, I followed Shane to the supplies tent to deposit them. As we walked, he told me about the events of the day. Or should I say the main event – the exit of the last married couple in the Village.

"We found them just after you left," he said. "Jane went to check on them since they hadn't made it to breakfast. She was the one that found them. Both curled up on the bed, holding each other's hand."

"Wow, man. That sucks," I weakly replied.

Although I felt like I should've given it more effort, I was bone tired. All the activity of the day – and mostly stress – had taken their toll. I was ready for the conversation, and the day, to be over. Shane picked up on it easy enough.

"Paul, we can discuss it in the morning," he said, then gave me a little punch in the arm when we reached my tent. That was his usual way of showing affection. That I was used to.

"Appreciate it," I managed, then added a quick, "Nite, man."

I don't really remember walking into the tent, closing the flap, or taking off my rig. The only thing I do remember was how good the pillow felt the moment my head hit it. Within seconds I was out like a light.

I'm not sure what time it was when I felt the first shove. Shane may have been jostling me for ten minutes for all I knew. The "Paul. Paul. Get up. Will you fucking wake up already?" I heard in Shane's whispering voice was the ship that cracked the iceberg – or the other way around.

"What the fuck do you …" I whined. Well, started to anyway. I would've said more but I suddenly felt Shane's sweat covered hand over my mouth.

"There's a group of guys coming up the hill. I need you on the wall," Shane whispered, scarcely audible. Seeing my acknowledgment, he removed his hand.

Sitting up, I tried to ask more. Shane's finger instantly shot up to his lips. Instead of answering the question he knew I wanted to ask, he waved for me to follow him, then turned and moved out the doorway. Or is it flap-way? Whatever.

Grabbing my jacket and holster – the only pieces of my apparel I wasn't still wearing from the day before – I put them on, holstered my 9, seized my AK and a couple clips, then followed after him.

As I approached Shane and Barb – both who were standing near the wall's front gate – I could see they were deep in a conversation. One would lean in to say something in the other's ear, then the other would lean in. It was super covert – and completely incomprehensible, especially with my tinnitus and all.

I stood next to the two for a few seconds while they finished their discussion. When they were done, Shane moved off to mount the west banquette. Which I guess is just a fancy way of saying he climbed up a ladder onto the raised walkway on the gate's west side. A walkway that ran the perimeter of the defense wall.

I was about to follow him to see what was up. You know, because he *asked* me to follow him. The moment I stepped forward, Barb latched onto my arm and pulled me close.

"I'm glad you made it back safe," she whispered, then smiled. I smiled at her in return.

Leaning in again, she added, "Shane says Bobby saw a group of Crazies headed this way. Maybe twenty of them. And they're armed."

Now, I gotta say, seeing Crazies on the road was nothing new. It happened from time to time – about once a week when I'd first arrived. But usually, if we kept things quiet and dark, they avoided coming up the road. I assumed wading through a bunch of trees and other foliage just didn't seem appealing to most. Because, really, that's pretty much all you could see from down at the bottom of the road. Or even from town, for that matter.

Except for one thing that was highly visible – the Village's broadcasting dish.

Because of it, we did get the occasional "visitor." A Crazy that would see the broadcasting dish way up on the hill and wonder if there was more to it than just the tower. You know, because a tower up on a hill might have a building. And that building might be filled with food … or guns.

But those ones were rare. Those visits only happened three times in my six months stay. And when they did, the "visitor" was captured and dealt with before they could reach the wall.

I know what you're probably thinking. That we'd offed those ones then bury them in a shallow grave never to be seen again. But, my friend, you'd be wrong. We, being Norms, were mostly passive, non-violent types … like most Americans. We didn't believe in killing people all willy-nilly. After all, as the Professor stated, everything would be returning to normal eventually. And, if she was right, our brain chemistry would be normalizing as well. So, no, in lieu of killing them we simply bound them, blindfolded them, and took them far away from the Village. One of us would drive them up the coast a piece to Valencia or one of its neighboring towns. There we'd drop them off then hightail it home.

And, you know what? None of them ever returned.

This little "visit" seemed different though. The sheer size of the group of Crazies approaching had everyone nervous … and downright scared. And there was only one reason I could think of.

Me. Somehow, they'd followed me there.

Before I could tell Barb my thoughts, Shane started frantically waving, motioning to men and the locations he wanted them to take. I knew that meant me as well. As I stood there waiting, he eventually waved at me, then pointed to a position on the east wall, next to Bobby.

After mounting the … err … banquette …

Okay. Sorry for that laughter. I'm back now. Excuse me for laughing … it's just that the name is so funny to me. I'm not even sure why, but it is.

Anyways, like I was saying, after mounting the banquette, I joined Bobby. He was focused, peering through his night vision scope at the road below. I tried looking out over the wall but saw jack shit. The night had gotten way dark. Too dark to see anything past the bend in the road. Maybe one-hundred feet away.

Wanting to know more – you know, like what he was seeing – I tapped him on his shoulder. The dude practically jumped out of his skin.

"What the fuck, dude!?" he spat – somewhat muted, but very pissed. I gave him a grimace and apologetic look. Seeing it was me, he calmed a little.

"Sorry, man ... just wondering what's going on," I whispered, pointing at the scope.

He leaned in. "What do you know?"

I shrugged. "Barb said there's a group of Crazies moving this way."

He nodded. "Band of maybe twenty. They look like they're getting ready to come up the hill."

"Do you think they know we're up here?" I asked. He paused for a moment before answering.

"If I had to take a guess, I'd say yes."

I gave him a look. "What makes you think that?"

"They passed the derelict a few minutes ago. Right now they're about halfway between it and us."

I gave a thoughtful nod, then asked a question that was probably rhetorical. "Did Shane tell you about my incident earlier?"

He returned a nod. I then asked what was first and foremost in my mind – and probably yours.

"Do you think it could be them? The ones from the studio?"

He did the only thing he could. He shrugged. Obviously, there was no way for him to know. But, again, I had that weird feeling floating through my brain, like I should know that answer. It was something that should've been as plain as the nose on my face. Yet was suspended somewhere above me, in the ether.

Before I could say anything else, Shane made a noise to get our attention. Bobby and I both looked towards him. Shane was gesturing over the wall. We both turned to see where he was pointing. Sure enough, that time I saw movement off in the distance. Not in one spot, but in two … or maybe three. People crouching and slowly making their way towards us – towards the wall.

Now, I feel like I've been negligent to this point. I never really described the place we were in. You know, the Village. Oh sure, I told you about the ten-foot-high gates and what they had inside – albeit abridged – but I didn't really describe what they had in the way of fortification.

A couple of the early contributors to the Village had been ex-military, like Shane and me. And, in their infinite wisdom, they'd made sure the place was safeguarded, and more so, defendable. At several strategic points along its length were embrasures – small openings in the wall made for guns to be fired through. And at each corner, and near both the front and back gates, were bartizans – small turrets for sentries to perch.

Obviously, with the few people the Village had left, only a few of these could be manned. But, in that instance – the instance of an assault at our front – the important ones were. And with each of those "important ones" came a small surprise.

But I'm getting ahead of myself. So, let me continue.

Seeing the people approaching, Bobby and I did as we'd trained. He moved to man one of the bartizans as I unslung my AR and made my way to an embrasure. The others – Tom, Mark, and even Barb – mounted the wall and took up their positions and prepared as Shane made his call.

“Who goes there?” he shouted into the darkness, then waited for a few moments for a reply. Hearing none, he called out again.

“Whoever’s out there, please state your intentions!” he yelled, then added, “Don’t come any closer! You should know, we’re armed!”

From out in the darkness I heard a muffled voice say, “Yeah, so are we, buddy.”

That was followed by a laugh, then quickly by another equally muffled voice saying, “Shhhh. Shut the fuck up, asshole. Let Hunter talk.”

There was a pause then. A silence that hung in the air like a frosty chill. A chill that was broken when a third, stronger voice, pierced the veil.

“Well, hello, hello, hello, all ye behind yonder wall!” the voice called, then went silent. It went silent as if waiting for us to react. But we didn’t. We just waited for the voice to speak again. When it did, it sent a shudder up my spine. It was a voice I’d heard before.

“No need to be shy in there! We’re new to the area and just want to meet our neighbors!”

I turned to look at Barb, to see if she was going to say anything. I knew that’s what Shane was waiting for as well. She was our founder and ambassador after all. But it didn’t look like she was going to live up to her titles. She was hunkered down in her spot, at the embrasure closest to Shane.

When it was obvious Barb wasn’t going to answer, the familiar voice outside called out again.

"Well, let me start by introducing myself. My name's Hunter, and I guess you could call me the leader of my merry band of misfits."

Again, I looked towards Barb. And again, she was doing nothing. She just remained in place, not even looking through the hole at the man.

Hearing no reply, Hunter spoke once more.

"Alright, now that I've introduced myself, don't you think it would be polite to introduce yourselves? I mean, you must have a leader in there, don't you?"

Hunter moved forward out of the shadows. And although it was almost pitch black out, I could see he was squinting. It was a squint I'd seen before. Only hours before ... in the basement of SiriusXM.

"What, no leader in there? No Sheriff of Nottingham?" Hunter barked, then let out a small laugh. As soon as the others in his group heard him, they also started laughing. Laughing that seemed to come from every direction. From the left. From the right. Everywhere. A laughing that went on for a bit, eventually growing in size.

Apparently pissed off by the hilarity, Barb finally broke out of her cocoon. Standing, she finally addressed the man.

"Ba-Barb. My name's Barb. I-I'm the la-leader here," she stated in a somewhat hushed voice. It was a miracle that anyone outside of the Village heard her. But they did.

Hunter raised his arms, then turned right then left. As he did, the laughter decreased, then abruptly stopped.

Lowering his arms, Hunter brought them together, interlocking his fingers in front of his groin.

"Well hello, Barb!" he replied as he slowly nodded. "It's nice to finally meet you! Damn nice to meet you, in fact!"

"Na-nice to meet you as well, Ha-Hunter!" Barb said, then quieted and waited for a response and, more so, a reason.

"Well, that's fine. That's fine," Hunter said, then looked right and left as if checking for something. Apparently seeing what he wanted to see, he turned back to Barb. "Alright, now that we have the pleasantries out of the way, don't you think it'd be nice if you maybe invited us in? It'd sure be great to meet you face to face, don't you think!"

Barb looked towards Shane as if to get confirmation. He just shook his head.

"I ... I don't think that's such a great idea. Tha-This is just fine for now," Barb replied.

There was a pause from Hunter. He stood there, almost looking perplexed. Eventually he just shrugged his shoulders and said, "Well, if you say so."

"I do," Barb quickly returned, finally starting to sound a little more confident.

Hearing this, Hunter emitted a small huff, then said, "You know, it's not very neighborly of you! Maybe I should just take my crew and go home!"

Hunter looked towards the wall, scanning it, as if looking for a rebuttal along its length. When nothing else came, he gave a small shrug, then turned and started away. After walking about ten feet, he stopped and called back over his shoulder, "Well, goodbye then, Barb!"

"Goodba ..." Barb started to say as the first shot rang out. A shot that caught her square in the neck. The force of the strike spun her around. She dropped like a rock, first to the walkway, then to the ground.

A split second later all hell broke loose.

A literal barrage of fire that seemed to be coming from every direction. It sounded like popcorn popping in a thinly lidded pan. Except it was louder. Much, much louder.

Hearing the salvo, all of us dropped away from the wall. Some of us manned their embrasures, some of us just cowered. Others ... well others just ran for their lives.

If it hadn't been for the shot that took out Barb, we may've stood a chance. Instead, everything quickly turned to shit.

Seeing Barb drop, Shane – who was supposed to be the general commanding our defenses – dropped down off the wall to see to her. Not that it did any good. She was dead pretty much the second the bullet struck. It was obvious. I could see it from my position twenty feet away.

Seeing Shane leave his post – and watching the rest scatter – I did what I could. As soon as I saw the hoard outside start running toward the gate, I yelled, "Lights!"

Luckily, Mark knew the plan as well. Hearing my shout, he jumped from the wall and ran over to the generator. With a quick jerk on the pullcord it started, which activated our small surprise – nearly a dozen spotlights, a few stationed at each of the bartizans.

Night instantly became day, and with it a halt to the rain of bullets. But that only lasted for a moment or so. Within seconds of the lights being triggered, those of us who'd stayed at their posts started firing upon the approaching hoard.

Hearing our shots ring out, some of those that had cowered rose and also started firing. It wasn't quite at the severity the hoard had generated. But having the high ground – the wall in front of us – we delivered uncompromising damage.

As I fired upon the approaching men and women, I watched as my shots and others found their marks. A lot of the Crazies – those blinded by the light, you could say – were dropped where they stood. Whereas others – the ones that kept their wits about them – turned and ran for cover. Within a minute of returning fire, we'd cleared the field of movement. Seeing this, a lot of us stopped firing.

And that was a huge mistake.

But it was a combination, really. The fact that Shane and Barb – our two leaders – were out of action. The late start on our secret weapon. Us thinking we'd stopped the onslaught. All of these things were huge errors in judgment. Errors that Hunter and his crew leapt on immediately. Within seconds of us letting up, we started seeing movement again.

Movement that came in the way of a school bus.

We heard it before we saw it. That familiar sound we've all heard as kids. A deep, almost grainy rumbling that slowly increased in volume as it approached.

The instant I saw it round the bend in the road, I started firing. Not that it did any good. I mean, maybe if I'd hit the radiator, I could've slowed it. Or maybe if a bullet had hit the driver. But even if those had happened, it might've still been too late.

As soon as the vehicle hit the straight stretch of road that led to the gates, I heard the rumble of the engine increase. And with it, its speed. It didn't take much. No more than ten miles per hour combined with the weight of the bus. Simple physics, if you look at it that way. There was a sudden crunch, then a snap, then the entire wall shook. And many of us – those close to the entrance, including me – were knocked from our posts and thrown to the ground.

After that … well … after that everything seemed to happen in slow motion.

Stunned by being suddenly thrown to the ground, it took me a few seconds to get my wits back. As soon as I realized where I was – you know, prone on the ground – I sat up, grabbed my AK, then got to my feet.

I peered to my right and left to see what was going on. It was like watching a shooting gallery, except from the target's side. Spotlights started exploding all around. People – those still on the wall – started falling as they were hit by gunfire. And the thunderous roar – both from Crazies and the firearms they were carrying – became deafening. A cacophony of noise that surrounded us like a shroud as the Village quickly dropped into darkness.

Knowing this was the end, and that there was nothing else I could do, I did the only thing I could think of. I ran over to Shane to see if I could help. He was finally on his feet and firing at Crazies as they started flooding through the Village's broken gates. His aim was brutal and spot on, taking out sunglass wearing enemies left and right. It was miraculous to watch … while it lasted. The Crazies eventually figured out where all their death came from. And they immediately turned all their efforts on that very spot.

When I was within, oh, maybe ten feet Shane, he suddenly lurched as a random shot bore into him. And then another. Then a third. I made it to his side just in time to catch his fall. Just in time to see his eyes roll into the back of his head.

Seeing their foe down, the Crazies instantly turned their attention away from Shane – away from us. This gave me the opportunity I needed. Moving behind him, I threw his arm over my shoulder then tried to lift. Feeling this act of comradery, Shane came back to himself … but only momentarily.

"Paul … you need to stop," he managed as he tried to pull himself free. Feeling this, I gently lowered him back to the ground. The moment he was down, he spoke.

"Leave me, Paul! I'm done. You need to run," he said, then grunted in pain as his eyes rolled into the back of his head once more. Seeing the whites of his eyes, images of that bird – the one with the white milky eyes – suddenly flooded into my mind.

But even seeing this – hearing this – I still tried to help. Rising slightly, I tried to lift him again. But again, he wriggled away. This time, he latched onto my jacket and forced me to meet his eyes.

"Paul … Pa-Paul. You need … you need to listen to me. You need … you need to run, man. You need to run and get yourself out of here. Tell … tell people … tell," was all he managed before he went silent. His eyes continued to meet mine, although I knew they now only saw darkness.

As he left me, I heard a round strike the ground next to me. Then I saw another hit Shane. Knowing what was coming, I did the only thing I could do. What Shane told me to do … even though I felt it was wrong. But I knew if I stayed, I would die along with all the rest.

From there on out, everything was kind of a blur. Everything continued in slow motion, yet not at the same time.

I ran towards the back of the Village, away from the action – away from the gunfire. Upon reaching the gate, I found it was wide open. As I ran past it, two others joined me. Cassandra and Mel. We all ran together for only a few seconds. Both of them were cut down before they hit the trees.

I'm really not sure how I survived. I remember running for a bit. Then I remember finding a small nook in a gulley. I hid there for a while and listened. Foot crunches came and went, but none got close. When the noises stopped – a good thirty minutes later – I made my way out of the gulley and continued up then down a hill.

It seemed to take forever, but eventually I found a road, and alongside it, an abandoned car. Lucky for me, after some prodding it worked. Once started, I drove … and I drove … and I drove. I didn't stop driving until long after sunup. And I didn't sleep until the sun was high in the sky.

That night I stayed in that same spot, too afraid to sleep, too afraid to move. I flinched at every noise, every sound. The only thing I did there, besides cower, was think.

I'm not sure how Hunter's "crew" found us. Did they track me down as I'd assumed? Or did they simply figure out that the satellite dish on top of SiriusXM was pointed at the Village? Or, hell, was it just dumb luck? Maybe fate!? I have no idea which.

And part of me … the greater part of me *never* wants to know the truth.

EPILOGUE

"And, I guess, that brings us to here. The Fall of 2025."

"After I calmed enough to drive again, I continued up the coast … up the PCH … looking for … something. Not that it mattered. I didn't see much. A few Crazies here and there, but no groups … and no Hunter, thank God."

"I also didn't find the main thing I was still searching for. What I was really looking for. A return to the life I knew before The Surge. But maybe that's a good thing. I … I just don't know."

"Well, by the time I reached Seattle, I'd grown tired. Deep in my bones tired. Tired of searching. Tired of living in fear. Tired of … well … everything, I guess."

"It didn't take me long to find this place. I saw the lights from a ways off and followed them here. Guessing you did too. The solar panels on the roof provide enough power for a few lights, and to keep my player playing. So, there's that."

"Even if it wasn't for the lights, this place would just stand out, you know!? The views are just, like … wow …"

"And here I am, sitting beach side … well, sort of. I'm sitting in a window seat that overlooks the beach. Just kicking back. Watching the water as the waves slowly make their way to the shore. It's … what … picturesque? I swear, one could write volumes about the scenery here. I'd be surprised if someone already hadn't. This place is a photographer's wet dream."

"Oh, and I've made sure I've got enough food and Monsters to last me a while. Yeah, I couldn't find any more Rockstars. So, that kind of sucks."

"My plan is to stay here for a bit and wait. Wait to be found. I'll be leaving the lights on, as they say. You know, like in that hotel commercial. When there were commercials, that is."

"It … my life … all of it feels like a dream now. JC … Lorie … The Surge. Just plain all of it. God, we had life by the balls then, didn't we!? But now … now … now there's nothing. Just simply nothing."

"Anyway, I know what you're thinking. Leaving the lights on is like putting a target on my back. But I tried it the other way. You know, traveling around. Until now though, I've never just tried sitting and waiting. The Village was what it was. But it wasn't … it wasn't this."

"I know, I know. Staying in one place goes against everything I've thought to date. But I just have to trust that eventually someone like me will see the house and wonder about it, like I did. It's not that far off the highway and, well, like I said, the views here are fantastic. Majestic even."

"To be honest, though, part of the reason I'm staying is because I no longer have the strength, or the stomach, to continue. The road … and what happened at the Village … have worn me out. Mentally … and emotionally."

"I figure if I rest up for a bit, maybe I can build up my … what? Fortitude? Haha! Yeah! That's a good a word as any, I guess."

"Shit! I think I've only got a few minutes of battery life left on this thing. Fucking flashing red light … it's dicking with my story."

"I guess after this thing dies, I'll have to venture out and find batteries… or something. If I don't, well, at least I'll still have my music to keep me sane."

"As I mentioned, I've always considered music to be the spark of life. Because it's always been there for me. From The Beatles to Boston, Bach to Beethoven, The Cure to Combichrist, Slayer to Slipknot. Oh, I could name so many. They're all my loves. All my dreams. But without them … well … what is life?"

"Okay, I'm gonna stop recording now … just for a bit. I'm really, really tired. I just need a short nap, then I can head out and find … what? I'm not sure …"

"I gotta say though, I like this spot near the window. A place I can look out and watch for people along the shore. And also see the waves. My God, the waves! The surf is absolutely gorgeous today! And the trees … all the colors … and the way the branches blow in the wind. It's like they're waving to me. Waving for me to follow them. To come visit them. And maybe I will in a bit. But first, I think it's time for a nap."

"You know, I do love this time of year. I mentioned that, right!? All the color changes and the way the birds sing! They're singing to me now, you know. Can you hear it in the background? It's like they're calling to me … calling to me now!"

"The Fall really is the best time of year, don't you think? I do … I do …"